MW00755275

YOLO COUNTY LIBRARY
226 BUCKEYE STREET
WOODLAND CA 95695

Forget-
Her-Nots

Amy Brecount White

Greenwillow Books
An Imprint of HarperCollinsPublishers

This book is a work of fiction. References to real people, events, establishments, organizations, or locales are intended only to provide a sense of authenticity, and are used to advance the fictional narrative. All other characters, and all incidents and dialogue, are drawn from the author's imagination and are not to be construed as real.

Forget-Her-Nots
Copyright © 2010 by Amy Brecount White

All rights reserved. No part of this book may be used or reproduced in any manner whatsoever without written permission except in the case of brief quotations embodied in critical articles and reviews. Printed in the United States of America. For information address HarperCollins Children's Books, a division of HarperCollins Publishers, 10 East 53rd Street, New York, NY 10022.
www.harperteen.com

The text of this book is set in 13-point Venetian 301. Book design by Paul Zakris

The lines from "somewhere i have never travelled,glady beyond" quoted on page 95, copyright 1931 © 1959, 1991 by the Trustees for the E. E. Cummings Trust. Copyright © 1979 by George James Firmage, from *Complete Poems, 1904–1962* by E. E. Cummings, edited by George James Firmage. Used by permission of Liveright Publishing Corporation.

Excerpt from *The Little Prince* by Antoine de Saint-Exupery quoted on pages 70–71, copyright 1943 by Harcourt, Inc., and renewed 1971 by Consuelo de Saint-Exupery; English translation copyright © 2000 by Richard Howard, reprinted by permission of Houghton Mifflin Harcourt Publishing Company.

Excerpt from "The Knight's Tale," from *The Canterbury Tales* quoted on page 231, translation copyright 1993 by Ronald Ecker and Eugene Joseph Crook, published by Hodge & Braddock. Reprinted by permission of Ronald Ecker.

Library of Congress Cataloging-in-Publication Data

White, Amy Brecount.
Forget-her-nots / by Amy Brecount White.
p. cm.
"Greenwillow Books."
Summary: At a Charlottesville, Virginia, boarding school, fourteen-year-old Laurel begins to realize that she shares her deceased mother's connection with flowers, but as she begins to learn their ancient language and share it with other students, she discovers powers that are beyond her control.
ISBN 978-0-06-167298-9 (trade bdg.)
[1. Flower language—Fiction. 2. Flowers—Fiction. 3. Magic—Fiction.
4. Boarding schools—Fiction. 5. Schools—Fiction.
6. Mothers and daughters—Fiction.] I. Title.
PZ7.W58176For 2010   [Fic]—dc22   2009007105

10 11 12 13 14 CG/RRDB First Edition 10 9 8 7 6 5 4 3
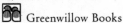 Greenwillow Books

To my husband, Pete,
I give a bough of blooming dogwood

"The more we learn about flowers, the less silent they are."

—SHARMAN APT RUSSELL,
ANATOMY OF A ROSE: EXPLORING THE SECRET LIFE OF FLOWERS

PROLOGUE

Lily reread the letter to her daughter and signed her name at the bottom. Her hands shaking from exhaustion, she dabbed glue on the top right corner of the stationery. She chose bell-like white flowers with slim leaves and pressed them gently into the glue.

Lily of the valley for the return of happiness, she thought. I've given her every clue I can.

PART ONE

The Language of Flowers

"When you take a flower in your hand and really look at it, it's your world for the moment."

—GEORGIA O'KEEFFE, AMERICAN PAINTER, 1887–1986

CHAPTER ONE
Spizzy, Tinny, Dingly.

A flash on the brown carpeting caught Laurel's eye, and she jumped mid-step to keep from crushing it. "What the—"

Three bright flowers tied with a shiny silver ribbon lay just outside her dormitory room. Her chest fluttered with excitement as she picked them up. There were two small white ones, a red one with a yellow center, and some feathery leaves. She looked both ways, but the hall was dim and empty.

She bit the inside of her lip. Pranking—according to her sophomore cousin, Rose—was one of the more popular hobbies on the campus of the Avondale School, outside Charlottesville, Virginia. Laurel listened for telltale giggles to break the silence, but all was still. And there was no note with the flowers.

Could a guy have left them? she wondered. Any time she saw Willowlawn boys on campus, she couldn't help double-taking. What had been a daily occurrence at her old school was now the exception, and she hadn't made any guy friends yet. Nearly everyone at both schools had started there in sixth grade, which left little room for newcomers like Laurel.

She lifted the delicate blooms to her face and breathed in. Sweetly spicy, the scents mingled in her nose and swirled through her head. Her body seemed to be floating up and spinning—light and dizzy. She threw out her hands against the door frame.

"Whoa." Laurel blinked while the hallway around her stabilized. She knew the white flowers were snowdrops—one of the earliest buds to bloom—but the red one and the feathery stuff were unfamiliar. Mom would have known their names, Laurel thought. She knew everything about flowers.

The squeak of another door startled her, and Laurel stepped out of sight. Twirling the flowers between her fingers, she wondered who to tell. She had no time to show anyone before class, not even Rose. Strangely, Laurel needed fresh flowers, different flowers, for an English presentation this morning. She was already carrying an empty basket, so she put the mystery bouquet inside it and hurried out of the dorm.

Spring was officially weeks away, but Laurel could sense its approach. The sky above her head was soft and pink. Drops of dew glinted on the grass like bits of crystal all along the path to the garden. The breeze that caressed her cheek was still cool, but the damp earth below her feet was warming and readying itself.

Taking out the list of flowers she needed, Laurel headed for a clump of purple-and-white pansies she'd found the day before. "Pansies for thoughts," she whispered, and picked a handful. Snowdrops, hanging like tiny white lanterns, dotted the brownness.

"Snowdrops for hope." She plucked a few, lifted them to her nose, and then wiggled her fingers. Her hand felt fuzzy inside and that whole arm was starting to tingle. "Dizzy, spinny, tingly," she whispered as her eyes scanned the landscape for color. "Spizzy, tinny, dingly."

Crisscrossing the mulched pathways, Laurel picked the rest of the flowers on her list, but she wasn't ready to leave the garden. Every branch, every bud seemed strangely fresh and distinct this morning, as if her vision had suddenly cleared. Everything unfolding and green seemed to shimmer and shine with newness. The garden felt almost magical, as if she might turn a corner and come upon lithe fairies dancing in a circle.

She'd just started down an intriguing path when a bell rang in the distance. Panic gripped her body like a hard pinch. *"Merde,"* she said, under her breath. She turned and sprinted back toward the main campus. Rose was right—there was something satisfying about cursing in French.

Laurel rounded the brick corner of Founders' Hall at full speed and crashed into a tight clump of classmates. Tara stumbled backward at the impact, and Laurel had to grab the nearest arm to stop her momentum. Flowers flew from her basket.

"Ahhh!" Tara screamed. Her pink cell phone spiraled out of her hand as she landed on a low bush. Nicole, a plump girl with brown skin and spiky hair, ran to pull her up.

Laurel's stomach clenched. "I'm sorry. I—I thought I was late."

"Watch it, Whelan." Tara shook out her long black hair and smoothed her uniform skirt. "I told you she's in la-la land," she announced to the circle of girls.

Laurel realized she was still holding on to someone's jacket and let go. "Sorry."

"No problem," said Kate, a tall blonde classmate who spoke with a southern twang. "But save your speed for soccer."

Laurel hardly knew Kate, but they were both trying out for the junior varsity soccer team, as was Tara. Before the tryouts Laurel had avoided the glare of Tara's attention.

Lately, though, Tara seemed to look for opportunities to knock her down a notch.

"Who are you supposed to be, anyway?" Tara's hands rose to her thin hips. "Little Red Riding Hood?"

Laurel frowned down at the oversized red windbreaker she'd grabbed from her closet without thinking. Pushing her too-long bangs out of her brown eyes, she noticed another snowdrop near Tara's foot and lunged for it.

Nicole's eyebrows lifted above the purple rims of her glasses. "Nice basket, too."

"It's for my report," Laurel said as she salvaged more flowers from the grass.

"You're going *today*?" Nicole said. "In English?"

Laurel glanced between the smirking girls. "Yeah. So?"

Tara giggled. "So . . . *nada*. Good luck, Little Red," she called back as she and Nicole headed into the classroom building. "Watch out for wolves."

To Laurel's surprise, Kate didn't follow the others but stood still with a few flowers she'd picked up in her hand. "Where d'you get these?" Kate said. "They're so . . . bright."

"The school garden," Laurel said. "You can keep those. I've got plenty."

"Thanks," said Kate. "You're pretty brave to go today."

Laurel trailed her into Founders' Hall. "Why?"

"'Cause it's Exchange Day," Kate shouted over her shoulder as they snaked through clusters of girls crowding the hallway. "Willowlawn guys come to our classes. Didn't you see the schedule?"

"Yeah, but I didn't know it meant *that*." Laurel's mind started to tick. She'd skipped breakfast that morning, so she didn't know if any guys had come to their dining hall or wandered into her dorm. But the idea of some secret admirer leaving flowers outside her door seemed like old-fashioned wishful thinking.

Laurel stopped outside the English classroom, pulled off her jacket, and stuffed it into her backpack. Inside, the desks were pushed together, and the rear of the room was jammed with lanky boys on folding chairs. She was surprised at how her heart sped at the mere sight of guys. Tara and Nicole had positioned themselves in the exact center of the room, while Kate claimed the last desk in the back. A balding man Laurel didn't recognize was standing off to the side.

"Please sit anywhere today," Miss Spenser called out above the din. She was past middle age and usually dressed in tweeds and bows. Most of the girls called her Spinster Spenser, but her voice sang when she read poetry out loud.

"Laurel, why don't you go first?" Miss Spenser tapped a desk. "You can sit here."

Laurel set her basket on the front desk and let her backpack clunk to the floor. Now she wished she'd chosen a normal topic, like the Globe Theatre or something about Charles Dickens. But ever since she'd opened that letter from her mom, Laurel couldn't get flowers out of her head. The letter had arrived on her fourteenth birthday out of the blue. Her mom had attached little white flowers to the top and written a puzzling inscription under them: "Lily of the valley for the return of happiness." Her mom's name was Lily, but Laurel had Googled the phrase. She was amazed to discover there was a whole language of flowers.

"Listen up, guys," the balding man said. "And settle down."

Miss Spenser cleared her throat. "I'd like to welcome Mr. Thomas's English class to our oral reports on history and literature," she said. "Our first presenter today is Laurel Whelan, and her topic is an unusual one: the Victorian language of flowers."

Her heart now galloping, Laurel fumbled with her note cards and wrote "The Language of Flowers" on the chalkboard. Behind her, someone whispered, and Miss Spenser's fingers snapped twice for silence. Laurel turned to face the crowd.

"Imagine"—she paused to steady her quivering voice—"imagine that you are a young lady living in the Victorian era."

Several boys snickered.

"Or a guy," Laurel added. "All the social events you attend are *strictly* chaperoned."

"Sounds like Willowlawn," a boy with thick sandy hair whispered loudly.

"Mr. Buchanan," said Mr. Thomas.

"Sorry," said the boy, but his blue eyes were unrepentant. Even Laurel had heard all about the infamous Everett Buchanan.

Ignore, she told herself, but her eyes kept straying back to his gorgeous face.

"Okay," Laurel said. "Now imagine that you're in love with someone, and you want to tell that person. Texting, Facebook, IMing, and even telephones haven't been invented, so you have to find other ways to communicate. *And* you have to do it while your chaperones are watching. You could send him—or her—a secret message in the language of flowers."

Laurel reached into her basket for a white flower. "In Victorian times," she said, "every kind of flower, even every herb and shrub, symbolized a different feeling or emotion. For example, if you gave someone a snowdrop that meant hope. Or you could give someone a whole bouquet of symbolic flowers, called a tussie-mussie. Each—"

"Fuzzy-wuzzy?" Everett said. "What-y?"

Tara's laughter shredded the air as she swiveled toward Everett.

Miss Spenser stood up. "Mr. Buchanan, *do* raise your hand if you have a question."

"Sorry." Everett held up both palms as if at gunpoint. "Excuse me, uh—Lauren?"

"Laur-*el*," she said firmly.

"Excuse me, Laur-elle. What did you call 'em?" Everett flashed a confident smile.

"Tussie-mussies. It's kind of a silly name, but that's what they were called back then." She giggled nervously.

"Thank-you-very-much," Everett said, bowing his head. "Laur-elle."

Laurel blinked at him because she didn't want to believe the sarcasm that slithered through his voice. She squeezed her cards and forced herself to read on. "Most Victorian girls had a language of flowers book for reference, like this one." She held up a pocket-sized paperback, *The Language of Flowers*, which she'd spied in the window of a florist shop near her dad's new town house. She'd hurried into the store and flipped its pages to the letter *L*. "Lily of the valley for the return of happiness," the book said—exactly like her mom's letter.

Skimming her next note card, Laurel crossed out the geeky words in her mind. "Lots of the meanings in the flower language come from literary sources, like the

Bible, Greek mythology, and Shakespeare's plays and sonnets," she said.

"Excellent!" exclaimed Miss Spenser.

"For example, if someone gave you a narcissus—that's the scientific name for a daffodil—that means they think you're narcissistic or egotistical." Laurel held up a photograph of a daffodil she'd printed off the internet because the buds weren't open yet outside. "In the Greek myth this guy Narcissus is really gorgeous. He sees his reflection in a lake and actually falls in love with himself." She shook her head. "You wouldn't want to get a tussie-mussie with narcissus in it."

"No way," whispered Everett. "That would suck."

Laurel winced as Tara laughed loudest of all.

"C'mon, man." An Asian guy kicked the back of Everett's chair. "Cut it out."

"Mr. Buchanan," the Willowlawn teacher said. "Final warning."

Everett nodded curtly. "Yessir."

Laurel met the other boy's eyes with silent gratitude. His shoulder-length black hair was parted in the middle and tucked behind his ears. When he gave her a quick nod back, her body relaxed a little.

Miss Spenser smiled at her. "This is fascinating, Laurel. Please continue."

Gathering herself with a slow breath, Laurel chose

other flowers and explained their meanings: pansies were for thoughts, crocuses for mirth, sprigs of green myrtle for love, and lily of the valley for the return of happiness. After her mom's cryptic reference Laurel *had* to have some lilies of the valley. It was too cold for them to bloom outside, but she found some online and ordered a potful. Her dad would never notice the expense on her charge card.

"And if you're really serious about someone," Laurel went on, "you could add ivy to symbolize marriage and fidelity." She tucked a few sprigs into the other flowers and wound strips of green tape around the stems. "So if you gave someone this exact tussie-mussie, you'd secretly communicate your hope for love and happiness in the Victorian language of flowers."

Everyone started clapping, but Laurel's eyes fell on the black-haired guy. She lifted the bouquet to her nose and breathed in. The honeyed fragrance swirled into her head and swept through her body, leaving a strange trail of lovely words she couldn't help whispering to herself.

> *"Bright cut flowers, leaves of green,*
> *bring about what I have seen."*

The instant Laurel uttered the words, a fizzy feeling sparked in her fingertips and whooshed up her arm.

"Ahhh!" She dropped the bouquet. Forty pairs of eyes stared, and her face flushed warm as she leaned on the desk. The scent of flowers was strong and dizzying.

Miss Spenser stepped toward her. "Are you all right?"

"It was a . . . a thorn," Laurel blurted out as she rubbed her arm. "It pricked me." All her flowers were thornless, but she hoped no one would notice. She couldn't meet her classmates' eyes. "So . . . uh . . . does anybody have any questions?" Like, What's happening to me?

Nicole's hand popped up, as usual. "How did you find out about this flower language?" she said in her breathy voice.

Laurel opened her mouth and closed it again. The birthday letter was a secret she needed to keep. "I found this book"—she lifted the small paperback—"at a florist shop called Say It with Flowers. It's in Georgetown."

Everett's hand waved at her. "Where can I get one?"

"You mean a flower book?" Laurel asked cautiously.

"No, a *luv* bouquet." Everett's grin oozed with self-satisfaction, and even the teachers smiled.

Laurel felt a flicker of resentment, but she'd known guys like him at her old school—guys so pretty they could get away with murder. She spoke deliberately, as if talking to a toddler. "If you *really* need one, Everett, like, desperately, you could make one all by yourself." She picked up the flower photo and laid it on his desk. "And why don't you start with this one? A narcissus is perfect for you."

"Ooooh," said several kids in the class.

"What's it mean again?" Tara said.

Laurel ventured a glance at the black-haired boy, who was grinning at her. "I found an antique language of flowers book in Avondale's library, too," she added with a sudden rush of confidence. "I'm sure they'd let you use that, if you ask nicely."

Everett slapped his desk. "I'll get right on it."

Tara pointed to the tussie lying on the desk. "What are you doing with that one?"

Laurel looked down at the bouquet, and her breath caught at its loveliness. "I—I don't know. Maybe I'll give it to someone."

"Someone you *luv*?" Nicole's eyebrows shot above her purple frames.

Laurel dropped her eyes at the scattered giggles so that guy didn't catch her looking.

"Do the fuzzy-wuzzy thingies actually work?" Tara smiled sideways at Everett, but he didn't seem to notice.

Laurel shrugged. "I guess if you gave someone certain flowers, and they knew the language, then they could decipher your message."

"That's way too complicated," said Nicole. "I'd rather text."

"Can I have *that* bouquet?" Tara asked in her most saccharine voice.

In your dreams, Laurel thought. But if she gave Tara the flowers, Tara might be nicer or leave her alone. Her fingers closed around the stems, and the words rose again: *Bright cut flowers, leaves of green*. . . . Tingling energy pricked at her fingers and swooshed up her arm, but this time she was ready. Within moments the sensation had spread so that every cell in her body tingled pleasantly, warmly—like a deep shiver that didn't end. *Spizzy, tinny, dingly.*

"I—I'll give this to somebody," Laurel said, mesmerized by the mingling scents, which were like honey on her tongue . . . honey to her soul.

Everett's hand sliced the air. "Me! Oh, oh, give it to me." Mr. Thomas stepped forward and bent over him.

Phrases from the language of flowers flitted through Laurel's mind: the return of happiness . . . hope . . . fidelity. She couldn't give the tussie to the nice guy; she didn't even know his name. Her eyes alighted on Spinster Spenser, who read them love poems with such passion. Laurel skirted the upstretched arms of Tara and Nicole as the tingling in her hand grew nearly painful. Passing the black-haired boy, she stumbled over nothing and then halted before Miss Spenser.

"These are yours." Laurel pressed the flowers into her teacher's hands.

"Mine? Good gracious!" Miss Spenser's blue eyes widened. "They're lovely. Thank you, dear."

A wall of whispers rose around Laurel as she walked to her desk. She could feel Tara's glare hot on her back.

CHAPTER TWO

Tingle and Hum

Laurel set her lunch tray at the end of a long wooden dining table and slid her basket underneath; it didn't fit in her locker. The cavernous hall was crowded with Willowlawn guys, but she didn't see her cousin Rose anywhere. Laurel guessed Rose was in a lab somewhere, probably eating lunch with her Bunsen burner.

Kate set her tray on the edge of the table. "It's sooo crowded with all these boys."

"Yeah," said Laurel. Her table was almost empty. "Really crowded."

"Have you seen Tara or Nicole?" Kate scanned the crowd. "Some geeks are sittin' in our place."

"Nope," said Laurel. "Haven't seen them."

"I give." Kate slid her tray across from Laurel. "Can I sit here? I'm starvin'."

"Sure." Laurel watched Kate take an enormous bite of her sandwich. "So when do we find out about soccer?" It was a conversation starter, as her lobbyist dad would say.

"Two or three weeks." Kate set down the sandwich and finished chewing. "You all right? You seemed out of it in English."

Laurel stretched her hand underneath the table, but it felt normal now. "Just fine."

Kate squeezed ketchup over a mound of fries. "Your presentation was pretty cool. I like flowers."

"Thanks." The flowers she'd given Kate that morning were now wilting on her tray.

"Everyone kinda thought you were the shy, wallflowery type, but they're wrong, aren't they?" said Kate. "You dissed Everett good."

Laurel couldn't help grinning.

"But why did you give that bouquet to Spinster Spenser?" Kate lowered her voice. "Tara is totally annoyed, and she's sayin' you're a little brownnose."

"I am *not* a brownnose." Laurel ripped open a package of saltines and crumbled them into her soup.

"I'm just telling you what people are sayin'," said Kate. "Don't you care?"

Laurel wished she didn't. "Am I supposed to do what-ever Tara wants?"

"No. But she asked for that bouquet nicely."

"It wasn't hers," said Laurel.

Kate shrugged. "Why not?"

"Because she's a total pain." Laurel's body tensed. What if Kate reported this conversation directly to Tara?

"She's not *that* bad," Kate whispered. "But she's pretty worried about soccer. You're a decent wing, and that's her position."

"You know she plays prissy defense," Laurel whispered. "What am I supposed to do? Screw up my tryout?"

"No way," Kate said between fries. "I wanna win."

Laurel wanted to scream loud and long. She'd imag-ined that transferring to Avondale, her mom's dear alma mater, would be exponentially better than this. Several silent moments passed as she stewed in self-pity. Then Kate's hands moved to pick up her tray, and Laurel real-ized she was blowing what might be her one and only chance with Kate.

"You *really* want to know why I gave Miss Spenser the flowers?" she said.

"I asked, didn't I?"

"Okay." Laurel leaned closer. "So I had this bizarre feeling that the tussie—the flowers—belonged to her. That she *needed* them."

"For what?" Kate said. "A love bouquet? She's taught here forever, and I don't think she's ever had a boyfriend. Tara says—"

"I'm sure she's had a boyfriend at *some* point," Laurel interrupted. She was not about to let Miss Spenser's love life be dismissed so easily. When her teacher's voice rose and fell with the rhythms of a poem, Laurel felt a gaping emptiness she wished she knew how to fill. "Maybe Miss Spenser had a *secret* romance. I think she's pretty."

Kate's nose wrinkled. "With all that frizzy orange hair?"

"It's red." Laurel held up a strand of her own brown, shoulder-length hair. "And my hair is frizzy, too."

Kate shook her head. "No, yours is naturally wavy, and it matches your eyes. Mine's too straight."

Kate's thick blonde hair seemed perfect, like everything else about her. Laurel glanced up as a group of guys passed close to their table. Her heart skipped when she pointed discreetly to the black-haired one from class. "Hey. Do you know who that is?"

"Justin Takahashi." Kate's eyebrows lifted. "Are you interested?"

"No. I—uh—he seems all right." Laurel stopped herself, worried that she'd blabbed too much already. She watched Justin until he sat down on the other side of the cafeteria with his back to her. When she'd met his eyes during English class, she'd felt a twinge of connection, a rare feeling for her lately.

Kate's face softened into a smile. "Oh, riiight. Justin told Everett to shut up, didn't he? So you should thank him—maybe send him one of those flower messages."

"A tussie-mussie?" Laurel asked incredulously.

"Yeah."

Laurel shook her head. "No way. Maybe an e-mail, or I could text him." *Merde*. She kept forgetting that her cell phone was locked in the school office with hundreds of others. A drug scandal had roiled the campus the year before, and—Rose had explained—the principal was convinced that cell phones and BlackBerries made "illicit trafficking" of anything too easy. Avondale students were allowed to check out their phones only when they left campus.

"But Justin's kinda different," said Kate. "I bet no girl's ever given him flowers."

Laurel stared at the now-mushy crackers floating in her soup because she didn't trust herself to meet Kate's eyes.

"What does this flower mean again?" Kate pointed at a snowdrop on her tray.

"Hope." It had been a while since Laurel had dared to hope for anything good.

"What about my flowers?" Kate lifted the drooping bunch off her tray. "Are they a tuzzy-wuzzy?"

"Tussie-mussie, and they look parched. Here." Laurel scooped an ice cube out of Kate's water glass and onto her tray. Kate started to put the stems in the makeshift vase.

"Wait a sec," Laurel said. "You want some myrtle, too? It's for love." Pulling her basket up to the bench, she pulled out green sprigs, some ribbon, and scissors.

"Sure." Kate leaned over. "May I have a few of those little white ones, too?"

"That's lily of the valley, for the return of happiness." Like anyone can make that happen, Laurel added to herself. Pulling a few blooms out, she snipped half an inch off the stems, like her mom had always done, and handed the flowers to Kate.

"Thanks." Kate put them in the water, and Laurel glanced down at her own mystery bouquet in the basket. It was wilting, too. She snipped its stems and put it into her water glass, along with the other flowers left over from her presentation.

"Where'd that one come from?" said Kate, pointing to the mystery bouquet.

Laurel couldn't quite trust her. "I was just playing around—like for practice."

"I love that red flower," said Kate. "Do you have any more?"

Laurel shook her head. She wished she knew where

to find that one, but she hadn't seen any red flowers in the garden. And if this was a tussie-mussie, she couldn't translate its message until she knew all the names.

"Hey, look." Kate pointed across the room. "Spinster Spenser brought hers, too."

Laurel turned to see the teacher walking toward the faculty table with her tussie-mussie in a vase on her tray. "Why'd she bring it here?"

"Duh," said Kate. "She *needs* it. You just said that."

Laurel craned her neck. Directly across the table from Miss Spenser, a man with gray hair and a striped bow tie stood up and extended his hand. Laurel stood up, too.

"Where are you goin'?" asked Kate.

Laurel flexed the hand that was starting to tingle again. "I need to see. . . ." Dodging a noisy group of upperclassmen, she grabbed a mustard packet from the condiment cart as an alibi and walked toward the faculty table. Miss Spenser had placed her flowers in the middle, and the bow-tie man was leaning forward, so that his face hovered over the blooms. Laurel blinked in disbelief. She could practically see the swirl of fragrances streaming up, up, and into his nose.

Now! she thought. Her right hand seemed to lift on its own and reach toward the bouquet. "Bright cut flowers," she whispered, "leaves of green, bring about what I have seen." When the last word left her tongue, her whole body tingled and hummed, as if a note was reverberating deeply inside her. She closed her eyes and pictured the bow-tie man walking hand in hand with Miss Spenser . . . him taking her in his arms. *That* was what she wanted to see.

When Laurel's eyes opened, the air around the vase seemed to shimmer—like heat rising—with the sudden explosion of fragrance. Someone sneezed twice, and the professor slowly straightened and blinked at the flowers.

At the far end of the table a tall woman with olive-toned skin stood up and looked around urgently. She lifted her nose and then turned toward Laurel, who dropped her hand. The woman's eyes met hers in a question, but Laurel took a step backward.

"Ow!" cried a voice behind her. "My toe."

"Oops." Laurel turned around to face a seventh grader. "Sorry."

Tara was standing right behind her, holding salt packets. "Hi, Laurel. How's the weather in la-la land? Find some new friends there?"

Laurel realized that she was standing next to the seventh grade table. Most of the younger girls were staring up at her, and one pointed at her hip. Mustard had oozed between Laurel's fingers and splattered on her uniform skirt, even though she didn't remember squeezing the packet. Her face warmed.

"They're about your speed," said Tara as she walked away.

"Here." Another seventh grader handed Laurel some napkins.

"Thanks." Laurel wiped off the mustard and walked back to her table. Tara was already there, and at her approach leaned toward Kate to whisper. Kate covered her mouth but a loud giggle escaped.

Tara grinned smugly. "Later, Little Red."

Biting the inside of her lip, Laurel looped the basket over her arm and picked up her tray with the mystery bouquet still in the water glass. Tara's eyes darted from those flowers to Kate's, but Laurel swiveled out of Tara's reach.

Walking to the conveyor belt, Laurel stole a glance at Justin, but he wasn't looking her way. Hope he missed all that, she thought. At the faculty table the bow-tie man was still talking animatedly with Miss Spenser. Laurel tucked her flowers under her coat and hurried past the cafeteria monitor.

Thwump! Laurel trapped the loose soccer ball with the inside of her foot. She waited for the defender to rush two steps closer and then tapped the ball left and turned on the speed. She was flying down the sideline with the ball dribbled close. She heard her name and saw Kate running down the center of the field. Quickly judging the distance to make the cross, Laurel lofted the ball over a fullback's head. It landed just ahead of Kate, who dribbled around the last defender.

"Shoot!" Laurel yelled. Kate slowed to aim and then the ball sailed off her cleat. The goalie dove, but the ball landed neatly in the corner of the net.

"Yes!" Laurel threw up her arms and jumped into the air. Kate held out her fist, and Laurel tapped it with her own.

"That was awesome," Kate said. "Sweet pass."

"Amazing shot," Laurel said.

"You dusted Tara," Kate whispered.

Did I? Laurel thought. On the field she saw only shirt colors, cleats, and the checkered ball while the rest of the world fell blissfully away.

"Nice assist!" A tall girl with cocoa-colored skin yelled from the sideline.

"That's Tashi, the varsity captain," Kate said. "She rocks."

Coach Peters blew a long whistle, and the girls headed to the sidelines. Licking the sweat off her lips, Laurel reached for her water bottle and sat cross-legged in the grass next to a curly-haired forward named Ally.

"Great pass," whispered Ally. "You're way fast."

"Thanks." Laurel was thrilled that everyone had seen.

That assist had to get the coach's attention. She'd been a starter at her middle school, and she couldn't imagine spring without soccer.

"Fabulous practice, girls," said Coach. "I'm going to have to make some tough cuts, but I'll have the roster soon."

Laurel ripped off a fat blade of grass and rubbed it between her thumbs. Making the team was her best chance to break through some of the entrenched cliques. She knew she was better than several other girls—Tara, especially—but the newest building had been donated by Tara's dad.

"Hey, Laurel," Kate called. She, Tara, and Ally had started toward campus for dinner, but Kate had turned around. "You comin' with?"

"Sure." Laurel jogged to catch up, her spirits rising in a rush of gratitude. As soon as the coach was out of sight, Tara pulled out her cell phone and started texting someone. Laurel was surprised anyone was willing to risk the harsh punishment, a dorm-and-classroom-only suspension, but Tara seemed to get away with more than most.

"Does Everett *ever* answer you?" asked Kate.

Tara narrowed her eyes at Kate. "Not now," she said through clenched teeth.

Laurel looked away to hide the start of a smile. All was not perfect in Tara-land.

The shortest path to the dining hall took them past several teacher homes. Laurel's favorite was Miss Spenser's neat white cottage, with its purple shutters and a porch swing, but looking that way, she froze. Miss Spenser was standing on her porch with the bow-tie man, and the vase with Laurel's flowers was on a table next to the swing.

Laurel tugged on the back of Kate's T-shirt and waited for the other girls to move out of earshot. She pointed toward the porch. "Who's he?"

"I don't know," said Kate.

"Doesn't he teach at Willowlawn? He was in the dining hall."

"He was?" Kate shrugged. "I don't recognize him."

Kate kept walking, but Laurel hurried past the next cottage and then circled around the back to its other side. Ducking, she sprinted across a driveway and crouched behind a bank of azaleas not yet blooming. A piece of gravel skittered behind her, and Laurel turned to see Kate following her.

"What are you doin'?" Kate whispered. "Spying?"

Laurel had to nod. She peeked over the bushes, while Kate hunched at her shoulder. Miss Spenser's laugh, high and musical, rang through the silence. The late afternoon sun glinted off her red hair, and she smiled girlishly as she rocked backward on her heels.

Kate dropped to her knees. "My legs are killing me. What are they sayin'?"

Laurel peeked higher. "I have no idea, but I think she's actually flirting."

"Nooo." Kate bobbed her head for a better view.

The man glanced at his watch. Then, as earlier, he leaned into the vase of flowers.

"He's sniffing them again," Laurel whispered and wondered if he felt the flowers, too.

"Sniffin' what?"

"My—I mean, Miss Spenser's flowers."

Straightening, the man put out his hand, and Miss Spenser extended hers. In a chivalrous sweep he lifted her hand to his lips. Miss Spenser stood motionless until he released her.

"Saturday, then. At seven," he called out in a buttery Southern accent.

Miss Spenser managed a nod. "Yes, Luke."

The man started briskly toward main campus. Hugging the vase to her chest, Miss Spenser sat down on the porch swing and buried her nose in the blooms.

"Spinster Spenser has a boyfriend," Kate said in a singsong voice.

Laurel's eyes were wide. "And he got the message."

Kate tilted her head to the side. "What?"

"A hope for love and happiness. Remember? That was

the message the tussie-mussie was supposed to send," Laurel explained. "And now look. Total romance."

"Like love at first sight," said Kate as they slinked back to the path.

Laurel shook her head behind Kate's back, because that wasn't it exactly. It was the tingling and the humming and the explosion of scent. Something from the flowers—an energy, a power—had moved through Laurel and out of her, awakening romance. "Say it with flowers," she mumbled.

Once they hit the path, they started running and zipped past the bow-tie man, who was whistling merrily. Tara stood far ahead with her hands on her hips.

"Hey, keep this a secret, okay?" Laurel whispered. "About the flowers, I mean."

"Why?" Kate asked.

"Pleeease?" They slowed to walking. "What if your *whole* life you dreamed of love, like Miss Spenser? And what if this is her last chance?"

Kate looked at her quizzically. "Okay, okay."

"Where did you two go?" Tara frowned. "How did you get so dirty?"

Laurel and Kate looked at their matching, mulch-stained knees and laughed in unison. Laurel could practically feel Tara's darts of disapproval, but she didn't care one iota. A fabulous idea was germinating in her mind.

CHAPTER THREE
Ambassadors of Love

Botanical prints that had belonged to her mom decorated the walls of Laurel's small dorm room. She'd also brought her mom's favorite upholstered chair to campus, because she felt close to her mom when she sat there, as if the chair were hugging her. A textbook lay open in her lap, but Laurel couldn't concentrate on any history other than her own.

Setting her book aside, she reached for the flowers on her desk. Almost a week had passed, so their scents—those of the mystery bouquet and the leftovers—were faded. Holding the glass vase between her hands, she whispered the words that streamed through her head like song lyrics, "Bright cut flowers, leaves of green, bring about what I have seen."

Laurel waited expectantly—as she had all week—but nothing in her body tingled, and her fingers felt cool around the glass. She pulled out the dripping stems, repeated the words, and sniffed deeply. Still nothing. She shoved the flowers back into the vase.

If this mystery bouquet *was* carrying a message, then someone else on campus had to have known about the language even before Laurel's presentation. She knew it was next to impossible that Justin had left it, but she still wished she'd talked to him in the dining hall. He'd stood up for her, and Kate was right—Laurel should've thanked him. She had tried to talk to Kate about the flowers a few times, but Kate was almost never alone.

In the room next door Tara played her music far louder than the rules allowed. Not for the first time, Laurel wondered if the dorm mother, Mrs. Fox, who lived near Kate's room, was deaf. Or maybe her reaction time varied according to how much a student's family donated.

As Laurel banged her fist on their shared wall, her eyes strayed to the wooden wardrobe, which was stock furnishing in the dorms. Her dad had called it a wardrobe when he'd moved her in, and it made her think of the one in *The Lion, the Witch, and the Wardrobe.* Its doors were open, and she could see her "special stuff" box on the top shelf. She spread her hands against the solid wood at the back. She didn't expect the snows of Narnia, but touching the wood was like a ritual now. She desperately wanted to believe in other worlds—especially in a world where she had tons of friends who weren't scared off by the sadness she sometimes wore like a hooded cloak.

Laurel dragged over her desk chair and stood on it to reach the white cardboard box covered with large pink roses. Cabbage roses, her mom had called them when she had given the box to Laurel years earlier. Struck by a sudden thought, Laurel leaped off the chair and grabbed her paperback *Language of Flowers*.

"Cabbage rose," it said. "Ambassador of love."

Laurel's fingertips traced the paper blossoms—very persistent ambassadors. Her mom couldn't have known Laurel would put the birthday letter in this particular box. Her mom couldn't have imagined writing such a letter when she gave Laurel the box. The cancer had still been hiding then. And yet . . .

"You can't be dead," Laurel whispered. "You're still sending me messages." She took off the top and handled the letter gingerly so the flowers wouldn't crumble into meaningless bits. Her mom's voice filled Laurel's mind as she read.

Lily of the valley, for the return of happiness

Dear Laurel,
Happy fourteenth birthday! I'm so sorry I'm not there.

*I tried with every iota of my strength to fight this damn
disease. You know that. Know also that I'll be with you
always, like a stubborn guardian angel.*

*Now for my surprise. I've written you letters to be
opened on each of your birthdays. In them I'll focus on
"matters of consequence," to borrow a phrase from our
friend the Little Prince. People often disagree about what
matters and what doesn't. That's one of the essential tasks
in your life: to determine what truly matters.*

*Along your path, seek out "kindred spirits," as Anne
of Green Gables calls them. People with whom you share
an instant understanding. They can be guides on your
journey as you seek to matter in this world.*

*All of us have gifts we are meant to share, but you
have to discover what yours are. Nurture your gifts,
because only then will you bloom fully. Share your gifts,
and love will flower like a meadow around you. I pray
that God showers your life with blessings.*

Love forever and ever,
Mom

Laurel had read the letter every day since it first surprised her, but one word stood out now: *bloom.* Flowers
had been one of her mom's favorite things. Their restored
farmhouse in northern Virginia had been surrounded
by an acre of gardens, and her mom was always sending

Laurel to deliver little bouquets to friends or neighbors. Even now—though it seemed like eons since she'd lived there—Laurel could lose herself wandering through memories of that house. Year round, sunny flowers or branches bright with berries cheered the rooms.

Her dad had sold the house only one month after her mom's death.

"That house *was* your mother," he explained brusquely. "You can't expect me—us—to start over in that old place."

Everything had happened so quickly that it felt like someone else's life. Her mom had died late in July, and by Labor Day Laurel and her dad were living in a brick row house in Georgetown. Her mom's garden was sold, bulldozed, and replaced with four McMansions. Her dad had tried to keep Laurel in the same public school with her old friends, but he wasn't able to once they'd moved. He got her into a private school near Georgetown, but she felt like she was sleepwalking and couldn't summon the energy to smile or chat or care about clothes. For a while her old friends called or IM'ed, but she wasn't in the loop. Laurel felt like an outsider nearly everywhere she went.

Her dad had always worked late as a lobbyist on Capitol Hill, but after the funeral his hours ballooned. Laurel wandered the lonely rooms of his row house and felt like she couldn't breathe the city air deeply enough. Worst of all, she suspected that the barrage of women who called her dad "to check up on him" wanted more. Laurel begged him to let her board over two hours away at Avondale, where her mom had been happy once upon a time, where her Grandma Cicely had gone, and where her genius cousin Rose was a sophomore. Weeks of relentless nagging wore him down, and she'd moved into her dorm room at the beginning of the second semester.

"'Love will flower like a meadow,'" Laurel repeated. She couldn't believe that all this—the roses on the box, the mystery bouquet, Miss Spenser's new romance—was coincidence, but her mom had never mentioned a flower language when she was alive. It was pure luck that Laurel had seen the paperback in the florist's window. Her mom couldn't ever call or e-mail again, and yet Laurel wanted to believe that her mom had found other ways—antique ways—to send messages.

Could the mystery bouquet be from her, too? Laurel looked around the room, trying to see everything with fresh eyes. Messages could be anywhere. Suddenly the room felt unbelievably stuffy. The sky outside her window looked gray and wintry again, but it wouldn't be dark for several hours. Whoever had created the mystery bouquet had probably gathered snowdrops from the garden, so the red flowers might be there, too. Waiting to be found. She touched the window to guess the temperature and then pulled on mittens and her winter coat.

Her quick steps crunched across the frozen mulch on the way to the garden. Finding a few snowdrops still standing, she scanned the gently rolling landscape for the color red and hoped the flowers could survive the pinpricks of ice now hitting her face. She was just about to head back when a color caught her eye, and she ran toward a large shrub.

Many of its roselike blooms were lying frozen to the ground, but a few had been sheltered by glossy evergreen leaves. Breaking off a flower, Laurel lifted it to her nose. It had no scent at all, but it was the same kind. She walked around the shrub twice, but there was no marker to tell her its name, its meaning in the language.

Laurel frowned at the stiff petals. Someone had sent her this message, but it might as well have been written in Urdu.

Midway through the following Tuesday, Laurel was walking in a stream of girls when she spotted Justin on the other side of the quad. His black hair was glossy in the sun, and he towered over everyone around him. Her stomach fluttered, and she jumped out of the flow to watch him from the edge of the grass. His stride was confident, but it didn't seem like arrogance. He was talking to a guy with brown curly hair, and they were headed away from her. She thought about yelling out his name—*Justin!*—but everyone on the entire quad would turn, and he might not remember her. They hadn't actually said a word to each other.

Later in the cafeteria Laurel asked Rose why guys were on campus that day.

"Advanced Classical Seminar," Rose explained. "For Latin geeks. We have a fabulous Latin teacher, so some guys come here for a long class once a week."

"And it's the same schedule every week?" Laurel tried to keep her voice casual.

"Yep." Rose narrowed her eyes. "Spill, cuz. Who's beeping on your radar screen?"

Stifling the smile that might give her away, Laurel rearranged the items on her tray. "Nobody. I just saw some guys and wondered. I take Latin, too." If Laurel wasn't careful, Rose would launch into a frenzy of teasing, but Laurel made a mental note to walk down the quad at that exact time the next week. She'd looked up Justin's e-mail address and checked out his Facebook page. He'd friended her, but that didn't mean much.

As the week passed, Laurel kept expecting to hear the latest about Miss Spenser's love life, but so far she'd heard nothing. Miss Spenser seemed to laugh more often, and Laurel caught her smiling dreamily during a pop quiz. Rose told Laurel that the new Willowlawn teacher—Professor Featherstone—had come out of university retirement to teach Ancient Civilizations when a faculty member left unexpectedly. Rose was adding his course to her already heavy schedule. Laurel couldn't wait to give Miss Spenser more flowers she could carry, like ambassadors of love.

When the bell rang at the end of English class, Laurel waited for Tara and Nicole to exit the room first. "Kate," she whispered.

"Hey, Laurel," said Kate. "What's up?"

"I'm dying to know how Miss Spenser's date went. You know, last weekend."

"Oh, yeah. I totally forgot," said Kate, following Laurel to the front of the room.

"How may I help you, ladies?" asked Miss Spenser.

"We were just wondering if you had a good weekend," Laurel began.

"Like say, Saturday night," Kate added.

Miss Spenser looked at them over her reading glasses and straightened some papers on top of her podium. "Yes. I had a very good weekend. Thank you for asking."

That answer was far too generic for Laurel. "But did you have a good time with that professor?" she blurted out, half shocked at her own boldness.

Miss Spenser pursed her lips. "Who told you about that?"

Laurel couldn't think of an excuse that didn't involve eavesdropping, but Kate threw her a line. "News spreads like kudzu at Avondale," said Kate. "You know, that huge vine that takes over everything in its path."

Laurel had to bite her tongue to keep from smiling.

"I know what kudzu is," said Miss Spenser. "But who told you about my date?"

Kate tilted her head. "I don't exactly remember. Do you, Laurel?"

"Not exactly," Laurel said. "I guess it was somebody. Or other."

"Somebody," Miss Spenser repeated. "Or other." A corner of her mouth edged up.

"You had fun." Kate shook her index finger. "I know you did."

Miss Spenser's eyes were smiling, but she somehow held her mouth straight. "Now girls, enough." She took hold of Kate's shoulders and turned her toward the hallway. "This is not *Days of Our Lives*."

Laurel followed Kate but spun around at the door. "But did you take any of my flowers with you? Those ones I gave you in class?"

Miss Spenser smiled. "You know, I did put some in my hair. Some lily of the valley. They were so sweet, and

Luke—Professor Featherstone—likes that scent." She placed a light hand on Laurel's shoulder. "Thank you again for them. It was very thoughtful."

But Laurel had to know more. "Did my flowers make you feel anything?" *Spinny, tingly, dizzy.* "Like sometimes flowers make me feel all tingly."

"Tingly?" Miss Spenser's face reddened. "I suppose you could describe it that way. Receiving flowers gives any woman a certain"—she hesitated—"a certain confidence. Maybe that's why men have given women flowers for centuries."

"But *I* gave them to you," Laurel said.

"Yes," said Miss Spenser, suddenly confused. Girls were streaming between them into the classroom. "Excuse me. I have to prepare for my next class."

"For the return of happiness," Laurel said as she trailed Kate to their math class. "Miss Spenser seems happier, don't you think?"

"For sure," said Kate. "Maybe she'll ease up on the pop quizzes."

Laurel grabbed Kate's sleeve just outside their next class. "Please don't tell anyone about all this, okay? Not yet."

"But it's cool. She got all blushy." Kate's voice switched to singsong. "Spinster Spenser's in love. Nobody's gonna believe this."

"Please," said Laurel. Gossip spread *faster* than kudzu on campus. Whatever was happening with the flowers, she wanted to figure it out for herself before Tara—or anyone else—could mess it up.

As the bell rang, she and Kate stepped into the classroom together. Glancing at Tara, Laurel could see that she was taking it all in. Tara's mouth tightened as she ripped a square of paper out of her notebook for her weapon of choice: the private note. Between geometry proofs Laurel watched Kate open the note and skim its contents. Kate smiled, but Laurel cringed because it *had* to be about her.

After math they had a few extra minutes to grab a snack or switch books. Tara and Nicole flanked Kate like bodyguards, so Laurel sat cross-legged outside her locker and bit into an apple. It was still bizarre for her not to see guys in the hallways, not to sit next to them or talk between classes. It would be so simple for her to find a way to bump into Justin if he weren't three miles away on another campus.

Laurel used to be part of a group—guys and girls—who went to Starbucks or Baskin-Robbins after school or practice and hung out together at dances. After her mom's diagnosis, though, she always went straight home and skipped the dances. Then when her mom died, it seemed like most people didn't know how to talk to her anymore. They seemed afraid of her—like she might shatter if they said the wrong thing.

"I need some guy friends," Laurel muttered to herself. "This place is unnatural."

"Laurel?" Miss Spenser was beckoning to her. "Do you have a moment, please?"

"Uh, sure." Laurel gathered up her stuff, but her feet halted in the doorway of the classroom. A tall dark-haired teacher was standing at the windows. She wore large hoop earrings, high-heeled boots, and a flowing purple skirt. Laurel had seen her zipping around in a golf cart, but they hadn't spoken. She looked exotic and beautiful, and she was the one who had stared at Laurel in the dining hall the day Professor Featherstone came.

"Laurel, this is Geneva Suarez," said Miss Spenser. "She teaches many of our science classes."

Ms. Suarez's silver bracelets clinked as she held out her hand. "Hello, Laurel. I've been meaning to introduce myself." She spoke with a trace of a Spanish accent.

"Hello." Laurel shook her hand.

"Ms. Suarez also oversees our gardens," said Miss Spenser. "If you see flowers brightening any room on campus, she's usually the reason."

Ms. Suarez smiled at the older woman. "You know what I always say: no room is complete without flowers."

Laurel's head snapped sideways, and her eyes met Ms. Suarez's. That comment sounded *exactly* like something her mom would have said.

"I adore flowers," the teacher said softly. "Just as your mom did."

Laurel inhaled sharply. "You knew my mom?"

"Yes. You have her beautiful brown eyes." Ms. Suarez sat down in one of the student desks and crossed her legs. "Lily and I were here at Avondale together. She was a year older than me, but we had a lot in common. I'm very sorry for your loss."

"Thank you," Laurel said automatically. She'd heard a million condolences, but they never changed a thing.

Miss Spenser laid her hand on Laurel's arm. "Ms. Suarez was impressed with that lovely bouquet you gave me. She's quite intrigued by that flower language."

"Really?" Laurel looked at the teacher again.

"Yes. I've heard of it," Ms. Suarez said. "Did your mom teach it to you?"

Laurel hesitated. Her mom hadn't taught her anything, not directly, but her mom had left clues she was tracking. She could feel both teachers watching her. "Yes," she said. "I mean, kind of. She—we—used to make bouquets all the time."

Ms. Suarez nodded. "How old are you now?"

"Fourteen." Laurel glanced up at the clock. "I'm sorry, but I need stuff for my next class."

"I have to run, too." Ms. Suarez stood up. "I'd be happy to give you a tour of the conservatory sometime, if you'd like."

"Conservatory?" Laurel said, taken aback. "There's a conservatory here?"

Ms. Suarez nodded. "Behind a row of cedars off the main path to the gardens. It's easy to miss if you're not looking for it, or if you don't know it's there."

Ms. Suarez was out the door when Laurel thought of something else. "Ms. Suarez?" she said. "Since you know about flowers . . . I went to the garden and found a red one on an evergreen bush, and it had bloomed even though the weather was freezing. Do you know which one I mean? With a yellow center?"

Ms. Suarez seemed to study Laurel's face before replying. "It's probably a camellia. Many of them bloom early and can withstand the cold."

"Camellia," Laurel repeated carefully. "Thanks."

At the lunch break she grabbed a few granola bars, ran back to her room, and flipped through her flower book. Camellias stood for "unpretending excellence." So far the mystery message was "hope and true excellence." Nothing about love—so far. The bizarre part was that when she'd sniffed the bouquet outside her door that morning, when she'd traipsed through the garden, and then dissed Everett, she'd felt unusually hopeful and confident. And Miss Spenser had given her an A for "Excellent!"

CHAPTER FOUR
Rosemary to Remember

Friday afternoon, Laurel's fingers clutched the grass as Coach Peters read the team list.

"... Kate Samuelson, Gabrielle Tulum, Laurel Whelan, Ally Wilkins." The coach closed her notebook, and Laurel exhaled in a rush. She loosened her grip but didn't dare look around. Tara's name hadn't been called, along with those of several other girls. Coach was explaining how difficult the decision had been, but Laurel felt like doing a cartwheel. She low-fived Ally and hoped to walk back to campus with her new teammates.

It was Laurel's turn, however, to help Coach with the equipment. Kate, her arm around a weeping Tara, was long gone by the time Laurel set the last stack of orange cones in the coach's trunk. She slammed the door shut, grabbed her sweatshirt from the grass, and took off toward campus. She glanced at Miss Spenser's cottage as she passed, but the porch was empty.

The Avondale grapevine was failing Laurel. No one seemed to know anything about the budding romance. All anyone had talked about all day was pizza and movies tonight at Willowlawn. Laurel was positive that Kate, Tara, Nicole, and probably Ally would be going, but no one had invited her along.

Rubbing her goose-bumped arms, she yanked the dorm door open and trudged up four flights of stairs to Rose's lofty room. She rapped on the door, but there was no answer. She jogged down to the basement and peeked into the silent study room. Tall and pale with short brown hair, Rose was hunched over a book.

"Geek," Laurel whispered.

Rose smirked. "Takes one to know one."

"Yeah, yeah. You hungry?"

Rose's left eyebrow lifted. "Do I have to sit with the jocks?"

"Hardly." Laurel pushed Rose's backpack out of the way and sat on the table. "I made the JV team."

"Awesome," said Rose, lifting her right palm.

Laurel slapped it. "Everyone's going to Willowlawn for movie night, aren't they?"

"Everyone who's anyone," Rose said sarcastically. She

marked her place and set aside her book. "You should go, too, and meet people."

"Are you?"

Rose shook her head. "I already know everyone I want to."

I'm not going solo, Laurel thought. "What are you working on?" She turned Rose's papers around to face her. "Fi-toh-ree-med-tion. Huh?"

"Phytoremediation. It means using plants to clean up the environment," Rose explained. "There are these cool ferns that absorb arsenic out of contaminated soil. This science competition is coming up, and the winner gets an internship at the Smithsonian. I'm looking for ideas."

Laurel touched the picture of the fern; it reminded her of the feathery plant she still hadn't identified. She'd hung the mystery bouquet upside down in her wardrobe to dry.

Rose glanced at her watch. "I'm meeting Mina for dinner. Want to come?"

"Maybe, but I need to ask you something." Her name was Laurel, her mom was Lily, Rose was her cousin, and Rose's mom was Iris. Other than her mom's mom, Cicely, all the women of their family were named after plants and flowers. Laurel had once drawn their family tree for a project and traced the custom back generations.

"I know it's tradition and all, but why are we *really* named after flowers?"

Rose smiled too sweetly and batted her lashes. "Because we are fair and tender young things. And we smell good, too."

Laurel felt a wave of impatience. "Will you be serious for once? I need to know, and it's not like I can ask my mom about it." Silence reigned as she ignored "the Probe," the piercing stare of people—her dad, teachers, the dorm mother, and now Rose—trying to figure out whether or not Laurel was "recovering" from her mom's death.

"Sorry," Rose said contritely. "I can ask my mom. If you want."

Laurel knew her mom might have entrusted the birthday letters to Aunt Iris. "Ask her, but I want to know what *you* think, too."

Rose shrugged. "Somebody started it way back when, and it kept on going." She stuffed her book into her backpack. "But I've never felt like a Rose. They're too prissy and persnickety—"

"So be a *wild* Rose," Laurel said with a grin.

Rose nearly snorted. "Puh-leeeze. Any other burning questions?"

Laurel nodded. "Have you ever heard of the language of flowers? It's symbolic."

"Of flowers?"

"Each flower or herb stands for an emotion. It was big in the Victorian period."

"Which explains why I know *nothing* about it." Rose stood and swung her heavy backpack over one shoulder. "Not a fan of the Victorians."

Laurel hopped off the table and followed her cousin outside.

"You know, Grandma would know more about the flower names," Rose said quietly.

"So?" said Laurel. "When was the last time she picked up her phone or answered an e-mail?" Grandma had endured her daughter's funeral with stony and unrelenting silence, and Laurel hadn't heard from her since. Not a word.

"A valid point," said Rose. "You could talk to Mina. She likes flowers."

"Does she?" Laurel said as they reached an intersection of sidewalks.

"May Day is the only time people here pay attention to flowers, and that's over the top," said Rose. "People wear flowers in their hair and do this medieval skippy dance with ribbons around a big pole. I'm hoping they make it optional by the time I'm a senior."

May Day, thought Laurel. But it's not even April yet.

Rose bumped her arm. "Come with me. It's pizza night here, too."

Laurel was sick of people thinking pizza made everything all better. She wished she was on her way to Willowlawn chatting with Kate and Ally . . . keeping an eye out for Justin. A cool breeze lifted the hair off her neck and wafted a sweet scent to her. The sweetness spun gently through her head—just a hint of the tinglyness she'd felt around flowers lately. Somewhere an owl hooted, and she looked toward the garden.

Rose tugged on Laurel's arm. "C'mon. Don't be such a loner."

Laurel yanked back. She didn't feel like trying to fit in—yammering about nothing with Rose's friends on the fringe. "Next time. I'm really tired." She faked a yawn.

"I'm meeting Robbie for Sunday brunch at Willowlawn. Want to come?"

"I can't," said Laurel. "I'm at Westfall's table this week." Each Sunday after chapel the principal invited eleven girls from various grades to eat with her. Besides, Laurel would soon be spending spring break with Rose's annoying little brother—her dad was out of the country on business—and that was all the Robbie she could take. Still, visiting him might be the only way she'd get to see guys on a regular basis. Some girls bounced back and forth between the two campuses, but Laurel felt like she didn't have the secret password. Not yet.

"Rosie!"

They both turned to see Mina coming out of the dorm. The pink jewel in her pierced nose glittered against her mahogany skin.

"Hi, Laurel," said Mina.

"Hey." Laurel turned back toward the garden, where a radiant moon was rising above shadowy treetops.

"I adore full moons." Mina giggled. "Makes you want to howl . . . or something."

Rose held up her hand. "Be my guest."

Mina shrugged. "Maybe tomorrow night. You coming with?" she asked Laurel.

Laurel shook her head. "I don't feel like being inside." She lifted her face to the sky as Mina followed Rose. A translucent cloud blanketed the moon and divided its glow like a prism. A rainbow moon, she thought. Where's its treasure?

The garden lay beyond the lit sidewalks of campus, beyond the rounds of the night security guard, but Laurel walked toward it. Moonlight silvered the path at her feet. Like a nocturnal creature, she treaded lightly, her senses straining to make sense of the shadows. The owl hooted again, and her heart beat more urgently: *a-LIVE, a-LIVE, a-LIVE*, it seemed to say.

As she rounded a bend, her nose caught a sudden strong scent. It was fresh and invigorating, and she looked for its source. She rubbed the stiff branch of a low bush and lifted her hand to her nose. That's it, she thought. Crouching, she found a small marker spiked into the ground and read it by moonlight. "Rosemary."

A rosemary bush had grown by the back door of her old house, and Laurel could picture its tiny, purple blooms. Her mom had cooked with the herb and dried it for sachets. Laurel grabbed a branch but jumped back immediately. Something—or someone—had hummed. The low sound had vibrated through her body the moment she touched the rosemary. She looked around, but she was still alone.

"Mom?" she whispered to the sky. "What's going on? Help me. Please." She quickly broke off a branch and felt the hummy tingling start again.

Laurel took a deep breath and raised the rosemary with both hands. "Bright cut flowers, leaves of green, bring about what I have seen." Her fingertips seemed to spark with an energy she felt pouring into her, spinning her senses. "Yessss," she said as the fragrance transported her into . . .

Daylight. She was standing in her mom's garden. Her mom's hat was like a straw halo as she worked among velvety blossoms. Nearby, Laurel—a little-girl Laurel—dug in the dirt, hardly listening to what her mom chanted. She jumped up and filled her mom's outstretched hand with a shovelful of dirt. Her mom smoothed the soil between her fingers. Her smile was like a kiss, and her voice seemed to caress the air.

"Rosemary to remember,
With sage I esteem,
Thyme to be active . . ."

Thyme to . . . Thyme to be . . . Thyme to . . .

Time. Laurel's eyelids fluttered open.

"Mom!" she screamed, but she was all alone in the dark garden. She stared down at the rosemary she'd crushed in her hands.

"'Rosemary to remember,'" Laurel repeated. She'd remembered something she didn't even know she knew. She threw aside the branch in her hand and broke off a fresh one. Pressing it to her nose, she whispered her words, but nothing happened.

"Please," Laurel pleaded. "I *need* to remember." Her eyes scanned the moon-drenched foliage around her as she breathed in more rosemary. When she was little, she'd trailed her mom through countless gardens. She knew the soft fuzz of lamb's ears, the tang of mint leaves, and the stab of thorns. Her mom used to say the names of the plants and make Laurel repeat them.

"These are asters," her mom said.

"Astwews."

"Hydrangeas."

"Hydwanjus."

Her mother had sung and said rhymes about flowers all the time. Why can't I remember them now? Laurel thought. A rapid flapping above her head startled her, and she saw the silhouette of wings—the owl—flying away. She bent off several sprigs of rosemary and ran out of the garden.

As she hurried past a row of tall swaying evergreens, a high light seemed to wink at her. Laurel pushed aside the branches and stepped into a clearing, where a Gothic tower rose above an expanse of glass. The conservatory, she thought with a shiver.

Most Avondale buildings were symmetrical redbrick structures with white columns and trimmed pairs of boxwoods outside every door. The administration building had a white dome that copied Thomas Jefferson's nearby home, Monticello. In contrast, the conservatory seemed to be lifted out of a fairy tale. Moonlight gleamed on the copper roof and reflected off the glass surfaces. Gargoyles with fanciful animal faces stretched their mouths wide, as if awaiting a downpour.

Laurel looked back through the trees and could still see the path to campus. Taking a deep breath, she tiptoed to the front stoop to peer inside. The huge room brimmed with plants, so there had to be flowers. Laurel jiggled the knob, but the door was locked. Knocking loudly, she pressed her nose to the glass but saw no one. She'd waved to Ms. Suarez in the hallways, but the teacher hadn't mentioned a tour again.

Conservatories had always seemed like magical places to her. The outside world could be cold and dead, but whenever Laurel stepped inside the glass, the world burst into bloom. I need to be inside, she thought. She walked around the building looking for another entrance, until a gleam of reflected moonlight caught her eye. An engraved plaque was set high in the wall.

For dearest Gladys,

*May the rooms of your life be full of bright blossoms
and sweet scents, even in winter.*

*Yours always,
Edmund*

"Rooms of bright blossoms and sweet scents," Laurel echoed. "I like that." But she had no clue who Gladys and Edmund were. Clutching her rosemary, she jogged toward the artificial glow of main campus.

CHAPTER FIVE
Translations

The next Tuesday Laurel was ready and waiting. Every time anyone walked by her, she pretended to look for something in her backpack, but the landing where she stood had a perfect view of the sidewalk below. She'd see Justin before he saw her, jog down the stairs, and step right into his path.

But her plan was failing dismally, because he hadn't materialized. Her next class was on the other side of the quad and started in three minutes. Stifling a cry of exasperation, she grabbed her backpack and took off. The grassy quad was draining of students, and she heard a shout just as she reached the door of her building.

"Wait up, man!"

Justin and the guy with curly hair were dodging girls

as they ran toward the spot she'd vacated moments ago. His hair flew back from his shoulders, and he was laughing, taking long, steady strides. Laurel's heart beat as if she were running at his side.

The bell rang just above her head, and she covered her ears. "*Merde.*" Excessive crushing wasn't an accepted excuse for tardiness.

After class Laurel's Latin teacher asked to see her, and then she had to switch books at her locker. At every chance her eyes darted to the door Justin would use and down the sidewalk he'd come along, but she didn't see him again that day.

Nothing was going smoothly this week. Kate was the only person Laurel felt comfortable talking to about the flowers, but whenever she approached her, Tara or Nicole instantly appeared to whisk Kate off for some "emergency."

Laurel's rosemary experiments were failing, too. Since that evening in the garden, she'd tried to resurrect more memories of her mom. She tried rosemary with her special words, rosemary without her words, rosemary in the morning, rosemary at midnight, wet rosemary and dry, but she couldn't replicate the tingling or humming. Her paperback didn't list any other flowers for memory. Surfing online, Laurel had found long lists of flower meanings and sites about the language, but none mentioned tingling or humming or poetic words.

When she'd researched her English presentation, she'd had time only to glance through an antique flower book she'd found at the last minute. That book in the library tower was much larger and more detailed than her paperback and definitely deserved another look.

Soccer practice was canceled the Friday before spring break, so after class Laurel headed up the spiral steps of the library tower. Standing still in the quiet, turret-like room, she could almost feel her mother's sweet smile. Her mom had collected first editions of books, which were now prominently displayed at her dad's town house. The collection was one of the few relics of his former life that any stranger could see.

Setting her backpack on a desk at a narrow window, Laurel removed the heavy leather-bound book—*The Language of Flowers*—from its place. It was shelved in the reference section, so she wasn't allowed to check it out. Strips of ribbon, like the bookmarks found in the Bible, protruded from its bottom. Randomly she lifted one of the ribbons, turned to the marked page, and skimmed the list of floral meanings.

Liberty ⌢ Live oak
Love ⌢ Myrtle or rose

Love, forsaken ⌣ Creeping willow
Love, returned ⌣ Ambrosia
Maternal affection ⌣ Cinquefoil
Maternal love ⌣ Moss
Melancholy ⌣ Dead leaves
Mental Beauty ⌣ Clematis

Laurel guessed that moss might be for maternal love, because it hugged the coldest part of a tree. What were cinquefoil and ambrosia, though? How was a live oak different from a regular one? And *memory* wasn't even on the list. She reopened the book to another page marked by a ribbon: the author's acknowledgments. She was about to flip the page when a name caught her eye.

> In addition, I am eternally grateful for the
> invaluable encouragement and assistance of
> Miss Violet Evelyn Mitchell. Her knowledge
> and personal experience were beacons of
> light, like heavenly spheres, to my wayward
> wanderings. To her I extend a bouquet of
> white bellflowers for everlasting gratitude.

"What?" Laurel said, too loud. Violet Evelyn Mitchell was her great-great-grandmother's maiden name on her mom's side. Laurel flipped back to the title page; this edition had been copyrighted in 1899. Jotting numbers in her notebook, she calculated back through the generations. In 1899, Violet would have been about twenty years old.

Laurel felt a mix of curiosity and hope churn inside. Only one person would know if it was the same Violet, and that was Grandma. But Grandma lived like a hermit now, consumed by grief. She might as well die and get it over with, Laurel thought, but felt an instant spasm of guilt. Grandma had been a different person before. She was quiet and dignified, but her garden was like an exuberant extension of her true self. When they were young, Laurel, Rose, and Robbie would spend hours chasing one another and playing hide-and-seek on its paths. Hopping on a rope swing, they'd sail out over banks of azaleas. In spring it was like swinging over a rainbow.

Laurel slumped back and threw down her pencil. Grandma had checked out of life, and there was no point in asking her anything. Still, Laurel browsed the ribbon-marked pages, but she couldn't find a clear pattern or anything that seemed like a clue. The illustrations of the tussie-mussies were as elaborate as her mom's botanical prints. She took out a notebook and copied down the entire text of the author's acknowledgments before she replaced the book on the shelf.

"Violet Evelyn," she whispered as she descended the

tower stairs. Did anyone ever leave flowers outside your door?

"Pssst."

The whisper startled her. Nicole was peering up through purple-rimmed glasses.

"Oh," Laurel said. "Hey." Her eyes darted around, but she didn't see Tara.

"What were you doing up there?" Nicole asked.

"Just some research."

Nicole leaned around her to look. "I've never gone up."

Laurel shrugged. "It's just a bunch of old books." She stepped aside to let Nicole pass up the stairs. "See ya."

"Later," Nicole said.

Laurel leaned against the heavy wooden doors of the library, which opened into the warmest day yet this spring. Girls were in shorts playing Frisbee on the quad, and a few had spread out blankets. Patches of daffodils and pastel hyacinths brightened the fronts of several buildings. Closing her eyes, Laurel raised her face to the streaming rays.

Make me bloom, too! she thought as the warmth penetrated her skin. Everywhere she turned, everywhere she walked these days, there was some new patch of color, some new fragrance to entice her. Colors, scents, petals were so much more vibrant this spring than ever before. She'd been surrounded by flowers her whole life, but they'd never made her body tingle and buzz.

Laurel craved flowers in her hand but hesitated to pick any publicly. Instead she headed to a strip of ground behind the library where a few days ago she'd noticed thick leaves poking through the mulch. Rounding the tower, she felt a sudden and soaring delight. A few red tulips had bloomed along its south-facing wall. She fell onto her knees and cradled a blossom between her hands. Its satiny petals were still closed, but she gently pried them open to breathe in a subtle but spicy scent.

"Mmm," she said. Red tulips were for a "declaration of love." She'd wanted some for her presentation, but they hadn't been blooming yet.

"What's with you and the flowers?" said a voice just behind her.

Laurel startled and turned. Nicole was standing only a few feet away.

"You scared me." Laurel spread her hand over her racing heart. This path was roundabout to anywhere. "Are you following me?"

"Why would I?" Nicole broke off a tulip stem. "Does this flower mean something? In that language?"

Laurel's eyes traced the lines of tulips. "Something about declaring love, I think."

Nicole lifted a flower to her face. "Are they supposed to smell good?"

"Here. Hold the petals open like this."

"I still don't smell anything."

"Let me try." Laurel bent toward the one in Nicole's hand. The scent was gorgeous, like simmering spices from faraway places. "Do you have a cold?"

"No," Nicole said sullenly.

Laurel stared at the red petals in confusion. "Are we allowed to pick flowers?" she said, and immediately wished she could unsay it. The question sounded so babyish.

"Who cares?" said Nicole.

Laurel winced as Nicole broke off another bloom. "I—uh—just wondered." She pulled herself away from the tulips and turned toward main quad.

"You're making another fussy flower thing, aren't you?" said Nicole.

"What?" Laurel turned around.

"At your presentation you said there was some old book in the library."

"So?"

"Sooo, if the book's really old, it's in the tower, and you were just there, probably looking at it. So you're making another bouquet," Nicole said smugly. "Right?"

"Wrong," Laurel said.

Nicole took a step closer. "You should make Tara one."

"Why?"

"She wanted that one in class."

Laurel threw up her hands. "But I'm not making any."

Nicole frowned. "Whatever. It's not like they matter." Striding past Laurel, she waved to someone else and hurried across the quad, still holding the two tulips.

Laurel turned back to the red blooms. The book said they declared love, but how could anyone translate? After one more whiff of tulip, Laurel walked back to the quad and scanned the patchwork of blankets for someone she knew. Dodging a whirling Frisbee, she spotted Rose.

"Hey." Rose looked up at Laurel through oversized sunglasses. "You look stressed, *mon amie.*"

"Always." Laurel threw her backpack onto the blanket and sat down cross-legged.

"Fifteen minutes of sun will promote vitamin D production and boost your mood."

Laurel had to smile. "Thank you, Dr. Rose."

"No problem." Rose lay back, her pale arms straight at her sides.

Laurel couldn't lie down or slow her thoughts. "Hey, do you know anything about Violet Evelyn Mitchell?"

"Who?"

"Violet Evelyn. Our great-great-grandmother."

"Enough with the flower names." Rose leaned on her elbows. "If I ever have a daughter, I am absolutely *not* naming her after a stupid flower."

"But there has to be a reason they *all* did it."

"Family pressure," said Rose. "My mom caved. Did you hear from her yet?"

Laurel shook her head. The only messages in her in-box were lame jokes her dad had forwarded from his BlackBerry. He required a daily e-mail exchange, but neither of them managed to talk about anything important.

"She's always swamped during tax season," said Rose. "Want me to remind her?"

"That's okay." Aunt Iris had said she needed to put in a full day at work, so she wasn't picking them up for spring break until the next morning. Laurel watched the Frisbee zoom back and forth. "So, does your mom ever hear from Grandma?"

Rose shook her head. "Mom says she's still grieving, but . . ."

"But what?"

Rose sucked in her lips. "I shouldn't talk."

"*Say* it."

"Well, it's like Grandma's punishing us. Mom said she didn't act like this when her own husband died. I mean, she has another daughter and grandchildren. Life goes on."

"Maybe she doesn't want it to." Laurel lay back on the blanket and closed her eyes.

"You are such a loser, man." A male voice yelled, so

nearly all the heads on the quad turned toward it. Laurel felt her hopes gather, until she recognized Everett.

"Spare me," said Rose, flipping onto her stomach.

Laurel took inventory of the quad. Everett and his gang were hanging out by the cheerleaders, who were yelling in unison and shaking their butts. Ally was attempting to teach Kate how to throw a Frisbee while Tara and Nicole lurked and whispered.

That makes *one* thing Kate's not good at, thought Laurel. A few more guys appeared intermittently, but none of them was Justin. Rose started snoring, so Laurel jumped up and yelled to Ally. The Frisbee came toward her fast and smooth, but she misjudged the timing and it hit her fingernails.

"Oww." Laurel shook her hand and picked the Frisbee up.

"Nice catch, Whelan," Tara snickered.

Laurel felt irritation flicker. She'd missed the catch, but she knew how to throw.

"Look out!" Nicole yelled. Tara barely had time to throw up her hands to block her face.

"Sorry," Laurel said. "I thought *you* knew how to catch."

"Perfect toss," Ally said, jogging over to Laurel. "Wanna play?" They threw the Frisbee back and forth until a bank of clouds gradually darkened and cooled the quad. Laurel woke up Rose as the first raindrops fell.

Back in her room Laurel sent a quick e-mail to Aunt Iris, asking her the questions Rose hadn't answered. Her aunt's response arrived a few hours later.

> I guess I named Rose after a flower because I didn't want to be the first to ditch tradition. She thinks that's idiotic, I'm sure, b/c I'm not into flowers. I always preferred numbers. :-)
> Why don't you send Grandma a letter or call her and ask? We can't give up on her!!!!
> You asked if I have the rest of the letters? What letters? I can't wait for your visit. See you tomorrow!
> Hugs, Aunt Iris

Laurel scowled at the screen. *But Grandma's given up on herself—on all of us.* Her aunt clearly didn't have the birthday letters, but Laurel would ask her about Violet as soon as they were alone.

One thing seemed certain to Laurel: her mom wanted her to wonder about the language. The lyrical words had popped into her head like she'd always known them, but she must have learned them from her mom. Other memories—vital memories—had to be buried deep inside her. She had to find her way back into her mother's garden, even if it no longer existed. She pulled a sprig of rosemary from a vase and closed her eyes. She had to make this memory magic—if it was magic—all by herself.

"Please let me remember something," she said. "Please, God, *please*." Holding the stem to her nose, she raised her eyes to a botanical print and stared until its colors blurred. "Bright cut flowers, leaves of green—"

Like a match struck into flame, the tingling sparked and spread through her body. Energy hummed into her, and she shut her eyes to ride its wave. . . .

Flowers—red, white, and yellow—next to the sickbed filled Laurel's vision. Her mom's pale forehead was wrapped in a bright scarf, and her eyes were closed. But she was smiling at something Laurel had said.

Laurel kept reading from the book in her lap, even when she saw the sheer curtains flap upward on an otherwise still day, even as the rasp that was her mom's breath ceased, even as the hospice nurse came to check her mom's pulse, and as the nurse's eyes fell heavy upon her. She kept reading when her dad came and kissed his wife's cold lips and didn't know what to do with his only child who was reading out loud to a dead woman. She kept reading because The Little Prince *was one of their favorites. Because throughout the dying months, her mom had asked for chapters from that book.*

"Read me the part about the geographer and what's ephemeral."
And Laurel read.

"Read me the chapter about taming the fox." And Laurel read.

When, on that last day, her dad took hold of the book and tried to pry it away, Laurel yanked it back and ran from the room and from their house . . . into the leaning sunflower tower they'd planted only months earlier when her mom was still strong enough to sit up in her garden and direct her daughter's hands.

Her mother's rosy presence, which Laurel sensed with every taut cell of her body, was still wrapped around her. Sheltered by the canopy of sunflowers, she read on, ignoring the urgent cries of her dad. She knew her mom was still listening, because her mom finished every book she ever started.

The familiar words on her tongue filled Laurel with peace and nearly hypnotized her into believing that her mom was still alive . . . still listening. The last picture. The last paragraph. Laurel read on more deliberately, savoring each syllable.

> "And if you happen to pass by here, I beg
> you not to hurry past. Wait a little, just under
> the star! Then if a child comes to you, if
> he laughs, if he has golden hair, if he doesn't
> answer your questions, you'll know who he
> is. If this should happen, be kind! Don't
> let me go on being so sad: Send me word
> immediately that he's come back. . . ."

"Come back." As soon as she'd released the syllables, Laurel longed to take them back forever unspoken —to hold them and her mom there. Come back. Laurel closed her eyes and held her breath for fear of reminding her mom where she now belonged.

But Heaven beckoned. Like a scarf unwrapping from her neck, the warmth, the peace slowly dissipated, leaving Laurel cold and exposed. She shivered and stared at the closed book in her lap. . . .

"No!" Laurel opened her eyes and hurled the rosemary across her dorm room. "I don't want to remember that!" she screamed.

PART TWO
ISO *Kindred Spirits*

"Flowers have spoken to me more than I can tell in written words.
They are the hieroglyphics of angels, loved by all . . . though few can
decipher even fragments of their meaning."
—LYDIA M. CHILD (1802–1880), AMERICAN ABOLITIONIST
AND WOMEN'S RIGHTS ADVOCATE

CHAPTER SIX
Red Tulips

New blossoms—pink, white, and lavender—blanketed the azalea bushes on the path back from soccer after spring break. It was a tunnel of flowers—a fragrant and magical pathway. Watching Kate's blonde ponytail swing from side to side, Laurel wondered if Kate—or anyone else—could smell the azaleas. She breathed in the fruity scent and wished, not for the first time, that whoever had left the mystery bouquet was at her side. That person *had* to be a kindred spirit. Those flowers had faded, and she'd told no one. Was that a mistake?

Over the break she'd asked Aunt Iris about Violet and if she knew the language. But her aunt had no answers and kept saying she was "knee deep" in tax returns. There were hardly any flowers growing in her yard or even in her neighborhood. Most nights Rose stayed up late watching sci-fi movies with Robbie and then slept until noon. Laurel's dad called from Brazil only once. Laurel took long walks by herself, searching for fresh rosemary, and even asked Aunt Iris to buy her some at the supermarket. But still she didn't remember anything important. Laurel had been surprised by her own eagerness to get back to Avondale.

Now she jogged to catch up with Kate. Ally wasn't back from break yet. "Hey, do you know any guys who like flowers?" she asked.

"You mean Willowlawn guys?"

"Yeah."

"None that would admit it."

Duh. Laurel switched tactics. "Have you ever had a class with Ms. Suarez?" She'd headed to the conservatory as soon as she got back from break, but no one had answered her knock, and the golf cart wasn't parked there.

Kate bounced a soccer ball off her thigh and caught it. "We had to take her earth science class last year."

"What's she like?" asked Laurel.

"Fine, but kinda out there." Kate bounced the ball off her other leg.

"What do you mean?"

"Sometimes I just don't get what she's talkin' about.

She gets all excited about stuff, like watersheds and butterfly migration. Tara says she had a nasty divorce right before she came here to teach."

"She's so nosy," said Laurel.

"Ms. Suarez?"

"No. Tara." Laurel grabbed the ball out of the air, dropped it, and dribbled ahead.

Kate caught up and stole the ball back. "But Tara knows a ton. It's . . . useful."

Cringing with impatience, Laurel booted the ball loose from Kate and ran after it as it rolled toward the teacher cottages. She trapped it and gestured for Kate to catch up.

"Look!" she whispered. "Miss Spenser's all dressed up." The teacher was wearing heels and pearls on a Monday evening. "Maybe she has another date. C'mon."

Miss Spenser was opening the driver's door of her car.

"Hi, Miss Spenser. Where are you off to?" Laurel called out.

"You look elegant," said Kate. "That lipstick's a great color for you."

"Why, thank you," said Miss Spenser. "A—um—a friend is cooking dinner for me."

"Who?" Laurel and Kate said simultaneously.

Miss Spenser shook her head. "You two pop up at the oddest times."

Laurel and Kate exchanged a knowing smile.

"You can't go *yet*," said Laurel.

"Excuse me?" said Miss Spenser. "And why not?"

"Because you need flowers," Laurel said. She pictured Miss Spenser carrying the red tulips that grew near the library.

"Riiight," said Kate. "Exactly. You *need* some."

"And why do I need flowers?" asked Miss Spenser.

Kate gestured like a game-show host. "Because they'll complete your ensemble?"

"And you can thank the friend who's making you dinner," said Laurel. "You know: 'Say it with flowers.' You look empty-handed."

Miss Spenser smiled. "Your earlier bouquet *was* lovely. How long might this take?"

"Ten minutes?" said Laurel.

"All right," said Miss Spenser. "I could use a sip of water."

"Great!" Laurel pulled Kate's arm and whispered as they hurried away. "Run to the bathroom and get some wet paper towels. Please."

"Cool," said Kate. "Got it."

Laurel let her legs lengthen into a sprint as she headed toward the library. She rounded the tower and gasped. Hundreds of tulips—red, yellow, and white—had opened their petals to the warming sun. Yellow tulips were for "hopeless love" or friendship, she remembered, and she wasn't sure about white, so she picked only red. A hint of their spiciness swirled around her, but she tried not to breathe it in. She gathered a dozen—enough to speak loudly for Miss Spenser's shy heart.

Moments later Laurel was dashing back to the teacher cottages. Nicole couldn't smell the tulips, but Laurel hadn't said her words then. In her mind's eye she pictured Professor Featherstone kissing Miss Spenser's hand, the two of them twirling and waltzing with happiness.

"Bright cut flowers," Laurel said, "leaves of green. Bring about what I have seen." The scented energy rocketed up her arm and flowed through her body.

Kate was just ahead on the path, but so was Tara. Breathless, Laurel held the flowers farther from her face and hoped no one else could hear the humming that filled her ears.

Tara shook her head. "More flowers? Are you playing Little Red again?"

Kate glanced anxiously from Tara to Laurel. She handed the wet paper towels to Laurel who—her hands shaking visibly—wrapped them around the stems. The humming, the tingling inside her was building.

"I *like* Laurel's flowers," said Kate.

"You're not supposed to pick them on school grounds," said Tara.

Laurel mirrored her glare. "Are you going to tell on me?"

"I'm no snitch," said Tara. "Just tell me who they're for."

Suddenly dizzy, Laurel looked pleadingly at Kate.

"Um," Kate started, "she's givin' them to Ms. Suarez . . . who needs them for some meeting thingy at the conservatory. Right?"

"Right," Laurel panted. Her hands were stinging, and she could barely stand still.

"La-ame," said Tara. "But why should I expect more from you?"

"Got to run." Laurel flashed Kate a look of gratitude and took off. Miss Spenser was waiting in her car, and Laurel almost tossed the tulips through the open window.

Miss Spenser caught them in her lap. "Oh! How wonderful. Where did you get these?"

The fierce energy sailed out of her, and Laurel sighed in relief. "By the library. There are tons blooming."

"You know, students aren't supposed to pick flowers." Miss Spenser tried to look stern, but her finger was stroking one of the velvety petals.

"Keep the bouquet with you the whole time," Laurel said. "Especially when you're with the professor."

Miss Spenser's eyebrows lifted. "How do you know that I'm seeing him?"

Laurel felt like her mind had stumbled. "But you *are*, aren't you?"

"Yes, but you're becoming quite dictatorial these days," Miss Spenser teased, suddenly girlish. "Thank you, dear. You're an angel."

Waving, Laurel watched the taillights disappear down the tree-lined road and crossed her fingers. This is so crazy, she thought, walking to dinner. But it feels right.

By the time Laurel reached the dining hall, Kate's table was full. Laurel had a quick meal with Rose and Mina and then headed for the dorm's basement, which held the mailroom. An occasional postcard from her dad was all she could realistically hope for, but she couldn't stop herself from checking. The other letters her mom had promised were somewhere in this world.

"Where's Tara?" Laurel whispered to Kate, who showed up moments later.

"Nicole's room," said Kate. She picked up a package and read the label. "Yay, it's for me. My mom's the queen of express mail."

Laurel's box was empty as usual. Her dad's easy smile flashed into her mind, and she couldn't help wondering if someone new was filling his time.

Kate also had a card in her box, which she handed to Laurel as they walked up the stairs. "My dad *adores* goofy cards," she explained. The card was funny, but Laurel had to fake a laugh. Kate's life seemed charmed. Tara's door was closed, a sure signal she was still elsewhere.

"You got the tulips to Spinster Spenser, right?" Kate whispered.

Laurel nodded. "Want to come in for a sec?" She shut the door behind them.

"Wow," said Kate. "Your room's so neat. Mine's a mess."

Laurel shrugged. Her room was one of the few things in her life she had complete control over.

Kate sat on the bed and opened her package. She pulled out a tie-dyed shirt with a scoop neck and held it against her chest. "My mom has awesome taste, doesn't she?"

Laurel could barely speak through the waves of jealousy. Her mom would *never* buy her another shirt. "Yeah. Great."

Kate met Laurel's eyes, and her mouth opened in recognition. "Oh. I'm sorry. You can borrow it any time, if you wanna."

Tara's distinctive laugh rang out in the hallway.

"Thanks for covering for me," said Laurel.

"I hope she doesn't find out," Kate whispered. "It's pretty rough on her bad side."

"I know. I'm there."

"All she talks about now is Everett. She's in *luv*." Kate wrinkled her nose and looked around. "Your room smells good. What is it?"

"Rosemary." Laurel broke off a piece and handed it to Kate. "Here."

"Mmm. It smells soft."

"'Rosemary to remember,'" said Laurel. The next phrases echoed through her mind. *With sage I esteem, thyme to be active*—but the last line still eluded her.

"'Rosemary to remember,'" Kate repeated. "Can it *make* you remember?"

"Maybe," said Laurel. "Here, smell it."

Kate bent over the herb and sniffed obediently.

"Now close your eyes," Laurel said. "Does it make you see anything or feel anything?"

"Like what?" said Kate, her eyes still closed.

"Like something you forgot about. Something you didn't even know you knew."

Kate blinked. "Is it supposed to?"

Laurel shrugged. "It's probably just an old saying."

"Can I keep it anyway?" asked Kate. "I need all the rememberin' help I can get."

"For what?"

"Pivotal dates in world history. That gigantic test is comin' up. Did you forget?"

Laurel shook her head as she glanced at her homework calendar. She had more important things to remember. "Ugh. I've got a Latin quiz tomorrow. Want to study together?"

Kate shook her head. "I don't take Latin."

"But it's required."

"No, it's not. I take Spanish."

"So do I," said Laurel, frowning. Latin had simply appeared on her Avondale schedule, and she hadn't thought to question it.

Movie night was on Avondale's campus that Friday. Tara had practically superglued herself to Kate, and Ally had a cold, so Laurel walked into the auditorium with Rose and Mina. She scanned the rows of heads for Justin. Kate—wedged between Tara and Nicole—waved as Laurel passed. Tara had stuck a red tulip over one ear.

Copycat. Laurel's stomach tightened in fear. Did Kate spill to Tara?

Some Willowlawn guys were turned around in their seats facing Kate and Tara, and Laurel recognized one of them. The gorgeous one.

"Hey! You're that flower girl," Everett called out. "Laur-*elle*. Qué pasa?"

"Hi. Uh, fine." Her face reddened as she sat down next to Rose.

To her surprise, Everett hopped over several guys, crossed the aisle, and knelt on the empty seat in front of her. "I'm kinda disappointed, Laur-*elle*."

Thinking she smelled a prank, Laurel looked around

suspiciously. She wanted him gone until she noticed Tara watching them. "Why are you disappointed, Ev-rett?"

"You didn't bring me a fuzzy-wuzzy." Everett shook his head in phony distress. "Again. You know, I was really hoping for more from our relationship. Flowers are sooo special to me."

Laurel knew better than to trust him, but she could play this game. "You call this a relationship? I haven't heard from you in weeks. Not even a dandelion."

Everett grinned. "You mean there's still hope for me?"

Rose leaned forward. "Not in this lifetime, Ev."

"Oh, hello, Rose." Everett bowed with mock formality. "Nice seeing you. You leave your broomstick in your locker?"

Rose slapped the chair in front of her. "Ha-ha. You're such a wit. Or is it twit?"

Everett held up his hands. "Oooh, Rose is thorny tonight. Get it?"

Laurel had to smile, but Rose scowled. "Like I haven't heard that one."

"Look, I'm just trying to get to know Laur-*elle* here," said Everett. "The new girl."

Rose shooed him. "Go sit with your little buddies, Ev. She's my cousin."

Everett glanced between them. "Now I see the family resemblance. Are you a flower girl, too, Rosie?"

"No," Laurel said with a firmness that surprised even herself. "She's not."

Rose's eyebrow lifted at her as the lights flashed.

"Got to go." Everett stretched his hand toward Laurel. "Later, Laur-*elle*."

But Laurel was struck with a jolting thought as she shook his hand. Everett was the only guy who seemed remotely interested in her flowers. Was there any way *he* had left the mystery bouquet? That made no sense.

"Congratulations," Rose whispered. "You've attracted the attention of the most obnoxious, arrogant fathead on the whole Willowlawn campus."

"Don't hold back now," Mina said.

"You know I can't stand him," hissed Rose.

Laurel tried to focus on the images flashing on the screen, but Everett's antics confused her. She half expected the whole room to turn around and start laughing at her, like this was some premeditated prank.

When the lights finally went up, she spotted Justin at the rear of the room, but it was too crowded for her to catch up. They followed everyone to the dining hall, where popcorn and sodas were being served. Laurel's eyes darted around as they grabbed bags and headed for some chairs in a corner.

"What's the deal with you and Everett?" Laurel asked Rose.

"That boy drives me insane," said Rose.

"I've heard this saga," said Mina. She wound her way back into the crowd.

Rose shook her head. "Last semester Everett and I got assigned to work on a project together because of this math test we both aced. He was less than worthless. I totally carried him, and then he bragged about the blue ribbon *I* won."

Laurel spied Everett with a red tulip between his teeth. Tara was pretending to be miffed. "So, he's actually smart?"

Rose threw a popped kernel up and caught it in her mouth. "Irritatingly so. He's gifted but totally lazy. He just coasts and mooches and gets away with it."

Laurel nodded, but the word *gifted* caught her attention. *All of us have gifts we are meant to share*, her mom's letter said.

Kate emerged from the crowd and sat down on the empty chair next to Laurel. "Y'all like the movie?"

"Just super," said Rose.

Laurel offered Kate some popcorn, but her eyes gravitated back to Everett. The tulip was tucked behind his ear now, and she wondered if he—or Tara—could smell its spicy scent. Is it sending any messages? she thought.

Kate leaned close. "So, what's up with you and Everett?"

"Huh?" said Laurel, but her face felt hot.

Kate elbowed her. "I saw you two chattin' it up before the movie. And you were just starin' at him."

Laurel shrugged. "He's . . . entertaining, but you said Tara liked him."

"She does," said Kate. "Do you, too?"

"Puh-leeeze." Rose's head fell backward. "Say it ain't so."

"It ain't so." Laurel said as she caught Tara watching them. "Why are you asking?"

Kate sat up straighter. "You talked to him a while, and I didn't know you knew him."

"We barely talked." Laurel felt a sudden flash of doubt about Kate's motives. "Did Tara tell you to quiz me?"

"No," Kate stammered. "I was just wonderin'. I thought we were friends now."

"I thought so, too," said Laurel. "But 'friends' don't report back to other people."

Kate's arms crossed tight on her chest. "So don't tell me anything."

Rose stood. "Let's get out of here, Laurel. It's too crowded."

Laurel stood uncertainly and then trailed after Rose. Halfway across the room she turned, expecting to see

Kate chasing after Tara, but Kate was still slouched in the chair.

Mina sat cross-legged on the floor outside the dining hall, and Rose sat down next to her. "You really think Kate's reporting back to Tara? I thought she was your bud," said Rose.

Laurel's spirits sagged as she slid down the wall beside her. "I don't know."

"You should have made something up—something juicy about you and Everett."

Mina leaned forward. "What's juicy?"

"Nothing." Laurel let her head fall back against the wall. "My life is not juicy." It's nothing like I thought it would be.

"Your life *could* be juicy," teased Rose. "But promise me you won't do anything moronic like liking Everett. *That* would send me over the edge."

Mina laughed. "You're already over."

Laurel crossed her heart. "I promise."

Mina elbowed Rose. "Even you have to give Everett credit for pulling off the mother of all pranks. Bubble gum and helium balloons: pure genius. Mr. Rodriguez was ready to call the SWAT team when the balloons started popping in rapid fire."

Rose frowned at her. "Just wait. I have two more years to top it."

Out of the corner of her eye Laurel saw several guys coming toward them, and Rose called out, "Hey, Justin. Alan."

Laurel's head snapped sideways.

"Hey, Rose," Justin said. "Hi, Mina." He was wearing jeans with holes at the knees and a black T-shirt. His eyes fell on Laurel, and his smile seemed to warm the air. "Hey."

"Hi," Laurel said. Her voice sounded squeaky.

Alan held up his hand and slid down the wall on the other side of Mina.

"This is my cousin Laurel," Rose said. "These guys are on the debate team with me."

Justin hesitated and then settled onto the floor near Laurel. "Victorian flower messages, right?"

Laurel nodded. "You saw my *amazing* report."

"Yeah. Tough crowd, but you hung in there."

"Did I have a choice?"

"Guess not, but Spinster Spenser's all right, isn't she?" he said.

"Yeah, I really like her. You should hear her read poetry." Especially *luv* poetry, Laurel thought, remembering an amazing poem about petals and fingers. She glanced at Justin's long smooth hands.

Rose tapped Justin's knee with her fist. "No more school talk, Geek-asaurus Rex. It's the weekend now. Laurel's a big jock like you."

"What do you play?" Justin asked.

"Soccer," said Laurel. "Left wing. JV. What about you?"

"I run cross-country." He pointed at the guy with brown curly hair who was talking to Mina and Rose now. "Alan does, too. What the—"

Justin jerked his head back as something flew past his nose and landed in Laurel's lap. It was a red tulip. Totally confused, Laurel picked it up and looked down the hallway. Everett waved to her, but Tara stood next to him, her face twisted in anger.

A declaration of love? thought Laurel. No way.

Everett gestured toward her. "She's the flower girl," he explained loudly. "She gets *all* the flowers."

Laurel's face was as red as the tulip, but she longed to breathe in its rich spiciness, for Justin to breathe it beside her. She ignored the question in Rose's eyes, because Tara was already glowering down at them.

"That one's mine," Tara said, holding out her hand.

"Uh, sure." Laurel thrust the flower up at Tara, who walked off in a huff. One of the petals had fallen into Laurel's lap.

Laurel's eyes flicked back to Everett, who was laughing loudly with his friends. "Is he drunk or something?" she whispered as she stroked the soft petal.

"Who knows," said Justin. "He's almost always a jerk."

"Always," added Rose.

"Great," said Laurel. "And he's weird about flowers, too."

"Hey, my mom's pretty into flowers," Justin said. "I should get her that book you mentioned. What's it called again?"

"*The Language of Flowers*," said Laurel.

"Can I get it online?" asked Justin.

"I think so. It would make a great gift, like for Mother's Day. And you could give her a tussie—" She stopped.

Justin was saying something else, but Laurel couldn't focus on his voice because of the sudden and searing pain in her chest as her own words sank in like a hatchet. I don't ever have to buy a Mother's Day present again, she thought. Ever.

Clutching her stomach and pressing her spine against the wall, she managed to stand up. *Merde.* She'd embarrassed herself in front of this crowd too many times already.

"Laurel? You okay?" Justin looked up at her. His hand reached toward her, but if she took it, she might disintegrate.

"I—um—" Her eyes burned as she pushed through a forest of bodies.

"Laurel!"

Rose's voice was behind her, and she heard Mina call too, but tears already streaked her face. No one could see her like this. She ran outside and collapsed behind a wide tree to gulp the cooling darkness and wait for the pain to weaken.

CHAPTER SEVEN
Wild Orchid

Saturday morning passed in a fog, but that afternoon Laurel crisscrossed the gardens in search of the feathery plant that *somebody* had included in her mystery bouquet. She had no luck there but was determined to resolve this once and for all. Finding an illustrated guide to herbs in the library, she narrowed it down to two: dill and fennel. She was pretty sure she'd recognize the smell of dill—like in pickles. Fennel, the flower book said, meant "worthy of all praise . . . strength."

"Hope, excellence, praise and strength." Laurel closed her eyes, but she couldn't barricade herself against the tidal wave of disappointment. Absolutely no one would choose those flowers for a *luv* bouquet. She blew out the last glimmer of hope she was still carrying for a secret admirer. All day long a tiny piece of her kept hoping

Justin would get in touch with her—to check up on her—but he didn't. I have too much baggage for anyone, she thought that night.

The next morning she was so wrapped up in her own misery that it wasn't until chapel was almost over that she noticed Ms. Suarez sitting in the pew next to Miss Spenser and the professor. Staring at the backs of the teachers' heads, she determined one thing: Ms. Suarez *had* to tell her more about her mom.

After dismissal from chapel Laurel waited by a large holly tree near the back door, but then she saw Ms. Suarez's golf cart already heading toward the garden. I'll look like a dork if I run after her, she thought. Miss Spenser's laugh rang out nearby. The professor was standing close to her, almost whispering in her ear, and her lips seemed about to smile.

My tulips rock, Laurel thought. Her favorite lines from the E.E. Cummings poem Miss Spenser had read bubbled into her mind:

> your slightest look easily will unclose me
> though i have closed myself as fingers,
> you open always petal by petal myself as
>   Spring opens
> (touching skilfully, mysteriously) her
>   first rose

What would that feel like? Laurel wondered. To be opened "petal by petal"? Miss Spenser was definitely blooming under the professor's attentions.

"Looks like their romance is—uh—*budding*." Kate gave Laurel a knowing look.

"I think geezer public displays should be banned," Tara whispered behind them. "Who'd want to kiss someone that ancient? And if I have to listen to another one of her stupid *luv* poems—"

Laurel spun around on Tara. "I *love* her love poems," she said. "They're sweet."

Tara smirked. "Like anyone cares what *you* think. You're psycho."

Nicole laughed, but Kate cleared her throat. "I like the love poems, too. It's not like we *all* have to like the same thing *all* the time." Kate went on. "That'd be lame."

All trace of triumph had vanished from Tara's pale face. "Whatever. Are you coming already, Nicole?" Nicole was trying not to smile, but followed her anyway.

Laurel met Kate's eyes. "Thanks," she mouthed.

Kate took a step forward. "I am *not* her puppet."

"I know," said Laurel. "Are you hungry?"

"Always," said Kate.

After brunch they walked back to the dorm together, and so Kate was standing at her side when Laurel found a note taped on her door:

Laurel:

Please come to the conservatory for dinner
tomorrow after soccer. —G. Suarez

"G.?" said Laurel, unlocking her door.

"Geneva Suarez," said Kate. "Must be nice. No teacher's ever invited *me* to dinner."

"She knew my mom," said Laurel. And she's going to tell me *all* about her.

"Really?" Kate followed Laurel into her room. "But you're not gonna eat *inside* the conservatory, are you?"

Laurel slipped off her uniform skirt and pulled on a pair of jeans. "Why not?"

Kate frowned. "'Cause there's this rumor it's haunted."

"The conservatory? You're kidding."

Kate shook her head solemnly. "*Tons* of people think so. Just get out before dark."

Every winter after the lights and warmth of Christmas had dimmed, Laurel's mom would stare out at the browns and beiges dominating her garden and throw up her hands.

"I can't take it!" her mom would cry. "I need colors! I need scents!" As soon as possible, she and Laurel would head to a conservatory. Their color-starved eyes would feast on shades of pink, red, lavender, and green on their "winter pilgrimage," as her mom called their road trips.

Over the years Laurel had visited so many conservatories on the East Coast that she wondered, as she walked to meet Ms. Suarez, why her mom had never mentioned Avondale's. In fact, her mom hadn't talked about the school much at all, other than to shake her head at the drug scandal that had made national headlines the year before Laurel arrived. They never once discussed her applying, maybe because both of them were clinging to hope for a cancer miracle that never came.

Outside the Avondale conservatory a tall woman dressed in shorts and hiking boots was cutting faded blooms off some bushes. Laurel's shoes crunched across the gravel driveway. "Ms. Suarez?"

"Excellent," Ms. Suarez said. She had a smudge of dirt across her cheekbone. "Thanks for coming." Taking off her gardening gloves, the teacher pulled the conservatory door shut and locked it. She picked up a backpack and handed it to Laurel. "Let's hurry so we have time to picnic." Ms. Suarez slipped another pack over her shoulders and walked around the building toward a path into the woods.

Laurel hurried to catch up. "But I thought you were going to give me a tour."

Ms. Suarez's pace didn't slacken. "It can wait. I want to show you something that can't."

"What?"

A smile flickered across the teacher's lips. "You'll see."

The trail sloped upward through a meadow and into cool, shady woods. The surrounding silence was broken only by the snap of twigs underfoot and the twitter of birds scattering before them. Laurel's legs were exhausted from soccer, and her stomach was tight with hunger, but Ms. Suarez's excitement was catching.

At the crest of the hill the teacher finally stopped and took out a water bottle. Laurel did the same and gazed at the vista spread before them. The valley below and the hills beyond were greening with the rise of spring. Worn to smoothness by seasons of wind, rain, and snow, the Blue Ridge Mountains receded in shades of grayish purple. Strands of white clouds streaked the evening sky like unspun cotton candy.

"Beautiful, isn't it?" whispered Ms. Suarez.

Laurel nodded. A red-tailed hawk glided into view as it rode the warm air currents swirling up from the valley. Ms. Suarez bent to pull a leaf off a plant, crushed it between her fingers, and held it to Laurel's nose.

Laurel sniffed. "Is it mint?"

Ms. Suarez nodded. "Some thoughtful person planted it years ago for refreshment. And over there's your namesake. It's evergreen, but it won't bloom for a while." She was pointing to a bank of shrubs covered with clusters of shiny, elliptical leaves.

Laurel walked over and cupped the waxy mountain laurel leaves in her hand. "My mom loved this plant," she said. "We used to hike whenever it was blooming."

"You should come back later this spring," said Ms. Suarez. "It will be lovely then. Speaking of lovely, have you ever seen a wild orchid?"

Laurel let her hand drop. "I don't think so."

"Then come on." Zipping her water bottle into her backpack, Ms. Suarez started down the slope below their feet, expertly zigzagging on a barely visible path. Loose stones rattled down as Laurel's feet slid, but Ms. Suarez didn't slow her descent. Like a grounded monkey, Laurel used both hands to grab one branch then another. Ms. Suarez was waiting for her halfway down the slope.

The damp ground sucked at their shoes as they walked across the hill, and Laurel breathed in a tangy, earthy scent. Suddenly the low sun slipped loose from a cloud, and the hillside was flooded with golden light. The sun cast its sheen onto every unfolding bud, every soft petal—enchanting the air. Laurel reached out to caress a fresh leaf on a curving branch.

Ms. Suarez turned around and smiled broadly. "Look."

Laurel followed the direction of her hand. At the center of wide green leaves, a flower glowed white as a summer cloud. Its silky petals stretched up from a green stalk like fairy wings unfolding. Its lower lip pouted pinkly. It was like a miracle, pure and luminous against the heavy browns of the forest floor.

"Wow!" Laurel crouched before it.

"Yes, yes!" Ms. Suarez nearly sang the words as she knelt next to her. "She is a queen. *Cypripedium reginae,* a queen lady's slipper."

"I've never seen one," Laurel said.

"They're rare in the wild." Ms. Suarez put her hand on Laurel's forearm. "But I'm bringing her back. I've colonized queen ladies in several places and protected them over the winter with a mini-greenhouse. This ecosystem just might work."

Laurel couldn't pull her eyes from the exquisite blossom, not even when Ms. Suarez started humming a lilting tune.

"She's blooming early this first year, but if she's discovered, she could be dug up by amateurs," whispered Ms. Suarez. "Promise to keep her a secret."

"I promise," Laurel whispered.

Ms. Suarez's fingers grazed a petal. "Unfortunately, she has no scent. The pollinators are already eager, so she doesn't need to exert herself to attract them."

Something this beautiful *has* to have a scent. Impulsively, Laurel leaned forward and sniffed a delicate fragrance. She closed her eyes and pictured a wisteria vine that had twisted through a trellis in her mom's garden. Purple flowers hung from it like airy grapes, and a delicious scent descended like rain.

"Mmm." Laurel's nose touched the orchid as she inhaled deeply.

"No!" Ms. Suarez's hand was on her shoulder, pulling her back. "Not too much."

The fragrance had somehow transformed. Its sweetness was cloying, like overripe fruit on the point of decay. Laurel stood up, but her body felt extraordinarily light. The hillside swam before her eyes. She staggered and grabbed the trunk of a small tree.

Not la-la land. Not now. "What's happening? I feel so weird."

"Oh, Laurel. I—" Ms. Suarez's hand covered her mouth, but Laurel could tell from her eyes that she was smiling—widely. "Wow."

Wiggles and flashes of light danced before Laurel's eyes, but a hand took hold of her arm to steady her.

"Let's sit over there," said Ms. Suarez. "Farther away."

Laurel took a tentative step forward, because the ground was coming at her in waves. "Whoa." She bent her knees like she was surfing.

"This way." Ms. Suarez led her to a wide log. "Okay. Now sit down and breathe slowly." She pulled off

Laurel's backpack and handed her the water bottle.

Ms. Suarez's face hovered above her, single then double. She spread a large cloth near Laurel's feet. "She's powerful, isn't she?"

"Wha-at?" Laurel's own voice sounded distant.

"The orchid—the queen lady's slipper." Ms. Suarez shook her head and laughed. "I think you're high on her perfume."

"High? Is this what it feels like?"

Ms. Suarez handed her a sandwich. "Here. You'll feel much better if you eat something. Now where's that orange?"

Laurel's mouth watered at the scent of food, and she bit into the sandwich eagerly. Ms. Suarez squeezed a piece of orange skin so that its zest squirted into the air.

"Perhaps I should have waited." Ms. Suarez passed an orange section to Laurel. "But the queen is with us such a short time."

The queen. Laurel squinted back at the glowing bloom, but she could smell only orange now. "But why did you say it doesn't have a scent?"

"It doesn't. Not for most people."

Laurel took a deep breath to clear her head. "What do you mean?"

"Not everyone can smell that orchid. I wanted to know whether or not *you* could."

"Why?"

Ms. Suarez met her eyes as they ate. "Because that tells me something—something important—about your nose. Yours is very sensitive."

Laurel rubbed the tip of her nose. "It is? Is that weird?"

"It's . . . unusual," said Ms. Suarez. "It's a real gift to be able to smell such a fragrance when most of the world can't. Now eat up."

A real gift. Laurel dutifully took another bite. Her mom had told her to nurture her gifts. *Only then will you bloom fully,* the letter said.

"Orchids are fascinating flowers." Ms. Suarez's dark eyes sparkled with enthusiasm. "Did you know that in Victorian times, professional orchid hunters would travel to the farthest, most dangerous corners of the world in search of exotic new species? The hunters were paid by wealthy collectors who wanted the prize orchids for their personal conservatories. Occasionally the hunters even died on their quests."

Laurel swallowed. "They *died* for a flower?"

"Not just any old flower." Ms. Suarez's eyes were dark and intense. "What if you discovered an amazing bloom that no one has ever seen before, whose scent no one has ever inhaled? Can you imagine the thrill of that?"

Laurel closed her eyes, but her head swirled. She threw her hands on the log to catch herself.

"Have some more." Ms. Suarez handed her a section of orange and bit into one slowly. "We all need a great love in our lives. Something to arouse our deepest passions. Something we might be willing to die for."

Laurel looked back at the luminous bloom. *To die for?*

"So," said Ms. Suarez. "Tell me about that bouquet you made for Miss Spenser."

Laurel sucked in her lips. "I didn't exactly make it *for* her. I mean, it was for my presentation, but I— it just seemed like the tussie belonged to her, that she'd like it."

"She did." Ms. Suarez's eyes lingered on Laurel's face. "And your mom told you about this language of flowers, right?"

Laurel stuffed the last orange slice into her mouth. "Kind of. I found out about it because of her—something she wrote me. And then I did some research."

"Has anyone else mentioned it?" Ms. Suarez asked. "Anyone in your family?"

Laurel shook her head. "It's so old-fashioned. Nobody even knows about it."

"True," Ms. Suarez said, frowning at the ground.

Laurel asked the next question on a hunch. "But *you* know all about it, right?"

Ms. Suarez rolled her napkin into a ball. "I'm familiar with it. But we should head back; it will be dark soon. How do you feel? You're still pale."

"Okay, I guess." Laurel could focus better now, on a slim distant tree, on the persistent tapping of a wood-pecker high above their heads. She stood up but had to step back to keep her balance.

"You sit. I'll clean up." Ms. Suarez shook out the cloth and repacked their things.

Laurel turned for a last glimpse of the orchid. What's the queen's meaning in the language? she wondered.

On the trek back they spoke only to direct each other's feet. Questions simmered in Laurel's mind, and images of the queen lady's slipper flashed before her, but she had to concentrate to navigate the darkness. If she twisted an ankle, soccer season was history.

When they finally reached the conservatory, Ms. Suarez put a hand on her shoulder. "Sure you're all right?"

Laurel nodded, but she wanted to collapse into bed. Her head was pounding.

"Can you walk back alone?"

"I'm fine."

"Good," said Ms. Suarez. "We'll talk soon."

Laurel was already underneath the evergreen branches when Ms. Suarez's voice turned her around.

"Wait!" Ms. Suarez jogged toward Laurel. "I—I think it's best for you to stay away from orchids. At least for now."

"Why?" asked Laurel.

"They might make you feel dizzy, like the lady's slipper did," explained Ms. Suarez.

Like *all* the flowers. Laurel reached up to push a long-needled branch out of her face. "What kind of trees are these?"

"Cedars," Ms. Suarez whispered. "Cedar for strength. Good night, Laurel."

"G'night, Ms. Suarez." Hidden by the cedars, Laurel watched the teacher hurry into the conservatory. She's not afraid of any ghost, Laurel thought. The inside of the building lit up, until the tower shone like a light-house above the wind-tossed trees.

CHAPTER EIGHT
A Certain Mystique

Holding the principal's note that had unexpectedly summoned her out of class later that week, Laurel
walked down the empty hallway. She heard voices in
Mrs. Westfall's office as she knocked.

"Come in," called Mrs. Westfall.

Laurel's mouth dropped open. Her dad, handsome in
his navy blazer and a red-striped power tie, was standing
beside the principal's desk.

"Dad!" Laurel said. "What are you doing here?"

"Can't a daddy surprise his little girl?" he said.

Laurel leaned into his open arms. His musky aftershave flooded her senses, but she hadn't seen him since
he'd moved her in, and she had no one to hug at Avondale.
He kissed the top of her head.

Mrs. Westfall stepped around her desk. "Your father has business in Charlottesville this afternoon, so I've given him permission to take you out of classes. I'm sure you'll make up the work promptly."

"Yes, ma'am."

"Laurel speaks very highly of her teachers here," said her dad.

She pursed her lips. He's such a politician, she thought. What's today's agenda?

Mrs. Westfall smiled. "I understand she's doing well in her classes."

"I'm not surprised." Her dad squeezed her shoulder.

The bell rang for the end of the period. "Let's go now," Laurel said. She didn't want hundreds of hallway eyes fixating on them.

"You'll want a coat," said Mrs. Westfall. "It's going to pour. April showers—"

"Bring May flowers," Laurel finished.

Tara was the first to spy them at the lockers. "Hi, Laurel," she said sweetly. "Is this your dad?"

Laurel felt only disgust at her phoniness, but her dad swallowed the bait.

"Are you one of Laurel's friends?" He shook the hands of Tara, Nicole, and some sophomore whose name Laurel couldn't remember. Her dad would have remembered. It was one of the reasons he was such a good lobbyist, her mom always said. Most Saturday evenings Laurel had sat cross-legged on her parents' bed while her mom slipped into silk and heels to dress for another "important" party.

"Every party's important," her dad said. "You never know *who* you'll meet."

"Whom you'll meet," her English-teacher mom corrected, and winked at Laurel.

With the guest list in hand, Laurel had often quizzed her mom. "Joe Mickleman."

Her mom's elbows thrust up as she fastened a strand of pearls. "Don't tell me."

"Want a clue?"

"Maisy," her mom said. "Maisy Mickleman. Sounds like a character out of a Dickens novel, don't you think?"

Laurel nodded. "Congresswoman Jeanie Gozanski."

"Married to Al Doorman, who sells real estate in—oh, Timbuktu?"

Laurel fell back giggling. "It's Al Bourman, Mom. Not Doorman. From Texas."

Now Laurel punched her hand through the sleeve of her raincoat. Did that happen before or after the diagnosis?

"She's a great wing, Mr. Whelan." Kate bumped Laurel playfully, and Laurel realized she'd zoned out.

Again. "Bring me back something edible," Kate added.

"Ka-ate?" Tara called from down the hall. "Are you coming?"

Her dad held out his arm, but Laurel waved it away. She almost pulled up her hood as they started across the grass toward the parking lot but stopped herself. She'd spoon-fed Tara enough material already, over the last few weeks.

"My car's there." Her dad pointed to a red convertible, illegally parked in the front circle.

Laurel stopped walking. "When did you get a new car?"

"Last week. She's nice, huh?" Her dad shrugged. "I'll put the top up."

Suddenly aware of a scent even stronger than his aftershave, Laurel turned in a slow circle, looking and sniffing for its source. She spotted a large bush in front of the domed building. Although it was leafless, its branches were entirely covered by coral flowers. When she leaned in, its blooms smelled like fresh peach juice running down her chin.

"Come here!" she yelled to her dad. "This bush smells amazing."

Her dad reached for a branch and then shook his hand. "Ouch," he said. "It's armed."

"But the flowers, aren't they delicious?"

Her dad leaned in cautiously. "I don't smell a thing, honey."

"But it smells like—" Laurel hesitated. Ms. Suarez must be right about her nose, her gift. She felt giddy with the fragrance. "Do you know what kind it is?"

He shook his head. "That was your mom's department."

Heavy raindrops began to dot the sidewalk, and they sprinted for the car. Her dad was uncharacteristically solemn as he navigated the curvy road to a nearby diner. Glancing at his profile, Laurel wondered again why he'd come.

"Hey, did you sign me up for Latin?" she asked as they entered the diner.

"Latin?" Her dad shook his head. "You filled out your own schedule. I trust you to do that stuff."

"But I didn't pick Latin. I thought it was required."

"Maybe it was a mistake."

"Maybe." Soon they were seated in a booth and ordered omelets. The silence felt awkward, until her dad reached across the table to squeeze her hand.

"Hey, I ran into Anna's mom on the Hill," he said. "Anna hasn't heard from you in ages. Did you all have a fight?"

Laurel shook her head. Anna had been one of her best friends in her old life. But she went to a different school, and Laurel wanted a new life. New friends. "We don't have much in common anymore."

"But you'll see her at home this summer. I'll forward her new e-mail to you."

"Fine." Once again the silence between them expanded until the waitress set down two mugs, and Laurel wrapped her hands around the steaming hot chocolate. Her dad took a sip of his latte.

"Earlier—" He cleared his throat. "When you stopped to smell those flowers, you reminded me so much of your mom. She couldn't walk by a flower without sniffing it."

Laurel ripped off a piece of her napkin and rubbed it into a ball. Her heartbeat quickened with her question. "Why did Mom like flowers so much?"

"Beauty. Fragrance. They seemed to have a certain mystique for her."

"Mystique?" she asked. "What do you mean?"

Her dad took another sip of coffee. "After your mom first convinced me to buy that rickety farmhouse, I used to sit outside and read the Sunday papers, beginning to end, while you napped in your stroller. We'd roll you into a shady spot, and Lily would wander off to find something in bloom. Then she'd tie the flower upside down above your head, like a talisman."

Laurel couldn't help smiling. "A talisman?"

"A good luck charm. Your mom was full of old-fashioned quirks like that." He seemed to look past her. "Some days she would just disappear into that garden."

Chocolatey warmth flowed down Laurel's throat as his memory became hers.

"Sometimes I called out her name, but she wouldn't answer. I'd look, but I couldn't find her." He shook his head. "It was like she became one with that garden."

Her dad met her eyes. "But as soon as you let out the tiniest whimper, she was there. Leaning over you and stroking your cheek."

The waitress set their meals on the table.

"Thank you." Her dad turned his plate halfway around. "Mothers have a way of materializing when they're needed."

Laurel stared at her plate. She couldn't count the number of times she'd desperately wanted her mom in the past year. "Not if they're dead," she whispered.

"Laurel," her dad chided. "She'd give anything to be here."

"But she's not." And she told me nothing about talismans, nothing about the flower language. Laurel picked up the salt and shook it over her eggs, but she'd lost her appetite. There was a pungent smell in the air, strong yet familiar. She scrunched her nose and glanced at the vase, but the flowers were fake. The only plant nearby was a bunch of leaves artfully arranged next to her omelet. She picked up the herb and sniffed. It was definitely the source.

"I'm glad to see you've made friends," her dad went on. "I was . . . concerned."

Laurel shrugged as she rolled the herb between her fingers. "Yeah, a few."

"And the soccer team—exercise is so important," he said. "It helps everything: your schoolwork, your emotions—"

"You sound like a pamphlet about teenage health," Laurel interrupted sarcastically. She felt a ripple of irritation, because she wanted him back on the topic of her mom and flowers. "Do you remember the rhymes Mom used to say when I was little?"

He shrugged. "Maybe."

"Not like normal rhymes, but ones she made up. Do you remember those?"

"Not off the top of my head," he said.

"But she used to give people flowers all the time, right?"

Her dad nodded as he speared a piece of omelet. "When we first dated, she'd slip a flower into my buttonhole or petals into my pocket."

Laurel sat up straighter. "Really? What kind?"

"Yellow ones and red—I'm not much good at their names. I used to tease her."

"Who else did she give flowers to?" she asked.

"Almost everyone. She was always generous with her garden."

Or maybe she knew people *needed* her flowers, Laurel thought. Like I know.

Her dad wiped his mouth. "You should ask Cicely about it. She brought a whole bushel of flowers from her own garden to the funeral, remember? She wouldn't let us throw the florist's onto the casket even though we'd already paid for them."

"Why not?"

"I have no idea," her dad said dismissively. "Have you heard from her at all?"

"No. *Nada.*"

"Damn. I was really hoping you would." He folded his napkin and set it next to his plate. "I didn't tell you this because you had enough to worry about at the time, but after the funeral Cicely went home and burned her garden."

"*What?*"

"She set every last plant on fire," her dad said. "A neighbor called the fire department, but most of the garden was ashes by the time they arrived. They could only save a few big trees."

Laurel was speechless. Photographs of Grandma's garden had appeared in national magazines, and she had shelves full of gardening prizes. She'd given tours every spring and designed a special "touch and smell" section for elementary kids to visit.

"Cicely should be on antidepressants," her dad said. "I've tried to call her, but I haven't heard back. Not since she wrote that letter."

"Letter?" Laurel's stomach dropped. "What letter?"

Her dad pushed his plate away. "I told you about that, didn't I?"

"No. You *didn't*." Laurel pressed the leaf between her fingers. Its scent seemed curiously stronger.

"Last fall I FedExed her a note saying that you were interested in Avondale, so she wrote a personal letter to Mrs. Westfall. They don't usually allow midyear transfers. She must have some clout as an alumna."

Laurel felt a flare of anger. "You *never* told me that."

"I thought I did," he replied.

"But you didn't," Laurel said, savoring the strange rush of emotion. Her blood was pulsing at her temples. "And it's totally important. You never tell me anything!"

Her dad frowned. "That's a gross exaggeration."

"No, it isn't. You didn't tell me about this letter or the flowers at the grave or Grandma torching her garden.

How am I supposed to connect with her if I don't know what's going on?"

Her dad's forehead creased. "You're right. I shouldn't be trying to shelter you, but God knows you've had to deal with enough already."

"More coffee, sir?" asked the waitress.

Her dad smiled up at the young woman—too widely, too happily, too handsomely for Laurel to take. She pushed her plate away. Her anger had never felt so pure and precise, like something she could aim.

"Grandma probably *tried* to call you," she said. "You're probably never home, and she hates answering machines."

Her dad turned his mug around. "Well, it's no fun coming home to an empty house."

"Empty?" Laurel said, mockingly sweet. "I'm sure you have all kinds of *friends* sleeping over now that I'm out of the way."

"What?" There was a warning edge to his voice. "You know I wanted you to stay with me."

"But your life is sooo much easier without me, isn't it? You can just cruise around in your hot little convertible and pick up—"

"Stop it, Laurel. This isn't what I came to do."

"What *did* you come to do?"

"Look. Can't we have a decent conversation without

accusations?" he whispered. "This is getting nowhere. Iris said—" He stopped himself, but it was too late.

"So that's why you're here." Laurel's anger flashed through her like a purifying fire. "Aunt Iris told you you *had* to come."

"That's not it. I've wanted to come. Truly." Her dad folded his hands together. "Please, Laurel. Life's too short to argue. Your mom wanted us both to keep living, to move on. I—I'm trying to do that."

Laurel tossed the mutilated herb onto her plate. "*Eventually* move on, Dad. Not immediately."

"Look." Her dad's voice was infuriatingly calm. "I'm sorry if anything I've done has offended you, but I am going to live my life as I see fit. Understand?"

Laurel's insides were boiling, but she felt sharp and potent. "And I'm going to live my life as *I* see fit."

Her dad shook his head. "You never used to be like this. Are you seeing the counselor like I suggested? Maybe you should ask her about antidepressants."

Laurel took a deep breath and screamed so that every head in the restaurant turned to look at them, "I DON'T NEED ANTIDEPRESSANTS!"

Her dad dropped Laurel off in the circle just as classes were changing. Her heart still beat fast, and her skin felt hot. She felt energized and powerful, because she'd said everything she *really* felt, the things simmering under the surface . . . the things she'd been afraid to say.

Justin was less than ten feet away before she noticed him. Her stomach clenched, and she stopped walking. What was he doing here *today*?

"Hey, Laurel," he said hesitantly. He crossed to her side of the sidewalk. His straight hair was pulled into a ponytail, but some of the strands had fallen out, framing his face. "How's it going?"

"Okay. But why are you here?" She had to calm down. She still felt tight and angry—exactly how she didn't want to be with Justin.

"We had a special speaker for Latin, and this was the only time she could come."

"Oh." Laurel suddenly realized she had no idea what Rose had told Justin after she ditched movie night or if he even knew about her mom. She took a step closer. "I'm really sorry I—uh—disappeared the other night."

"No problem. You didn't miss much."

She couldn't agree. "Is there a movie at Willowlawn this week? Maybe Rose and I could come over."

"Probably," Justin said. "But the track team's leaving at five A.M. Saturday morning for an away meet, so I'd have to skip it."

"Oh." She looked down at his sneakers, which were black with black laces. Across the quad a bus horn beeped three times. Why can't *anything* go my way? she thought.

Justin took a step sideways. "I've got to make that bus or I'll miss bio lab. See you around?"

"Yeah. Sure." Frowning, she watched him dodge clumps of girls as he jogged to the circle. Does he just feel sorry for me? she wondered.

There was a pop quiz on top of every desk in her world history class, and several girls looked stricken. Laurel was sick of pretending to care about civilizations dead for thousands of years. The only history she really wanted to know about was the flower language and how it was woven into her mother's life. That wasn't on anyone's syllabus, and there was only one person on campus who knew anything about it.

After classes Laurel waited until the last girl had left Ms. Suarez's room before she slipped inside. Leafy plants sat on a shelf built along the length of the windowsill. "Ms. Suarez?"

The teacher looked up from her grade book. "Laurel, hi. How are you?" She closed the book and glanced at her watch.

Laurel turned to make sure they were alone. "May I talk to you?"

"Sure, but I just have a minute. I need to copy something for a meeting."

Laurel slid into a desk, and Ms. Suarez sat nearby, crossing her boots under a crinkly velvet skirt. "What's up?" the teacher asked.

Laurel picked the easy question first. "You know those azaleas on the way back from the soccer fields?"

Ms. Suarez nodded. "Avondale's azaleas are spectacular, aren't they?"

"The flowers smell fruity, but I thought azaleas didn't have a scent."

"Most don't," said Ms. Suarez. "Modern breeders tend to emphasize the size and color of the bloom, but wild, native azaleas will smell delightful."

Laurel concentrated on the next question that beat in her mind.

Ms. Suarez stood up and grabbed a packet of papers. "The same is true of petunias. Modern varieties have had the scent bred out of them, except for the purple ones. For some unknown reason purple petunias have held their fragrance. Now I—"

"One more thing." Laurel stood in her path. "Someone left a bouquet with three flowers outside my door in March. Do you know anything about that?"

Ms. Suarez smiled. "You found me out."

Laurel's face flushed with a mixture of relief and embarrassment. She felt stupid to have held on to the hope of some mysterious guy for so long. "Why did you do it?"

"Your mom was my friend, and I thought you could use a boost."

"But why didn't you sign your name?"

Ms. Suarez shrugged. "You didn't know me then. Besides, everyone loves a little mystery in her life, right?" She lightly touched Laurel's shoulder. "We'll talk soon."

"I still want to see *inside* the conservatory," Laurel said petulantly.

"Come by any time." Ms. Suarez called as her heels clicked down the hallway.

At soccer practice Laurel ran hard and took out her frustrations on the ball, but on the way to dinner her energy began to ebb. Then nagging doubts sneaked in as her mind replayed the scene at the diner. It had felt so good, so cleansing, to say every single thought that had popped into her head, however mean. But she couldn't believe she'd actually screamed at her dad in front of all those people. She felt all twisted up and wrung out. Nobody seemed to have room for her in his or her life, not her dad or Grandma, not Justin or Ms. Suarez.

Even though it was still light outside, Laurel undressed and pulled a threadbare nightgown over her head. It was tight across her chest—she never wore it in the hallway—but it was one of the last things her mom had bought for her. She curled up in her mom's chair and pulled an afghan across her lap.

Laurel's memories were a mix of good and bad, light and dark. She had no idea how to dispel the darkness and summon the light. Tonight she needed to remember something—anything—to tell her what her mom wanted her to do. She twisted some myrtle—which also meant "pleasing reminiscences"—around a stem of rosemary.

Dear Lord, Laurel began as she rubbed the leaves, thank you for my blessings. Please—She stopped. What she truly wanted was impossible. She lifted the plants to her nose and whispered her words.

As she closed her eyes, her chest ached to be held against the emptiness widening inside. Sometimes she could barely remember what her mom looked like or how her mom's hand felt sifting through her hair. Now Laurel felt herself drifting on the scents ... spinning ... and her mom's face was ...

leaning close to kiss her tingling cheek. Her mom's fingers were warm as they closed around Laurel's hand, pulling her from the chair.

Up . . . up, and they were flying into the moonless night beneath a luminous lace of stars. Below them flower buds glowed like colored Christmas lights. A hillside of forsythia branches shone in tufts of yellow fluorescence. Her mom grasped her other hand, and they twirled around and around, their feet dancing above the golden blooms. Her mom began to laugh, and her laughter was like bells ringing: peals of resonant silver. Laurel threw her head back to spin faster and faster.

But her mom stopped and pulled her away. They were sweeping through the sky again but faster now, and her mom seemed intent on some distant matter. Emptiness streamed through Laurel like ice water, and she shivered. In one smooth and gentle gesture her mom pulled her close, so that warmth flowed from her body. They halted midair above rows of gray buildings and slowly descended into day-time. Not buildings—tombstones. Laurel tried to twist away, to go back to the dance, but two faces fixed her attention.

Grandma and Ms. Suarez stood above an open grave, holding buckets that brimmed with flowers. When one spoke, the other threw a bloom onto the casket.

"Amaranth for immortality," Grandma said in a voice worn brittle by grief. Ms. Suarez threw a rust-colored bloom. "Flowering reed for confidence in heaven to come."

"Zinnia for thoughts of absent friends."

The voices continued the litany, but Laurel's eyes were drawn to a flash of light behind them. The brightness coalesced into a shim-mering column, a lovely, ethereal being whose colors shifted like light from a prism. More of these creatures appeared and surrounded the grave. Her mom reached for her hand, and together they wove in and out of this circle of radiance. The creatures sang, and their song sparkled over Laurel like sunlight on water.

One being extended something to Laurel as she passed, and she reached for the flower. Fiery energy exploded up her arm, but she couldn't let go. She held a rose, a perfect rose that shimmered all colors. Laurel could feel its pulse, its power seeping into her, synchronizing with the rhythms of her body.

"What is it?" she asked her mom, who was becoming sparkly, too . . . pearl-like . . . peaceful. She kissed Laurel's cheek, and her image wavered. . . .

"No!" Laurel screamed. "Come back! Please!"

There was an awful noise, and her eyes blinked open. Someone was banging on her wall, on Tara's side, and she sat up. The fingers of her hand were tightly bent, as if still clutching the flower the angel—Were they really angels?—had given her.

Laurel shivered, and a seam in the nightgown ripped. She closed her eyes and tried to imprint an image into her memory—the image of the two of them dancing above the forsythia. Her mom had loved to dance. Every year Laurel could remember, they'd danced barefoot in their garden on the vernal equinox. It was the first day of spring when the sun hung directly over the equator, and the hours of light and the hours of night were nearly equal. After that equinox the light lengthened, and the northern hemisphere bloomed.

Even when winter was reluctant to loosen its grip,

their bare feet would melt dark footprints as Laurel and her mom danced on a thin layer of white frost. Around and around their footprints circled, but they never felt the cold through their laughter.

But the vernal equinox had already passed this year.

Next year, Mom, Laurel promised. I'll dance for both of us.

CHAPTER NINE
Matchmakers

Laurel couldn't believe Grandma had burned her garden, that such an Eden was now ashes. One night she called and let the phone ring forty-two times before hanging up. She sent an e-mail to the only address she had, but it bounced back. Still, Grandma had written a letter to Avondale, so she wasn't completely beyond reach. Lying on her bed, Laurel stared into a coral flower she'd cut from the bush near the front circle.

Bright cut flowers, leaves—the words tumbled into her mind, and she grinned. In her dream Grandma had thrown flowers on the grave and knew the language. Laurel hadn't found the name of this coral flower yet, but pansies were still blooming. She ran outside, picked a perfect one, and glued it to a piece of stationery. Just under the petals she wrote:

Pansy for thoughts of you.

Dear Grandma,

I found an antique Language of Flowers *book in the Avondale library. The author of the book thanked Violet Evelyn Mitchell for her help. Do you know if that is our ancestor Violet? I'd love to know more!*

Love, Laurel

P.S. If you don't know about the language, I'll explain it.

Please, God, make her answer, Laurel prayed as she dropped the note in the campus mailbox on her way to Saturday brunch later that day.

"Hey." Kate ran down the library stairs toward Laurel. "Have you eaten yet?"

Laurel shook her head. "What are you doing in the library so early?"

Kate rolled her eyes. "Extra-credit project. I hadn't done the reading for that pop quiz, but I did ace that huge test. Your rosemary was awesome."

"Really?" said Laurel.

"For sure. I felt all confident," said Kate. "I always study, but then I second-guess myself and change my answers all around. Can I have some more?"

"Rosemary? Sure." They walked into the dining hall together.

"Hey, what's up with Spinster Spenser?" Kate grabbed a tray and piled on some food. "I haven't seen that professor around."

"I don't know." Laurel's eyes found Miss Spenser at the faculty table reading the paper alone. Was it time for another tussie? "Let's go find out." They carried their trays to her.

"Hi, Miss Spenser. May we join you?" Laurel asked.

The teacher smiled. "Of course. Quite a few teachers are away."

"So, how are you?" asked Kate.

"Just fine." Miss Spenser folded her paper. "But if I know you two, you're up to something. Honestly, girls, you're like a couple of matchmakers."

Laurel and Kate grinned at each other.

"So you're having fun?" asked Laurel.

Miss Spenser couldn't keep her lips straight. "It's written all over my face, isn't it?"

"He liked my red tulips?" asked Laurel.

"Oh, yes!" said Miss Spenser. "I've never encountered tulips with such a marvelous scent."

Laurel felt a thrill of triumph. "I'll find you more for your next date."

Miss Spenser dabbed her lips with a napkin. "That's very kind but not necessary."

Yes, it is, Laurel thought. She wanted her teacher to find love almost as much as she wanted it for herself.

"The professor's a busy man, you know." Their teacher's face seemed to droop a little. "He had to go back to Richmond unexpectedly to take care of some business and isn't sure when he'll return."

"But he'll be back?" Laurel had seen the flash of doubt Miss Spenser was trying to suppress.

"He *has* to come back," said Kate. "Then Laurel will give you tons of flowers."

"Exactly," Laurel said. "Your life should be full of 'bright blossoms and sweet scents.'"

Miss Spenser's coffee mug stopped halfway to her lips. "'Bright blossoms and sweet scents,'" she repeated. "That's what Gladys's plaque says."

Kate tilted her head. "What plaque?"

"It's outside the conservatory," Laurel explained. She turned to Miss Spenser. "You knew Gladys and Edmund?"

Miss Spenser frowned at her. "I'm not *that* ancient."

"I didn't mean—" Laurel began, but Miss Spenser waved away her apology.

"Gladys was my great-grandmother, and Edmund was her husband," said Miss Spenser. "I'm very proud of her, because she was quite the feminist for her day. She's the one who insisted they build a girls' school along with Willowlawn."

"What about the conservatory?" Laurel asked. "Was that her idea, too?"

"Possibly. If I remember the family lore, that was Edmund's gift to her," Miss Spenser said. "Her family—she came from England—had marvelous gardens and a renowned conservatory. He tried to recreate that for her here."

"Cool," said Kate.

"Laurel, you should speak to Ms. Suarez about this," added Miss Spenser. "One of her ancestors was involved with Gladys's conservatory. He had something to do with our orchid collection."

"Orchids?" An image of the lady slipper in the woods flashed into Laurel's mind. *Stay away from orchids,* Ms. Suarez had said. At least for now.

"What about orchids?" Tara knelt on the bench next to Kate, and Nicole slid next to Laurel, who now felt surrounded.

"Avondale's orchids," said Miss Spenser, glancing at her watch. "When it was first built, our conservatory was renowned for its collection. However, I have an appointment to make. See you soon, girls." She picked up her tray and left.

Tara took a blueberry muffin from Kate's tray and broke off a piece.

"Hey," said Kate. "I'm starvin'."

"Like always," said Tara. "What were you all talking about? You never sit here."

Laurel spoke before Kate could. "Avondale's history. I find it fascinating, don't you? Miss Spenser was just telling us—"

"This place sucks." Tara threw down the muffin and stood up. "You coming?"

Kate shook her head. "I'm still eatin'."

"Later, ladies," said Nicole as she trailed Tara.

"You gonna eat that biscuit?" Kate reached toward Laurel's tray.

"It's all yours." Laurel's mind puzzled through this new information about the conservatory.

Kate broke the biscuit in two and poured honey on half. "Gladys is the ghost."

"What?"

"That ghost in the conservatorium. Everyone calls her Gladys."

"After the founder?" Laurel frowned. "You really believe there's a ghost? Have you ever been inside?"

Kate nodded as she chewed. "Ms. Suarez took us there to study some plants, but it was during the day. I wouldn't go into that spooky place at night." She exaggerated her shiver so Laurel had to smile.

They finished eating and headed outside. Tara and Nicole were sitting on a bench farther down the quad, so they cut diagonally across the grass.

"Tara knows something's up," Kate whispered.

"We can't let her find out about Miss Spenser's flowers," Laurel insisted.

"She hates being left out," said Kate. "And she'll find out. She always does."

"Not this time," Laurel said, trying to sound more confident than she felt.

"But she might be able to help," said Kate. "She knows a ton."

"She'll try to take over," snapped Laurel. "She's critical of everything I ever do."

"Wait a sec." Kate stopped and skipped a circle on the green. "I'm brilliant."

"What?"

"The professor's *got* to come back on May first. Everybody from Willowlawn comes here for May Day."

Laurel nodded, catching Kate's enthusiasm. She'd forgotten about May Day. "But he's new, right? He might not know about it."

"Miss Spenser could call him," Kate suggested.

"We have to make sure he finds out. Do they send out invitations?"

"The alumni office might. Want me to go by tomorrow and see?"

"Perfect," said Laurel. She was already wondering if Miss Spenser would prefer a tussie in her hand or flowers for her hair.

"Hey, um, can you make a tuzzy-muzzy for me, too?" said Kate.

"Tussie-mussie. You really want one?" said Laurel.

"Duh. Almost everybody will have flowers," said Kate. "It's not like I understand what's goin' on, but I might as well have *your* flowers."

Laurel nodded thoughtfully. "It could be like an experiment."

"How?"

"To see whether *my* flowers are really different from everyone else's."

As May Day approached, Laurel looked for ways to rekindle the professor's feelings. Miss Spenser seemed almost depressed in class, and Laurel couldn't bear the finality of her loneliness. She headed to the conservatory whenever she could but kept missing Ms. Suarez. She couldn't help feeling that the building held an answer to something—for her or Miss Spenser—if she could get inside.

Laurel had just stepped out from the cedars after

another futile attempt when someone called her name, and she cringed. She wanted a flower in her hands—a talisman against Tara and her mind games, but nothing was within reach.

"I *need* to talk to you," Tara said. "Now."

"I've got practice soon," Laurel protested.

"Just a few minutes of your precious time," Tara said sarcastically. "Nicole says you're making more of those bouquets."

Laurel's mouth tightened for the lie she was about to tell.

"And I saw all those red tulips you gave someone," said Tara.

"So?"

"So, I want some, too," said Tara, taking a step closer. "You know that guy Everett?"

"Yeah?"

Tara twisted strands of her long hair around her fingers. "I've decided I like him, but whenever I go to Willowlawn, he's totally surrounded. I need something to get his attention. Prom's coming up, and he really liked that fuzzy-wuzzy thing."

"It's called a tussie-mussie, and he was making fun of me. Just call him."

"He never answers, but I *know* he has a thing for flowers. Remember, he grabbed that tulip from me at movie night?"

Laurel refused to agree. "Look, I'm really busy. Soccer takes up a ton of time."

"Yeah, I wouldn't know about that, would I?" Tara crossed her arms. "Maybe I'll make a tuzzy thing myself. Nicole told me about that book in the tower. How hard can it be?"

Panic ripped through Laurel's chest. What if it's not just me? she thought. What if anyone who says my words can do it? She hadn't seen those exact words in the antique book, but she wouldn't be surprised if they were there. "Okay, okay. I'll do it," she said.

"Yes!" said Tara. "So, can I get it soon? Everett's got a rugby match I'm going to."

Laurel hesitated. "It's not that easy—"

"It *is* that easy," said Tara. "Just give me one like Spinster Spenser's."

"But some of those flowers aren't blooming anymore, and I had to order some online. There's no—"

Tara waved both of her hands. "Way too much info. Just make sure I get it by May Day, okay?" Her long hair swung out from her hips as she walked away.

Laurel walked to a nearby tree and laid her forehead against its bark.

CHAPTER TEN
Into the Conservatory

The tulips had all dropped their petals, but pink and white dogwood blossoms were unfolding on bare branches that raised them, like an offering to the sun. Laurel was feeling panicky because May Day was only a week away. Scanning the first floor of the library, she hurried up the steps of the tower. Her hand froze as she reached for the antique book, because its title was upside down. Laurel was compulsive about replacing books correctly, as her mom had been. She looked around, but the stacks were silent.

Was it Tara or Nicole? she wondered. She shook the book gently, but nothing fell out. The ribbon was still marking Violet's name, so she moved it to another page. Settling in at a desk, Laurel turned to the list of flower meanings and got to work. She made a wish list for Miss Spenser, but she had no idea what was blooming.

Before she left, she looked up one more flower: Cicely, Grandma's name. She found it under "sweet cicely, for gladness and comfort." She almost snorted, because Grandma's name was so wrong. Hugging the book to her chest, she crept around the tower and slid it underneath a stack of yellowed newspapers. *They won't find it again,* she thought.

As Laurel hurried down the stairs, a set of old-fashioned portraits near the checkout desk caught her eye. She stood under the couple and gazed up. *Gladys du Valle,* said one card. *1878 to 1932. Avondale Founder and Benefactress.* Gladys's red hair reminded her of Miss Spenser, but Gladys was young in the portrait and held her head high. She was holding a bouquet, a blur of bright colors, in her hand.

Laurel stepped sideways and met the gaze of a handsome man with a kind face. *Edmund du Valle, 1868 to 1924. Founder of Willowlawn and Benefactor of Avondale.* A hundred years earlier he'd built Gladys a conservatory and a school and filled her life with "bright blossoms and sweet scents."

"Psst."

Laurel turned toward the sound. Rose's friend Mina

waved to her from behind a pile of books. She had a few violets stuck behind one ear. They were blooming all over the quad, but Laurel couldn't remember their meaning.

"Whassup?" said Mina.

"Nice flowers," Laurel whispered. "Hey, have you ever been in the conservatory?"

"Sure. Lots of times."

"What's it like inside?"

"It's soooo beautiful. Flowers bloom there in winter, and it's always warm."

Laurel hesitated, but she could never ask Rose. "What about the ghost? I heard—"

A hand clamped down on her shoulder. "This is not social hour," said the assistant librarian. "Please stop the chatting."

"Sorry," Laurel and Mina said in unison. Mina stared down at her book, and the ghost question hung unanswered between them. Frustrated, Laurel gave Mina a quick wave and headed out to the library steps. With a glance at the waning sun and a shiver of indecision, she ran toward the cedars.

Every time Laurel saw the gaping gargoyles and Gothic tower, she thought of foreign lands and fairy tales. She half believed that anyone who stepped into that fanciful building would be transported into another world. She knocked on the glass door and felt a wave of relief as she saw Ms. Suarez walking toward her.

"Laurel." Ms. Suarez smiled warmly. She was wearing old jeans and a stained apron. Her hair was pulled back, but dark wisps hung loose through her silver hoop earrings. "Come in. I've been thinking about you."

Finally. Laurel breathed in the heavy moist air. Plants, vines, and small trees were hanging from hooks and rods, stacked on shelves, and even winding through a wrought-iron circular staircase that led to the central tower. She couldn't wait to explore.

Ms. Suarez leaned against a table. "Did you come for your tour?"

Laurel wanted to phrase this just right. "Sure, and I want to make another tussie-mussie—like I did for my presentation—but I don't know if the flowers I want are in bloom."

"What do you have in mind?" said Ms. Suarez.

Laurel took out her list. According to the antique book a flower called cape jasmine was for "ecstasy and transport." "What I really want is some cape jasmine," she said.

Ms. Suarez's eyebrows drew together. "Cape jasmine?"

"Is it really rare?"

Ms. Suarez shook her head. "Not at all. It's the old-fashioned name for gardenia."

"Really? That's great!" Laurel knew that scent. Her dad had given her mom a huge gardenia every Mother's Day, and her mom always acted surprised. "I need just two."

"Two whole plants?"

"Oh, no. Two flowers, and maybe some cabbage roses, too."

"I'm curious," asked Ms. Suarez. "Where did you learn about cape jasmine?"

"There's this old language of flowers book in the tower," Laurel explained. "I have a paperback, too, but it's not so detailed."

Ms. Suarez smiled. "It's a lovely book, isn't it? Quite rare and full of fascinating stuff." She scanned the room around them. "Let's see. I don't attempt roses inside, and it's too early outside. You know the scent of a gardenia?"

"Yes."

"They're here." Ms. Suarez's eyes twinkled as she swept her arm in an arc. "You find them."

Laurel turned around in the mass of plants. "Here?"

"Think of it as a treasure hunt." Ms. Suarez touched her nose and walked away.

"Oh-kay." A citrusy scent hung on the air, and Laurel could feel a breeze stirring through the open windows. She turned in a circle and sniffed. Although few plants were labeled, her nose quickly found open gardenias. *Ecstasy and transport.* The scent was so delicious that she shivered wordlessly with delight. The professor won't be able to leave her side, she thought.

Laurel considered taking a bloom now, but she didn't have permission, and it would wilt before May Day. She opened her mouth to call Ms. Suarez, and then closed it. Stepping softly, she followed the whims of her nose up and down the aisles. She found strange and lovely blooms redolent of lemon, while others exhaled cinnamon or licorice. Her head swirled with the giddy mingling, and she felt like she was flitting, floating in a dreamy cloud. She was about to lean into a large white lily when she heard footsteps.

"That's a lily," Ms. Suarez said flatly. "Do you need some help?"

"No." Laurel smiled blissfully. "I already found the gardenias. I've just been . . . exploring."

"Oh." Ms. Suarez's red lips parted in surprise. "Please show me them."

Laurel turned toward the circular staircase to gain her bearings. She retraced her steps and leaned into a creamy gardenia, but the teacher's hand pulled her back.

"Not too much," Ms. Suarez said. "Remember the wild orchid? Gardenias are potent, and I don't want"— she paused—"you to feel dizzy again."

Laurel straightened. "Oh."

Ms. Suarez reached for some drooping petals and pulled them off. "You're fourteen now, right?"

Laurel nodded.

"I know this is personal, but I assume you've started your period?"

Startled, Laurel took a step backward but nodded.

"I thought so," said Ms. Suarez. "Your sense of smell has improved, hasn't it? The world is rich with scented delights, and you'll come to—" She tapped her fingertips on her mouth. "But maybe it's not my place to say," she whispered, almost to herself.

"Your place to say what?" asked Laurel.

Ignoring her question, Ms. Suarez took small scissors from her apron. "Have you ever heard of the Hupa?"

Laurel shook her head. "No."

"It's a tribe of Native Americans in northern California. They've lived in the same, isolated canyon for thousands of years," said Ms. Suarez. "When a girl of the Hupa tribe becomes a woman, the tribe holds a Flower Dance for her. Their dancing and flowers and singing summon the Spirits to welcome her womanhood."

Ms. Suarez snipped off a gardenia. "Welcome, Laurel, to your blooming."

Laurel flushed red as she took the flower. "Uh, thanks."

"And I have another idea." The teacher motioned for Laurel to follow her to a desk in a corner. Crouching, she took a colorfully woven purse from the lowest drawer.

"We don't know each other that well, but I'm going to trust you," Ms. Suarez said as she unfastened the purse's flap. An ornately wrought silver key fell to the bottom of a chain. She held the chain wide, and Laurel bowed her head as she slipped it over her hair.

"It's a key to the conservatory," said Ms. Suarez. "An original. But tuck it under your shirt. I don't want it to fall into the wrong hands."

The key hung cold between Laurel's breasts. "Thanks," she said, although she had no idea whose were the "wrong" hands. "Does this mean I can come whenever I want?"

"Yes."

"And may I take *any* flowers?" Laurel stared down at the single gardenia.

"No," Ms. Suarez said solemnly. "I cultivate many for their seeds, so the flowers shouldn't be cut. But you wanted gardenias, right?"

"Yes, but not for me."

"Who?" Ms. Suarez's voice cajoled. "Who needs gardenias?"

"Miss Spenser." And Kate, Laurel added to herself.

She didn't want Ms. Suarez to think she'd take too many flowers.

"Sheila?" Ms. Suarez's eyes scanned Laurel's face. "You gave her that bouquet you made in class. Have you given her anything else?"

Laurel nodded. "A few weeks ago when she went to the professor's for dinner."

"Which flowers?"

"Red tulips."

"To declare love," Ms. Suarez whispered. "But they just met, and you . . ." Crossing her arms, she gave Laurel a look resembling the Probe. "To be honest, I wasn't expecting this—not so quickly. You seem more . . ."

"Quiet and well behaved?" Laurel finished for her. "Shy and boring? Everyone thinks that, but it's not who I am."

Ms. Suarez lifted her eyebrows. "Then I'm excited to know the *real* Laurel."

If I could only figure out who that is, thought Laurel. I used to know. "So, can I have gardenias for Miss Spenser? The book says they're for ecstasy and transport."

"Yes, but the book won't tell you everything," Ms. Suarez said.

"Then how do I find out more?" Laurel asked.

Ms. Suarez pinched off a few browning petals. "You have to study and spend time with the blooms to learn names and scents. It will take time, Laurel. And patience."

But May Day was looming. "Don't you want me to give her flowers?" Laurel asked. "You left some outside *my* door."

Ms. Suarez pursed her lips. "I wish this could be simpler, but you shouldn't rush things. You need to know the blooms better . . . and yourself."

Laurel couldn't bear Miss Spenser being empty-handed on May Day. "Can't I have just a few more gardenias? Or even one? *Please.* It's practically an emergency."

Ms. Suarez looked at her skeptically. "A flower emergency?"

Laurel nodded. "Really. And I need them to be fresh on Saturday."

"That's May Day."

"Yes. The professor's coming back for it."

Ms. Suarez exhaled audibly. "All right. Leave a note in my box to remind me, and I'll set a gardenia plant near the front door on Friday. But be careful who you give them to, okay?"

"Thank you sooo much," said Laurel. "You're awesome." She headed for the door, but then spun around and retraced her steps. She couldn't let go of an image from her dreams—of flowers falling into a grave.

"Excuse me, Ms. Suarez?"

The teacher was opening a cardboard box. "Yes?" she said without looking up.

"Do you know my grandma?" Laurel asked.

Ms. Suarez pulled the flaps apart. "I met her when I was a student here. Why?"

"I had this dream," Laurel said softly. "About you and Grandma throwing flowers on my mom's grave."

Ms. Suarez's head snapped up, and she dropped what was in her hands. "What?"

Laurel took a step back. "It was just a dream."

Ms. Suarez shook her head. "No, it wasn't. We threw Cicely's flowers onto your mom's grave. You must have seen us."

Laurel shook her head. "I didn't see you there. I left when my dad did."

"Dreaming can be a way of seeing, too. You have to tell Cicely. She'll—"

"She won't care. She never talks to me, and my dad said she torched her garden."

Ms. Suarez's hand covered her mouth. "Nooo," she whispered.

Laurel nodded. "After the funeral, she set it all on fire."

Ms. Suarez leaned heavily against a table. "I've been too out of touch."

"I just found out," Laurel said. "I've tried to call her,

but she doesn't answer me or call back. I think she wants to die."

Ms. Suarez rubbed her forehead. "There are ways to die even while your body lives on. But, Laurel, we can't let her slip through our fingers."

"I sent her a letter," Laurel said.

Ms. Suarez nodded pensively. "Then I will, too."

PART THREE
Romance in the Air

*"Flowers leave some of their fragrance
in the hand that bestows them."*
—CHINESE PROVERB

CHAPTER ELEVEN
Rite of Spring

"*Wow*," Kate said as she lifted her tussie to her nose. "These smell amazin'. But you have some, don't you?"

The scents of gardenia and lilac—for the first emotions of love—filled Laurel's room. She'd been feeling a little dizzy ever since she dropped off Miss Spenser's tussie at her cottage. She nodded at Kate as she took the last gardenia out of her refrigerator.

"That's all you have?" said Kate.

"That's all that's left," Laurel explained. She'd kept adding more flowers to her teacher's bouquet, and the rest were for Tara and Kate. She followed Kate out the door.

Kate knocked on the frame of Tara's open door. "Flower Delivery."

"Enter." Tara was leaning toward the mirror, puckering her lips. Her smile was almost believable when Laurel handed her the bouquet. "Mmm. This will get Everett's attention, right?" Her eyes fixed on Laurel.

"It should," Laurel said, reluctant to predict anything about Everett.

"Let me see yours," Tara said to Kate.

Kate held up her bouquet for inspection.

Uh-oh, Laurel thought.

"What's that flower?" Tara pointed at the white one in Kate's tussie.

"Ask the expert." Kate gestured toward Laurel. "I sure don't know."

Laurel cupped her single, lonely bloom behind her back. "It's just a gardenia."

"And I don't get one?" asked Tara.

Laurel made her voice light. "I'm all out. But next time. For sure."

Tara's pink lips straightened. "Oh. I get it now."

Kate shrugged at Laurel. "You want mine?" she asked Tara.

Tara looked at the floor. "No, thank you."

"Please." Kate pulled the white flower out of her bouquet. "I don't need it."

Tara's chin lifted as she shoved the flower into her tussie. "You're such a sweetie."

Laurel cringed. I can't believe this, she thought.

"Where's Nicole?" asked Kate.

"She's meeting us there." Tara locked her door behind them.

Laurel pulled on Kate's arm as Tara strode ahead. "Why'd you do that?"

"She was about to go off on you," Kate whispered. "I can't let her spoil the day."

"But your tussie's trashed. Here." Laurel pushed her own gardenia into the empty space. "That's better."

"That's your only flower," Kate protested.

Laurel shrugged. "I'll find something." Something for Justin.

Outside a warm breeze ruffled the flowering trees. Grinning, jostling Willowlawn boys seemed to pour off the buses, but Laurel didn't see Justin yet. A painted pole with multicolored ribbons streaming down towered over her head and into the cloudless sky. Clad in gauzy white blouses and flowing skirts, senior girls ran by barefoot, laughing and whispering. Their heads were wreathed by pink roses and baby's breath.

"Here comes another bus," said Kate.

"Let's go," said Tara.

Laurel's bouquets began to disappear into the crowd, and she was gripped by sudden panic. I never said my words! she thought. "Kate, Tara, wait up!" Whether it was the flowers alone or the rhyming words or both that made the world shimmer with fragrance, Laurel wasn't going to risk not saying them today.

"I need to see the tussies again." Pretending to straighten them, Laurel held her hand over Kate's and sent the thoughts she wouldn't speak—not around Tara. She pictured Kate flirting with someone tall at her side and then did the same for Tara. The rise of scent was swift and bold.

Kate pumped her shoulders and looked around. "What the heck was that?"

"What?" said Tara.

"Kinda like a shiver?" Kate looked at Laurel expectantly.

Laurel hid a smile behind her tingling hand. "It's just a bloomin' breeze."

"You are so weird sometimes," Tara said. "To the bus?"

"Go ahead," said Laurel. "I—uh—have to check on something."

Kate and Tara dashed away, but Laurel had spotted Miss Spenser on the steps of a building, holding her tussie: three perfect gardenias woven with ivy for matrimony. Rose was also standing nearby, next to the professor, and waved her over.

"Professor Featherstone, this is my cousin Laurel," said Rose.

"I'm very pleased to meet you," he said with a deep Southern accent.

Laurel shook his hand. "Thank you. Me, too."

"I've missed your lectures," Rose told him. "I'm so psyched you're back."

"So am I." Miss Spenser's fingertips lightly touched the professor's arm.

"The substitute was way lame," Rose added.

"Now Rose," began Miss Spenser, but Laurel didn't hear the rest. She was staring into the ivory petals, raising her hand, and sending her words over the gardenias in barely a whisper. The burst of fragrance was intense. Laurel stepped back and held her breath.

"Oh!" exclaimed Miss Spenser, looking unsteady on her feet. "Oh."

Laurel reached for her, but the professor had already flung out his arms.

"Sheila—are you all right?" He supported her as they moved toward a bench.

Miss Spenser blinked rapidly and felt her forehead. "I'll be fine in a moment." She stared at the tussie in her lap. Its lush scent hung on the air.

Bull's-eye, thought Laurel.

"Would you like a glass of water?" the professor asked.

"No, I'm fine now. Really." Miss Spenser held up

the bouquet. "Smell this nosegay, Luke. It's incredible. Laurel gave me those lovely red tulips, too."

Rose turned to Laurel with one eyebrow arched.

"They're magnificent," the professor said dreamily. "What an unusual hobby for someone your age."

"They're from Avondale's conservatory," Laurel explained.

"You have a conservatory here on campus?" said the professor.

Miss Spenser nodded. "It's one of the original buildings."

"I'd love to see it," he said. "I had a little corner at our university greenhouse."

Rose elbowed Laurel. "Busy, busy," she whispered. "What's with the flowers?"

"LADIES AND GENTLEMEN," the principal's voice boomed. "PLEASE CLEAR A CIRCLE AROUND THE MAYPOLE. OUR FAIR MAIDENS ARE READY TO DANCE."

"Let's stand," said Miss Spenser.

"Are you sure?" The professor extended his arm. "Lean on me to be safe."

Two rows of senior girls encircled the Maypole and picked up ribbons from the grass. They faced opposite directions as a fiddle and tambourine began to play. With their flowered heads held high, the girls danced in and out of one another's lines, weaving the bright ribbons on the Maypole. Laurel watched with fascination. None of her former schools had celebrated anything like this.

Miss Spenser leaned toward the professor. "This is a lovely tradition that my great-grandmother, Gladys du Valle, brought from England. Girls have been dancing on this green on May Day for more than a hundred years."

The professor nodded. "I believe that Maypole dances originated in the ancient Roman holiday of Floralia, honoring Flora, goddess of the flowers. A May queen was chosen as a symbol of fertility to promote a bountiful harvest."

Goddess of the flowers. The words echoed as Laurel watched and realized that her mom must have danced on this green. And she kept dancing all her life, she thought.

The tempo of the music quickened, and the senior girls nearly tripped over one another to keep up. Then one did. One of the popular seniors, Whitney, plummeted forward, dropping her ribbons. Several girls almost fell on top of her, and the tambourine player stopped jingling.

"Oops," whispered Rose. "That doesn't bode well for the harvest."

A loud guffaw escaped from the professor, who cleared

his throat and smiled appreciatively at Rose. Principal Westfall came tearing across the green, and Ms. Suarez appeared out of the crowd with a large pink flower behind one ear. Like puppet masters, they set the dance in motion again.

Laurel had a sudden thought. "Professor, do you know anything about Native Americans doing flower dances?"

"That's not my area of expertise, but I'd be interested in knowing more," he said.

"I think they're called the Hupas. They do flower dances to welcome girls when they—" Laurel hesitated. "When they become women. Ms. Suarez told me about it."

The professor nodded. "Cultures in all times and places have drawn connections between maidens and flowers. Most of their ceremonies include dancing, too."

Ceremonies, thought Laurel. My mom made up her own on the vernal equinox.

"Look, there's Robbie," said Rose. "He's such a goober. What's he doing, eating Tara's flowers?"

Uneasiness rippled through Laurel as she stood on her tiptoes to see. "What?" Robbie was standing close—too close—to Tara. Tara stepped away, but Robbie followed like a smitten puppy.

"Uh-oh," said Laurel. "I think Robbie might—um—need us."

Rose squinted at her. "He's irritating the heck out of Tara. No worries there."

"I have to check it out," said Laurel, jogging down the steps. The crowd was swarming in every direction now.

"So, what's the deal with all these flowers?" said Rose, right on her heels.

"Later. This way." Laurel shot through an opening, twisted around clusters of people, and froze.

Robbie, a dreamy smile glued to his face, was centimeters away from Tara. When she moved, he followed as if attached by strings.

"Robbie, man," said Rose. "Whassup, dude?"

"Hey," Robbie said in a deep voice that didn't sound like his own.

Tara scowled at Rose. "Call off your brother. He's like Velcro."

Rose grinned. "You should be flattered."

"Hardly." Tara looked at Laurel. "Did you put him up to this?"

Laurel shook her head, but she thought it served Tara right for wheedling the gardenia from Kate. From her.

"He's messing up all my plans." Tara tried to pull away. "Call him off."

"I'm not my brother's keeper," said Rose. "Hey, Robbie, you hungry? I'm buying."

"Sure." Robbie's eyes didn't leave Tara's face. "I want a hot dog."

"C'mon, dummy." Rose pulled his arm. "You have to come with me to get it."

"Can Tara come, too?" said Robbie.

"No! Can't you turn it off?" Tara yelled at Laurel.

"Wow." Rose put her hands on her hips. "Tell me this is not my brother. Do you understand what's happening?"

Laurel's shoulders rose toward her ears. "Kind of."

"Then make it stop," said Rose. *"Puh-leeeze."*

Tara tried to hide behind a huge oak tree, but Robbie chased her around it. "Go away!" she shrieked at him.

"Okay. You tackle him, and I'll tell her to bolt," Laurel said to Rose.

"LADIES AND GENTLEMEN," the principal's voice boomed across the quad. "IT IS NOW TIME TO ANNOUNCE THIS YEAR'S MAY QUEEN. THE AVONDALE MAY QUEEN EPITOMIZES THE VIRTUES . . ."

"Now!" Laurel whispered.

Rose grabbed Robbie and locked him in a half nelson as Tara dove into the crowd.

"Let go or I'll scream," hissed Robbie, trying to twist away.

"THIS YEAR'S MAY QUEEN IS . . ."

Robbie opened his mouth, but the cheering drowned

his cries. As soon as Rose loosened her grip, he took off after Tara again.

"Um, Laurel," Rose began. "Why is my brother acting like a total moron? Be straight with me now."

"I will, I will." A brilliant idea was taking shape. Maybe Laurel *could* turn it off. "I've got to check on something—for Robbie."

She spotted Justin with his friends as she hurried across the quad, but she couldn't stop now. Robbie had fallen deeply under the spell of her flowers, and Tara's anger could be dangerous. The silver conservatory key bounced against her chest as she ran into her room and grabbed her flower book. There had to be something in the garden that could help—some antidote to her love flowers. She sped out of the dorm, past the cedars, and into the center of the garden.

A heady, plumlike fragrance scented the air, and Laurel's nose led her down a windy path to a tree. Its branches held hundreds of white blossoms, and its perfume streamed into her like mist. All her worries seemed to loosen as she exhaled. She wanted to lose herself in this scent and flit from flower to flower like a butterfly. She wanted to dance on May Day.

Spreading her arms, Laurel pointed her toes and sprang lightly down the path. She felt free and floating as she whirled in a blur of color and sensation. Again! she thought. Again! She was dancing—like her mom and the maidens. Again! Again! She spun and spun, but suddenly there was only brownness. Her hands barely caught her before she fell face first. She stared at the dangling key and tried to remember why she was in the garden.

May Day! She brushed the mulch off her hands. Robbie was making a fool of himself, and Rose would be livid. Tara would be out to get her. Laurel dug her fingernails into her palms, held her breath, and headed away from the tree.

A shiny watering can sat near rows of tender plants in the herb garden. She knelt and read several names on the markers: lemon thyme, marjoram, basil. She picked one of each, rubbed its leaf, and lifted her fingertips to her nose. The scent of basil was the most familiar, but she couldn't remember where she'd last smelled it. She flipped through her paperback. Basil was for "hatred."

"Hatred?" Laurel said in astonishment. Her mom had cooked with the herb and grown it outside their kitchen in the summer. How could it mean *that*? But it might be perfect for Robbie. She plucked several leaves, sniffed them again, and remembered. Basil was the herb on her plate in the diner with her dad.

Weird, she thought as she sprinted back to the quad. Rose was scouting from the library steps.

"Where's Robbie?" Laurel said, panting.

Rose shook her head despondently. "I lost him. He's possessed."

"Not exactly." Laurel pressed some of the basil into her hand. "Here. Find him and make him smell this."

"What is it?" Rose lifted the leaves to her nose, but Laurel pushed her hand down.

"Basil, but it's for him, not you," Laurel said.

Laurel took a direction opposite Rose's. Just ahead, a girl shrieked, and Laurel was nearly knocked over by Everett, who zipped through the crowd holding a senior wreath above his head like a trophy. A flowerless Whitney was chasing him.

Following the path they'd created in the crowd, Laurel found Robbie on the outskirts and grabbed his arm. "Here. Tara wants you to smell this." She held the basil leaves under his nose and said her words quickly.

Robbie batted her hand away. "I can't find her."

"No, seriously," said Laurel. "Tara *really* wants you to smell this." She bent a leaf and rubbed it against his upper lip.

"Yuck," said Robbie. "What is it?"

"Basil. Tara really likes it."

"She hates me." Robbie rubbed his forehead. "My head hurts."

"Sniff again," said Laurel. "It's good for headaches, too. You want something to eat?" She led him to the food tables and pressed a hot dog into his hand. She crumpled the rest of the basil and pushed it close to his nose.

"Cut it out!" Robbie pulled away from her.

"Where's Tara?" Laurel asked.

"Who cares?" Robbie's mouth was jammed with hot dog. "Can I have 'nother?"

"Have all you like." My antidote worked perfectly, she thought.

"Laurel!"

Turning toward the voice, Laurel saw Kate waving both hands at her. She was standing in a group of five boys, including Justin and his curly-haired friend. Laurel's stomach fluttered, and she dropped the basil as she threaded her way to them.

Kate sidled close. "Your flowers are awesome." Then she turned to the curly-haired boy, twirling her bouquet. "Alan, have you met Laurel? And this is Justin. And Ben. And Casey. And Hugh."

Omigod, Laurel wanted to say. The guys were literally hovering around Kate, jostling for her attention. Laurel's hands were empty and smelled like basil. She wiped them on her jean skirt.

"Hey, Justin?" she said, leaning into his line of vision. "How's it going?"

Kate noticed her and smiled mischievously. "Here."

She pulled out one of her lilac fronds and tucked it behind Laurel's ear. "You need a flower, too."

Laurel's face flushed, and her hand shot up to catch the bloom as it fell from her hair. She could kick herself for not grabbing something in the garden.

Justin turned toward her. "Is that lilac?"

"Yeah," Laurel said. *For the first emotions of love.*

"My mom has lilac bushes," he explained. "She puts the flowers all over the house."

"Cool." Laurel raised the flower to her nose, but its scent seemed muted.

Kate touched Alan's arm as she laughed. He's winning, Laurel thought. Suddenly jealous, she wanted to move closer to Justin, to touch him and laugh together at private jokes, but he'd turned back to Kate. Laurel frowned at his ponytail as someone grabbed her from behind.

"Robbie ditched me," Rose whispered. "I can't find him anywhere."

"I took care of that problem," said Laurel, keeping an eye on Justin. "He's fine."

Rose's eyebrows drew together. "You're positive? He's totally not himself."

"Positive," said Laurel. "I'll explain later."

"You've got an awful lot to explain," Rose said. "This better be—"

Justin lunged to grab a yellow Frisbee that had shot across the quad.

"Did someone just aim that at my head?" Rose craned her neck.

Laurel stepped back to Justin's side. "Nice catch," she said.

Justin flipped the Frisbee between his hands. "I play Ultimate sometimes. It's all in the wrist." He flicked his hand, and the Frisbee glided smoothly away.

"Cool," said Kate. "Can you teach *me* to toss like that? I stink."

"Sure," said Justin, smiling only at Kate. "When do you want a lesson?"

"I play Ultimate, too," said another boy, whose name Laurel had already forgotten. "I'll teach you."

"Or I can," said Alan, putting his arm around Kate's shoulder.

Kate was beaming, but Laurel felt a wicked glare rise up. This was too much. Kate's smile faltered when she met Laurel's eyes.

"ATTENTION WILLOWLAWN STUDENTS. THE FIRST SHUTTLE BUS WILL DEPART IN FIVE MINUTES."

"Uh, sorry, Kate," said Justin. "We've got to go. Alan and I have a massive project due Monday, but we couldn't skip May Day. Can we do a lesson later?"

"For sure," said Kate. "And Laurel will come, too."

"Yeah, sure," Justin said, but he didn't even glance Laurel's way. He punched Alan's arm. "Yo, Alan. We got to go, man."

"I'll catch up," said Alan, his eyes on Kate.

"You can't," said Justin. "We have to meet with Snarly Yarley in half an hour. Chemistry project?"

"Why are all these guys hanging on Kate?" Rose whispered to Laurel. "It's like she has pheromone perfume."

Laurel blinked at the tussie. Pheromone perfume? Chemistry project?

Kate waved to Alan as Laurel stood frozen. Justin had never even looked back.

"Oh, Justin," Rose said in a high, mocking voice, and clasped her hands together. "You're so big and strong and talented. Will you teach little me to play Frisbee?"

"Shut up," said Laurel. Kate lifted her tussie to her face, but Laurel pushed it down. "Careful. That thing is dangerous."

CHAPTER TWELVE
Ivy for Matrimony

"*Don't* you think Alan's adorable?" Kate said between bites of hamburger. She'd used the I-have-to-go-to-the-bathroom excuse on the leftover guys, but she, Laurel, and Rose were hiding behind some bushes anyway. Laurel didn't want to be harassed by Tara, either, and she made Kate throw away her tussie.

Kate went on. "He's so funny and—"

"But does he have good teeth?" asked Rose.

"Huh?" said Kate.

"She's making fun of you," said Laurel.

"Am not," protested Rose.

Laurel scowled at her.

"Okay, a little."

Laurel was finishing an ice cream cone, but she felt

ready to snap at anyone. Part of her was excited that their experiment had been a success, but most of her wasn't. She tried to convince herself that Justin was attracted to Kate *only* because of the flowers, but Kate was tall and blonde and gorgeous. The flowers were like icing. Laurel couldn't help wondering if her life would be entirely different now if she'd kept that gardenia.

Rose bumped Laurel's arm. "So start explaining. What happened with Robbie?"

Laurel held up her palm for silence. "Wait a sec." The professor and Miss Spenser were walking toward the forest. She was still holding her tussie, vibrant with gardenia magic.

Kate clapped her hands. "They're goin' to the gazebo—to the kissin' couch."

"You've got kissing on the brain," said Rose.

Kate grabbed Laurel's arm. "Let's follow. Aren't you dyin' to see if he got the message?"

"Yeah," said Laurel, but she couldn't shake her disappointment. Romance and love were swirling all around, yet nothing seemed to touch her. "I just—"

"Come on." Kate tugged on Laurel's arm. "We have to get there first to hide."

"Stop!" Rose said. "Will someone puh-leeeze explain what's going on?"

"Later," said Laurel impatiently.

"But—but—" Rose sputtered.

Laurel and Kate ducked low behind the bushes and hurried toward the gazebo.

"This path is shorter," said Kate. The pine needles were soft beneath Laurel's shoes, and the crisp scent of the trees was energizing. She took a deeper breath. A stick snapped behind her, and she turned to see Rose rushing after them.

Laurel felt a pinch of guilt about spying, but she was too curious to stop now. She plunged into the high meadow moments after Kate. Pastel wildflowers dotted the knee-high grasses. At the top of the slope, the green-and-white gazebo stood unoccupied.

"Quick," said Laurel. Kate squealed as they scrambled into a tangle of branches.

Rose arrived seconds later. "What are we doing?" she begged breathlessly.

"Spying," Laurel whispered. "Shhh."

With its privacy and views of the Blue Ridge Mountains, the "kissing couch" was the most romantic spot on campus. Tales of amorous conquests—of both victories and defeats—zoomed through the corridors with fiber-optic speed on most Mondays.

Just then they heard voices, and footsteps echoed on the wooden steps. The wicker couch creaked above their heads, and they all hunkered low.

"This is a lovely spot," Professor Featherstone said in his genteel drawl.

"It is," said Miss Spenser, whose voice had more of a lilt than usual. "You should see the sunsets from here."

Laurel longed to peek even though she could picture Miss Spenser sitting ladylike straight with her knees pressed together and her feet crossed.

"There's also a marvelous view of the valley from the other side of that hill," added Miss Spencer. "Would you like me to show you?"

"Some day, Sheila," said the professor. "But not now. Now we have something far more important to discuss."

Kate's mouth sprang open, and she squeezed Laurel's hand too tightly. Laurel pressed her index finger to her lips.

"Sheila . . ." The professor cleared his throat. "After Dolores died, I had few expectations for the rest of my life. But when I first saw you in the dining hall with that bouquet, you looked like a portrait. You look like one today with these gardenias."

Kate pumped her fist, but Laurel was concentrating. *Bright cut flowers, leaves of green, bring about what I have seen.* She closed her eyes and imagined a wedding in a grand church, with sunlight slanting through stained glass windows.

"My soul smiles whenever I see you," he said. "This may be sudden and impulsive, but Sheila Spenser, will you honor me with your hand in marriage?"

There was complete silence. Neither Laurel nor Kate nor Rose dared to breathe for fear of interrupting the spell.

"Of course, Luke." Miss Spenser's voice quivered with emotion. "Of course."

Laurel clamped both hands over her own mouth to keep from exploding with delight.

"Omigod," Kate mouthed silently to her.

"Now, now," said the professor. "No tears. Aren't you happy?"

Miss Spenser was sniffling. "So happy."

The girls below squeezed themselves into silence as the crying above transformed into a peal of laughter. Rose huddled quietly, tracing patterns in the dirt with a stick. Footsteps echoed down the stairs, but Laurel held Kate back and counted to a hundred before peeking out. "All clear," she whispered.

Kate popped out, trailing a stray vine from her shoe-laces. "I can't believe they're gettin' married already. Your flowers are awesome."

Laurel picked a leaf out of Kate's hair and hurried up the steps to watch the path the couple must have taken. "They're old. They can't waste any more time."

Kate sat down and spread her arms along the back of the kissing couch. "But none of this would be happenin' without your tussies."

"It must be just coincidence, right?" Laurel said, hoping Kate would contradict her. Rose followed them into the gazebo and sat down on the railing.

Kate smiled. "C'mon. I don't believe that and neither do you."

Laurel had to smile back, because Miss Spenser's life was forever transformed. There was a power in her blooms, in her words—a force that could awaken and sway sleeping emotions.

"You think he kissed her?" asked Laurel.

"Why do you think it got all quiet?" said Kate.

"Passionately?" asked Laurel.

"Passionately."

"Stop," said Rose. "Enough with the girly-girl talk. Will someone please explain to me what all this flower crap has to do with my brother freaking out?"

Laurel and Kate exchanged a glance.

The couch creaked as Kate moved. "Laurel makes bouquets that are like magic."

"Magic?" Rose folded her arms on her chest.

Kate nodded. "*Luv* magic."

"Not really magic," Laurel said, leaning against a post. She knew Rose would never buy that explanation. "The flowers just seem to—to influence people's feelings."

"Their *romantic* feelings," interjected Kate.

Rose shook her head. "So you actually tried to make Robbie fall in love with Tara?"

"No way." Laurel straightened defensively. "Tara was after someone else."

"Those flowers were meant for another guy," Kate added.

"Enough with the flowers," Rose said angrily. "My brother acted like a total ass in front of the entire school!"

Kate waved her arms. "Whoa. Rose, please try to open your mind."

"I am completely open-minded," said Rose. "About rational things."

Laurel took a deep breath. "Remember that language of flowers project I did for English?"

"Not so much," said Rose.

"So, I made this bouquet following the language and gave it to Miss Spenser."

"Actually, you gave her three," said Kate. "And now they're happily ever after in *luv*."

"It's like the flowers were saying the things she was too shy to say," Laurel explained. "And the professor could sense that—the flowers speaking."

"Flowers speaking," repeated Kate. "I like that."

Rose walked to the other side of the gazebo. "Okay, maybe some pretty flowers got his attention, but you can't *make* someone love another person."

"Not just pretty," whispered Kate. "Powerful."

"Oh, I get it." A huge grin spread across Rose's face as she looked around. "Major prank, right? You guys are doing a great job for newbies."

"This is *not* a prank," said Kate. "You're smart, but you don't know everything."

Rose crossed her arms. "I never said I knew *every*thing."

"Stop," Laurel said. "Rose, you know people have always used flowers for medicines and messages. Greek mythology has tons of flower stories."

Rose lifted one eyebrow. "So?"

"Right," said Kate. "People are always turnin' into flowers or constellations or something."

"And my name, too," said Laurel. "Apollo fell in love with Daphne, a beautiful huntress—"

"A *virgin* huntress," added Kate.

"And he chased her until she cried out to her river-god father, who changed her into the laurel tree," Laurel said.

Rose circled her hand impatiently. "Then the laurel was Apollo's favorite, and winners wore wreaths of laurel. Blah, blah, blah . . . It's just a myth."

Laurel bit her lower lip. She couldn't bear Rose's scorn. "Look, one time my mom took me to hear a scientist who lived in the rain forest. He talked about how the natives use plants and flowers to heal people."

"Those shamans use plants as cures, not to play around with emotions," said Rose.

"But the Victorians believed flowers were magic," Kate said, "didn't they?"

"I think so," Laurel said.

"The Victorians were also fond of tight corsets and bleeding with leeches," Rose said.

Laurel scoured her mind for proof. "Think about how Robbie was—a different person. The only explanation is that he inhaled Tara's love bouquet."

Rose frowned across the meadow. "That was scary."

"What about Kate and all those guys?" added Laurel. "You even said something about pheromone perfume."

"I was joking." Rose's face twisted in disgust. "You didn't buy some pheromone crap on the internet, did you?"

"No way," said Laurel. "But it's like that, except it's the natural scent of the flowers."

Kate shook her hair. "You've lost me. What are pheromones?"

"Chemicals released by an organism that allow it to

communicate with other members of its species," Rose recited quickly.

"In English, please," said Kate.

Rose sighed. "Okay, so scientists have discovered that animals release certain chemicals, like smells, that signal other animals that danger's near or that they're ready to mate."

"For real?" said Kate. "Do humans do it, too?"

"Yep." Rose nodded. "Big research topic now. Biologists are trying to figure out how it all works."

"So." Laurel stepped forward. "Scientists think that what you smell can affect your behavior, right? Tara had a gardenia, which means 'ecstasy and transport' in the flower language and some purple lilac, which means 'the first emotions of love.' And that's exactly what happened. Robbie acted like he was *ecstatically* in love with her."

"Ecstasy?" said Kate. "Like the drug? Can flowers make you high?"

"Poppies can," said Rose. "That's where opium comes from."

"High on *luv*?" Kate giggled.

"No," said Rose, "just stoned. Opium fries your brain, and it's seriously addictive."

"Please. Let's focus here." Laurel took a deep breath. "Rose, you know my mom used to give people flowers all the time."

"She always had so many," Rose said wistfully.

"But I think it was more than that," said Laurel. "I think she was speaking to them—to their souls—in this language. Maybe trying to make their lives better."

"With flowers?" said Rose.

Laurel nodded solemnly. "And the messages can come true."

Rose's eyes were cool with skepticism. "Did she tell you this? I mean, before—"

"No," Laurel said. "But I'm positive she knew it and that she wants me to know."

Rose hesitated. "Just don't use Robbie as a guinea pig next time."

Laurel lifted her right palm. "Promise. That was a total accident, but we could use your help figuring this all out."

Rose rubbed her forehead. "It's a little outside my range of expertise."

"But what about that fern you told me about?" said Laurel. "The one that takes poison out of the soil?"

"Arsenic," said Rose. "The fern absorbs it. Phytoremediation."

"Exactly," said Laurel. "Plants have *tons* of powers we don't understand yet."

Kate stood up. "And Laurel has powers, too."

Rose held her palms outward. "C'mon. How do you

know Miss Spenser and the professor wouldn't have fallen in love anyway?"

"You kinda had to be there," Kate explained. "The flowers did something. Laurel felt it."

"He couldn't stop sniffing them," said Laurel. "We believe my flowers helped make it happen."

"Believing is completely different from knowing," Rose said. "And why would anyone use *flowers* to communicate? It's totally inefficient."

"It's retro," Kate said with a smile. "Laurel's flowers are *beyond* retro."

Rose was fighting back a smile. "Okay, so there's nothing weird about carrying flowers on May Day, but what about the other three hundred sixty-four days?"

"Flowers are always part of special occasions," said Laurel. "Valentine's Day, Mother's Day, lilies for Easter—"

"And corsages for prom," added Kate. "Everyone's gonna want flowers like mine."

Prom? Laurel wasn't sure if the feeling that rippled through her was excitement or fear.

Later that evening Laurel pasted blue violets—for faithfulness—to another note for Grandma. She'd promised herself that she'd send them until Grandma responded, but it seemed like an "exercise in futility"—one of her dad's favorite expressions about life on Capitol Hill.

When someone knocked on her door, Laurel put a heavy book on top of the note. "Come in," she called out, and immediately regretted it.

"Hope you had a good laugh," Tara sneered, and shut the door behind herself.

"What?"

"Don't act all innocent," said Tara. "You and Rose set up the whole Robbie thing to make me look like an idiot. Congrats. You win prank o' the month."

"But Rose would never want Robbie to—" Laurel hesitated.

"Never what?" asked Tara.

"She'd never want Robbie to look like an idiot, either. He was in the wrong place, and he smelled—" She stopped herself before she gave anything else away. "I mean, he *saw* . . . the flowers. Maybe if you had shown them to Everett first."

Tara lifted one palm. "It's not a wise move to treat me like I'm stupid. And, BTW, that old book is missing from the library tower."

Laurel cleared her throat to make her voice light. "What book?"

"The really old flower one." Tara squinted at Laurel's bookshelf. "Is it here? I told the librarian it was gone, but I didn't tell her you stole it. Not yet."

"I didn't steal it."

"Then where'd it go? Nicole saw it awhile ago." Tara picked up a remnant of purple lilac from Laurel's desk. "There's more of this in the garden, right?"

"We're not supposed to pick them," said Laurel.

"*You* do."

"Uh, Ms. Suarez gave me special permission," said Laurel. It was almost true.

"Ms. Suarez? Is she involved in this, too?" Tara asked.

Laurel wished she could keep something to herself. "She just likes flowers."

Tara plopped down on Laurel's bed. "Alan's called Kate like six times, and other guys asked her out."

Other guys? Laurel thought. Would Kate tell me if Justin called her?

"I never got close to Everett." Tara punched Laurel's pillow. "He followed Whitney around, and she has a boyfriend. I'm totally in love, and Ev hardly knows I exist."

Staring at Tara's curtain of dark hair, Laurel wished she could read her mind. Any pity, any help she offered could be twisted to explode in her own face.

"You have to help me," Tara pleaded softly. "You're my only hope."

Laurel wanted to laugh and kick Tara out, but she couldn't bring herself to do it. "Maybe there were too many people around. Maybe if we tried it again—"

"Then he'll get the message?" Tara finished. "That would be so awesome."

"Yeah." But Laurel's own thoughts moved back to Justin. Would fresher flowers have worked? Different flowers? She had no idea how long the effects of Kate's tussie would last. The love between Miss Spenser and the professor had taken root, but maybe Justin's feelings for Kate wouldn't—not if they weren't reciprocated.

Tara sat up straighter. "So promise me that your flowers will work right next time."

Laurel stood up. "I can't. Besides, they worked perfectly *this* time."

"On the wrong person," said Tara.

"I can't control that," said Laurel.

"Why not?" said Tara.

Laurel opened her mouth but didn't have a satisfying answer. "You have to go now," she said, suddenly flustered. "I have a huge project for . . . Latin."

"Fine." Tara spun around at the door. "Is Robbie going to stalk me next time I see him?"

Laurel shook her head. "He's fine now."

Tara took a step closer. "What I really want is for Everett to ask me to prom."

"But he's a freshman. He can't go, can he?"

"Yes, he can," said Tara. "Edmund du Valle thought

all 'proper' young men should dance. You missed the ballroom dance classes in PE last fall. The guys have to go to two dances a year, and lots go stag."

Laurel had never been to a real dance, not one with a date. "So why don't you invite Everett, then?"

"Duh," said Tara. "It's Willowlawn's dance, not ours. Ours was the semi-formal in December. We switch off every year."

Laurel frowned. "But you just said Everett doesn't know you exist."

Tara's look was steely as she left. "We'll have to fix that, won't we?"

Laurel locked her door. She wanted sharp thorns and dead leaves for Tara's tussie, but that would be too obvious. Her head throbbing, she walked back to her desk and picked up the heavy book that had pressed the violets onto her note. She tossed the book onto her bed, picked up a pen, and scrawled across the back of the envelope:

Lily doesn't want you to be like this!!!

CHAPTER THIRTEEN
Flower Fame

Forty-eight hours after May Day nearly everyone at the school knew that Miss Spenser was engaged, and strange rumors about Laurel's flowers were starting to fly.

"I didn't tell anyone," Kate insisted. "I mean, I didn't mean to. Everything's happenin' at once, and everyone wants to know all about Alan. Ally thinks we're nuts."

"Really?" Laurel asked, disappointment creeping into her voice.

The hum of voices paused and heads turned when she and Kate entered the dining hall for dinner. She heard her name whispered as she slid onto the bench. She bowed her head during the blessing, but her skin prickled with the thought of eyes watching.

"Is it true?" several girls finally asked. "Spinster Spenser's really getting married?"

Kate nodded. "We heard it all. . . ." Two seniors suddenly appeared at their table.

"Which one of you is the flower girl?" asked Whitney. Her thick dark hair and pale skin reminded Laurel of Snow White, but Whitney always wore lots of eye makeup and red lipstick. She dated Ricky Pavotti, a popular senior at Willowlawn, and his letter jacket hung on her as low as her uniform skirt. Her tall friend Amanda was with her.

"You must mean Laurel." Kate flipped her hand across the table.

"Hi." Laurel waved the fingers of one hand.

Whitney's voice was low and hoarse. "You gave Spinster Spenser flowers, right?"

"She's the one," said Kate. "We heard the—"

Laurel kicked her under the table.

"Ow," Kate said.

Whitney scanned the freshman faces that were straining to hear every syllable. She leaned closer, and Laurel inhaled an unpleasant mix of cigarettes and mint gum.

"We need to talk," the senior whispered. "Alone. Meet me at Bill's bust at seven."

"Tonight?" Laurel's voice squeaked.

"Past your bedtime, punkin?" Whitney said, unsmiling.

Laurel blushed. "No, I have to have tea with Mrs. Fox. It's my turn."

Whitney frowned. "Dorm mothers are a major nuisance. So tomorrow afternoon?"

"I've got soccer practice."

"Aren't we Little Miss Everything!" said Whitney.

Tara laughed. "Hardly."

Laurel glared at her. "What about Wednesday? I could get there by six."

"Okay," Whitney said. "Bill's bust. Wednesday."

"I'll be there," Laurel said.

Whitney whispered something to Amanda, who snickered as they walked out of the hall.

"They didn't even eat," Nicole said. "No wonder she's so skinny."

"She's skinny because she smokes," said Tara. "My mom smokes like a chimney when she's trying to lose weight. It takes away your appetite."

"That's brilliant." Rose squeezed onto the bench between Laurel and Kate. "Pump your body full of carcinogens just to lose a few pounds. What's a few years off your life span, anyway?" Her fist pounded the table. "Better to be thin."

Tara glowered at her, but Rose smiled widely. "Hello, Tara, and how are we today?"

Tara and Nicole picked up their trays and moved to the other end of the table.

Rose shook her head. "It's such a drag being popular. What did Whitney want?"

"She says we haaave to talk," Laurel said. "I'm meeting her Wednesday."

"Why?" Rose shook her chocolate milk carton.

Kate leaned around Rose to whisper to Laurel. "I told you everyone would want flowers. You're famous now."

Rose frowned. "Princess Whitney's not known for her benevolence. She must want something *baaad* to talk to a lowly freshman."

"Thanks a lot." Laurel elbowed her.

"You want me to come?" asked Rose.

"That's okay," Laurel said. Rose was sure to say something to irritate Whitney.

"I'll go," announced Kate.

"Hey," Laurel whispered to Rose. "You didn't tell Robbie about the flowers, did you?" She was dying to know if anyone was talking about her at Willowlawn.

Rose sniffed. "How can I begin to explain what I don't comprehend myself?"

Laurel held on to one question until Rose left. "So, Ally thinks we're nuts?"

Kate nodded and took her last bite of cherry pie. "She tries to be so frickin' rational all the time. Typical math geek."

"Like Rose," Laurel said. "What about you? Do you think my flowers are illogical?"

Kate crumpled the napkin onto her tray. "Love isn't supposed to be logical, is it? And I'm havin' a great time."

Laurel matched her smile. "Me, too."

The next day Laurel hurried from her class to the library tower. In all the excitement she'd forgotten about Tara's threat to snitch. Her hands shook as she unearthed the antique book from the newspapers and slid it back into its slot. Now no one could hassle her about the book.

"Yes, of course," a familiar voice said from the stairs. "I'll look, too."

Sucking in a breath, Laurel threw her backpack onto a table, grabbed a random book, sat down, and pretended to read.

"Laurel?" whispered Ms. Suarez, coming around a bookcase.

"Oh, hi, Ms. Suarez." Laurel struggled to keep her voice even. "How are you?"

"Fine." Ms. Suarez's beaded earrings brushed her shoulders. "Come here often?"

"Pretty often." Laurel giggled nervously. "The dorms get so loud."

"I love the scent of old books." Ms. Suarez walked directly to the shelf, which once again held the antique flower book. "Ah. She has magically returned. The librarian told me this book was missing even this morning."

Laurel stared down at the scramble of words on the page, but Ms. Suarez pulled out the chair directly across from her and placed the antique flower book between them.

"We need to talk." Ms. Suarez's face was solemn. "I'm sure you're relieved that this rare and valuable book has returned."

Laurel knew she'd never get away with playing dumb, not with Ms. Suarez. "Yes."

Ms. Suarez leaned forward and whispered. "I don't know exactly what happened, but this book cannot leave this library again. Okay?"

Laurel twisted a string that hung loose from her backpack. "Maybe it never left the library. Maybe it got misplaced, and then someone found it and put it back."

"Ah." Ms. Suarez seemed to be waiting for more, but Laurel needed to shift the conversation. She lightly touched the book between them.

"Did this one belong to Gladys du Valle?" she asked.

"No. She would have had her own copy. What do you know about Gladys?"

"Not much. I—I think she's interesting," said Laurel.

Leaning back, Ms. Suarez started to toy with a pendant she was wearing. "She was a fascinating woman. Troubled but fascinating."

"Troubled?" Laurel pressed. She could feel the tension dissipating.

"I'll tell you what I know of her story." Ms. Suarez took the deep first breath of a practiced storyteller. "Over a hundred years ago there was a family in England with three daughters named Daisy, Lavender, and Gladys."

Two flower names, Laurel thought. Like mine.

"Their mother had the gift of flowers, but she could be careless. She—"

Gift? Laurel leaned forward on her elbows. "You said something about my gift before—in the woods with the orchid. Should I call it that? The *gift* of flowers?"

Ms. Suarez looked down at the table. "Have you heard from your grandma yet? She should be the one—"

"No." Laurel jumped to her feet. "She might as well be dead."

"Laurel!" Ms. Suarez admonished. "Don't talk like that. She's one of our elders."

"*Our* elders?" Laurel sat down.

"Yes." Ms. Suarez looked around and lowered her voice. "The elders are ones who have mastered *all* the flowers and herbs after many years of study and practice."

Laurel folded her hands together like she was praying. "*Please*, Ms. Suarez. I need to know more about the flowers and my gift. I can't stand this anymore!"

"Shhh." Ms. Suarez nodded solemnly. "You are the youngest in an ancient line of Flowerspeakers. Your gift has been passed on through many, many generations."

"But what does that mean, flowerspeakers?"

Ms. Suarez tilted her head. "It means what you *know* it means. Flowers respond to your summons. You draw forth their scent and true meaning."

"In the language?"

"Yes." Ms. Suarez patted the book between them. "That's why this book is so valuable. It holds one key to our gift."

"Like a translation? But I found lists of flower meanings all over the Web."

"Yes, but many of them are wrong. Besides, just knowing the meaning isn't enough." Ms. Suarez held her fist to her chest. "You have to have the magic inside you."

"Like you do?"

"Yes." Ms. Suarez smiled. "And like your mom did."

Like my mom, Laurel's mind echoed.

"And like your grandma," added Ms. Suarez. "Cicely is one of the wisest and most respected Flowerspeakers."

"Why?" Laurel said. "She does *nothing*. She won't even answer her phone."

Ms. Suarez leaned forward. "But you should have seen her before, what she could do. I haven't given up hope, and you can't, either. Promise?"

Laurel shrugged. She didn't want to ruin this moment with thoughts of Grandma.

Ms. Suarez spread one hand on the flower book, as if she could absorb its wisdom.

"And Gladys must have had the gift," said Laurel, "right?"

"Sadly, no. It runs in families, but not everyone is blessed with it," said Ms. Suarez. "Only her sisters, Daisy and Lavender, had it."

"But that's *awful*," said Laurel.

Ms. Suarez nodded. "Gladys was very jealous and blamed her mother for not naming her after a flower. But having a flower name never guarantees the gift. It's just tradition. I've watched Rose, but she doesn't have it."

"Aunt Iris doesn't, either," Laurel added. "She doesn't even have a garden. So, what did Gladys do?"

"Gladys's sisters could be condescending," Ms. Suarez continued. "They teased her, but Gladys was a fighter, and she vowed to master the flowers. When she was seventeen, she met Edmund du Valle, the oldest son of a new American millionaire. He'd come to their estate to meet and court Lavender. Despite Lavender's best efforts Edmund fell in love with fiery Gladys. Her parents refused his proposal—they wanted to marry off an older daughter first—so Gladys ran away with him. One morning she took her daily horseback ride, galloped off to meet Edmund, and they eloped." Ms. Suarez's dark eyes sparkled. "It was quite the scandal."

"How do you know all this?" Laurel asked in amazement. "Are you related to her?"

"No." Ms. Suarez smiled to herself. "It's strange, isn't it, to speak the secrets of the dead? I know her story because of my great-grandfather Juan José Suarez. He was an orchid hunter—Gladys's orchid hunter. He traveled the world seeking jewels for her conservatory. At home he tended her blooms and listened to her stories.

"Whenever she visited her flowers, Gladys talked. 'The flowers are her confessors,' my great-grandfather wrote. He kept a detailed journal of everything that happened here. I found it behind some rotted boards when I was restoring the conservatory."

"Cool." Laurel pictured Edmund's handsome face from the portrait in the library. "So, did Gladys really love Edmund? Or was she just dissing her sister?"

Ms. Suarez laughed. "She must have loved him deeply to risk such scandal. She was disinherited, but Edmund gave her everything, including our splendid conservatory."

Laurel nodded. Edmund had filled Gladys's life with flowers and scents, and the whole campus was fragrant with descendents of those blooms. "So if your great-grandpa worked here, then did your mom and grandma come here like mine?"

Ms. Suarez shook her head. "Juan José was an employee, so his daughters weren't the proper social class. It was a different world then."

"Oh." Laurel frowned and traced a ray of sun shining through the slim window onto the table. "So Gladys *never* got the gift?"

"No. It can't be forced. It can't be bought."

"Did Juan José have it?"

Ms. Suarez smiled broadly. "Yes. He was a rare and talented man. In his journal he even sketched the bouquets he made for Gladys."

"Can I see—" Both of them startled as the bell rang for the end of lunch.

"So much for eating." Ms. Suarez stood up. "There's one more thing you might be interested to know. One of *your* ancestors was good friends with Gladys."

Laurel's eyes widened. "Really? Who?"

"Her name was Violet."

CHAPTER FOURTEEN

The Flower Seekers

"*Bill's* bust" was a life-sized statue of William Shakespeare at the front entrance to Avondale. Gladys had named the school after the River Avon, which runs through the bard's birthplace. Laurel was hurrying from the soccer field with Kate to meet Whitney, and she'd finally worked up the courage to ask Kate if Justin had called.

"No," said Kate. "He only sent me one e-mail, about playin' Frisbee, and I put him off. Alan's called nine times and we're texting all the time. I would've gone there for dinner tonight, but they had an away meet."

"So, you've answered all of Alan's messages?" asked Laurel.

"Definitely," said Kate. "He's adorable!"

"What about the other guys?"

"I didn't answer, and they didn't write back."

"So, it wears off," Laurel whispered. *Thank God.*

"What? You mean the flower magic?" asked Kate.

Laurel nodded. "It must."

"But I wanna keep Alan around." Kate stopped walking. "Do you think he likes me only 'cause of the flowers?"

"No way," said Laurel. All guys seemed to be attracted to Kate.

"But all the other boys have moved on," said Kate. "I need more flowers! Now."

"Calm down already," Laurel whispered. "Even if the magic is temporary, I think the feelings only last if they're really real. Miss Spenser and the professor aren't going to stop loving each other when my flowers aren't around."

"No way. They're gaga."

"Like you and Alan. Maybe none of the other guys were in love with you, but my flowers made them feel like they were. And Robbie can't possibly love Tara."

Just ahead of them Whitney took a long drag and flicked a cigarette butt into the grass. "Hey," she said.

"Hey," Kate and Laurel responded in chorus.

"Who's the chaperone?" Amanda nodded at Kate.

"This is Kate," said Laurel. "We're on JV soccer together."

Whitney straightened her lips into a wry smirk. "Can you keep a secret, Kate?"

"Of course," Kate said eagerly. "I *never* tell anybody anything."

Laurel had to suck in her lips so no one would see her smile.

Whitney shoved her hands into Ricky's jacket. "So you've done this flower thing a lot?"

Laurel shook her head. "Only once."

"Nooo." Kate bumped her. "At least four times. You gave three bouquets to Spinster Spenser, and one to me at May Day. I had guys hangin' off me."

Laurel shot Kate a look of caution. She wasn't sure how much she wanted these seniors to know.

"Really?" Whitney's eyes appraised Kate. "Are the guys still around?"

Kate shook her head. "Just one—the one I want."

"Interesting," said Whitney.

"Bogus," said Amanda. "I can't even believe we're listening to freshmen, Whit. I'm calling him now." She took out a cell phone but didn't dial.

Whitney stared hard at Laurel. "This isn't some moronic prank, is it?"

Laurel and Kate both shook their heads.

"'Cuz you can just leave this school now if it is," Whitney finished.

"Of course it is," said Amanda. "You can't think some stupid flowers—"

Whitney glared at Amanda. "So. If your flowers can make somebody fall in love, could they make somebody fall out of love?"

"Maybe," said Laurel. Basil had cured Robbie's obsession almost instantly.

"And is it permanent?" asked Whitney. "What the flowers do?"

"Permanent enough," said Kate. "Spinster Spenser's gettin' married."

Whitney turned to Kate. "You mind giving us space? I need to talk to Laurel alone."

Kate's face fell. "Uh, sure," she said. "Whatever."

Laurel thought about protesting, but she was too curious. She followed when Whitney started down the lane toward school. Amanda stayed behind, as if guarding Kate. The sun was low, and the air was cooling. On either side of the road the trees were covered in snowy blossoms that took on the pink cast of the evening.

"Promise me no one will ever find out about this," Whitney whispered.

Laurel nodded.

"Say it," said Whitney.

Laurel rolled her eyes at the ground. "I promise no one will ever find out about this. You want me to cross my heart and hope to die, too?"

Whitney frowned. "I'll know if you tell anyone."

"I said I won't."

"Okay." Whitney took a deep breath. "Everybody says Ricky and I are destined to be prom king and queen. I don't want to mess with that, but Ricky and I don't exactly have the same agenda."

Laurel shook her head. "What do you mean?"

Whitney pushed back her thick hair. "Ricky's dad reserved a hotel suite for after prom, and Ricky says he's kicking everyone out so we can spend the night together."

"Ohhh." Laurel glanced sideways at the senior. She's treating me like I'm her best friend or something, she thought.

"I mean, it's not like I'm an angel," said Whitney. "Ricky's totally fun, but I don't love him. And my sister got pregnant at her prom. That can't happen to me."

"So why don't you just break up?" said Laurel. "Or say no?"

Whitney shook her head. "Everybody loves Ricky. They'll think I'm a bitch if I dump him, and then no way will I be queen. Trust me; it will be so much easier if he doesn't want to, you know?"

Not really, thought Laurel, but she nodded anyway. "So what do you want me to do?"

"I was thinking"—Whitney stopped walking—"you could have flowers ready and give them to me right after the announcement. Flowers to turn him off."

"But I'm not going to prom."

"Yes, you are," said Whitney. "I put your name on the list of freshman hostesses. You can even ask that Kate girl to help."

Laurel said little as they walked back to where Kate and Amanda stood. Whitney's request was bizarre, but she didn't see a way out of it. The senior's bad side could be even worse than Tara's, she'd heard.

Amanda handed a cell phone to Whitney. "He says two minutes."

"Cool," said Whitney, waving them off. "Y'all run along back to campus. Wouldn't want you to get into any trouble."

Laurel felt too curious to move far. She and Kate walked away and then hid behind a shrub, so they heard and then saw Ricky's red Wrangler as it crested a hill and screeched to a stop. After the seniors climbed inside, the car did a tight U-turn and sped away.

Kate stood up and stretched. "How do they get away with leaving campus?"

"Maybe the rules are different for seniors," said Laurel.

"Maybe just for them," said Kate.

They started walking back. "How well do you know her?" Laurel asked.

"Whitney? Only what I hear, but everybody says Amanda does weed."

"I thought the school had really cracked down?"

"They did," said Kate. "Remember? Everyone has to sign a release form sayin' they can search our lockers. So what did Whitney want? Another hot boyfriend?"

Laurel hesitated. "I—uh—promised her I wouldn't say anything."

Kate stopped and put her hands on her hips. "Laurel Whelan, you can't possibly be more loyal to her than you are to me."

"She made me swear. She'll *kill* me if it gets out."

"But I thought we were friends now. I thought we trusted each other."

"We do," said Laurel. "We are. But please don't make me tell."

"Can't you give me a little clue?" Kate pressed.

Laurel shook her head.

Kate looked away. "I'm gonna skip dinner. I'm not hungry anymore."

"Come on." Laurel grabbed Kate's arm. "You're always hungry. You wouldn't want me to tell anyone your secrets."

"But I don't have any juicy ones," Kate said despondently.

"Sure you do," said Laurel. "About *Alan*. Is there movie night this weekend? Want to go together?" Justin was likely to be there.

Kate shook her head. "Tara already called dibs, and I know you don't wanna hang out with her. Sorry."

Laurel frowned at Kate's ponytail as she walked ahead toward the dining hall. "Wait a sec!" Laurel yelled and caught up. "Whitney said we could be freshman hostesses for prom."

Kate stopped walking. "Both of us?"

Laurel nodded.

"Well, why didn't you say so? That changes *everything*."

Laurel and her flowers were gossip topic number one on campus. Kate and Rose kept her informed on what was said:

"She made that all up to get attention."

"Does she *actually* think this flower stuff will make people like her?"

"Are you kidding me? Enough already with the Harry Potter magic crap."

"How do I get some?"

So far, ten notes asking for flowers had been shoved through the slits in her locker or under her door. Most of them wanted to snag a prom date. Laurel had e-mailed back promising to help, even though she'd have to do a lot more research. And Kate was now asking for rosemary before even minor quizzes.

"You're Laurel, right?" a voice whispered behind her as she switched books at her locker on Thursday. Susan Monroe, a sophomore cheerleader, was leaning over her.

"Hi, Susan." Laurel turned and stood up.

"I have this favor to ask," Susan whispered as she ran her fingers through her streaked hair. "I blew off my homework last night, and I just found out we have this chem quiz next period. Someone said you have some lucky flowers or something that makes you remember better. Can I have some?"

Kate and her big mouth. "You need it now?"

Susan nodded. "Right now."

Laurel frowned into her locker. After the history test she'd emptied the contents of her pocket onto the top shelf. The stems of rosemary were dry and browning.

She put one into Susan's outstretched hand. "This is all I have, but it's kind of dried up. I don't know if—"

"I'll take anything." Susan stared into her cupped palms. "That's it?"

"Wait." Laurel held her hand over Susan's and said the words to herself. "That's it."

"I totally owe you for this," Susan said, and then ran down the hallway.

Fear flickered through Laurel. Nothing in her body had tingled.

Miss Spenser caught up with Laurel as the girls were fil-
ing out of her class. "Could you wait a minute, Laurel?"
she said. "I have a favor to ask."

Laurel smiled in anticipation. I'll make you the perfect wedding bouquet, she thought.

"Have I told you that Luke and I've decided not to
wait?" Miss Spenser asked. "I know it's impulsive, but
it's so lovely out now. We'll be married in two weeks and
would be delighted if you could be our flower girl."

Laurel choked back the "yes" that was poised on her
tongue. That's for little girls, she thought.

"I picture you strolling down the aisle strewing petals on the grass." The teacher's hand swept out to
illustrate. "White and pink and red rose petals. I'm not
having bridesmaids, but I am indulging myself with a
flower girl. Luke says your bouquets drew him to me. I
just never imag—" Her voice faltered as her eyes filled.

"Okay." Laurel squeezed Miss Spenser's hand. "Yes.
I'll be your flower girl. I—I'm honored."

Rose flagged down Laurel and Kate outside the dorm.
"Hey, I want to show you something I found," she said.
"Let's go back to Laurel's room."

"I have a big quiz tomorrow," Kate whispered to Laurel.
"Do you have any more rosemary? Or something newer?"

"I have rosemary," Laurel said, glancing at Rose, who was obviously listening.

"Hey, what about forget-me-nots?" said Kate as they filed into the room. "Could they help me remember, too?"

"Maybe." Laurel pictured clusters of tiny blue blooms, one of her mom's favorites.

"Forget-*who*-nots?" said Rose.

"Forget-*me*-nots," said Kate. "I don't want to forget my Spanish vocab words."

Rose sat down on Laurel's desk, grinning. "Okay, so forget-*you*-nots."

"Forget-*her*-nots," Laurel said. And I don't want to be forgotten, either, she added to herself.

Rose's eyebrow arched. "Flowers for quizzes, eh?"

Laurel tried to silence Kate with a look. "To help remember. Some girls have asked for some."

"Older girls," said Kate, bouncing on the bed. "Tashi wants some, too."

"*Older* girls," mimicked Rose. "That explains everything. I had no idea you were so *pop*-ular, floral Laurel." She pulled out a paperback and flipped through it, looking for something.

"Tashi, as in the varsity center forward?" Laurel asked, sitting down next to Kate.

"Exactly." Kate bounced again. "Floral Laurel. I like it."

"What does Tashi want?" asked Laurel.

"She needs help with her evil Spanish teacher," said Kate. "I promised her some flowers for friendship or something by tomorrow."

"Ka-ate," said Laurel. "Friendship flowers?"

"It's got to be easier than *luv* flowers," said Kate. "Or whatever *Whitney* wants."

Laurel sighed, because Kate wasn't easing up about Whitney. "I don't even know which flowers are for friendship."

"You'll figure it out." Kate waved her concerns away. "Hey, you're goin' to the wedding, aren't you?"

"Stop bouncing," Laurel said as she stood up. "Miss Spenser asked me to be the flower girl." She could already see the wicked grin breaking out on Tara's face.

"The flower girl?" said Kate.

Rose looked up from her book.

Laurel frowned. "It's not like I could turn her down. She's too . . . happy."

"Well." Kate bit her lip. "I have this great light purple dress—"

Rose waved her hands. "Stop. Cease. Girl talk later. I found the passage, and I only have a few minutes."

Kate tilted her head to read the cover of Rose's book. "Shakespeare?"

Laurel took a step closer to Rose. Her mom had adored Shakespeare.

Rose nodded. "We're reading *A Midsummer Night's Dream* in Honors English. Listen to these lines.

"Fetch me that flower; the herb I showed
    thee once:
The juice of it on sleeping eyelids laid
Will make or man or woman madly dote
Upon the next live creature that it sees."

"Huh?" Kate shook her hair. "Read it again."

Rose read more slowly.

Laurel sat up. "If you dote, you love that person like you're obsessed, right?"

"Exactly," said Rose.

"Wow. So, Shakespeare's talking about a flower juice that makes people fall in love," said Laurel. "Who says those lines in the play?"

"Oberon, king of the fairies," said Rose.

"Fairies?" Kate's face lit up. "You think Laurel is part fairy?"

"Kate, puh-leeeze," said Rose. "Lay off the fantasy novels and live in *this* world. This is Shakespeare, and these lines seemed relevant."

Kate scowled at her.

"So Shakespeare believed in flower magic?" said Laurel.

"At least in fairyland," said Rose. "Oberon has the

fairy Puck squeeze the flower juice into Titania's eyes—she's his queen—while she's sleeping. When she wakes up, she sees this mortal who has a jackass's head. She falls in love with him and makes a total fool of herself until Oberon gives her the antidote."

The antidote, Laurel repeated to herself. Like basil.

"Wait. The mortal has a jackass's head?" asked Kate.

Rose nodded. "He's under a spell, and his name is Bottom."

"Bottom?" Kate laughed.

"And in another scene," Rose went on, "Puck—he's like Oberon's head fairy—is supposed to put the love juice on this guy Demetrius's eyes so he falls for Helena. But he also accidentally puts it on another guy's eyes. So then they both act like they're in love with Helena, and the other girl's out in the cold. It's total chaos."

"Then everyone's in love with the wrong girl?" asked Laurel.

"Yeah, but it gets straightened out in the end." Rose closed the book. "I'm not saying this is proof of anything, but it's interesting."

"Very," Laurel said. Greek mythology, the Victorians, and now Shakespeare. Flowerspeaking was woven throughout human history.

Kate turned to Laurel. "That's kinda like what

happened on May Day, isn't it? With all those guys hangin' around me?"

Laurel didn't want to be reminded. She hadn't managed to talk to Justin since then.

Rose hopped off the desk. "But all this messing around with people's emotions seems kind of risky. And now quizzes?"

Laurel held up her hand. "Don't tell anyone else about this, okay?"

"But we all need some special flowers for the wedding," said Kate. "Rose, too. I'm sure Miss Spenser's invited Willowlawn guys."

Rose shook her head. "Uh, no, thanks."

Kate's foot nudged Rose's leg. "C'mon, you could use a spicy romance."

Laurel pressed the back of her hand to her forehead dramatically. "Rose has too many equations to solve, too many diseases to cure, too many—"

"*Shut* up," said Rose. "Just because I have a master plan for my life doesn't mean I can't have fun."

"So have some," said Kate.

"I will." Rose slung her pack over her shoulder. "I do. And I don't need any of your forget-her-nots."

Laurel shrugged at Kate as Rose closed the door behind herself. Is my genius cousin actually jealous? she wondered.

CHAPTER FIFTEEN
Scents and Sensibility

Just before the bell rang on Friday, Miss Spenser called Laurel to her desk. After all the other girls had left, the teacher shut her door and turned around with her arms folded. Her face was strangely grave.

"Earlier this morning I intercepted a note that's troubling me, Laurel. It mentioned 'Miss Spenser's magic flowers.' Have you heard anything about this?"

Laurel's mind raced. "I—uh—I think people noticed how quickly you and the professor fell in love, and then they saw that you had flowers with you. And you two just seem like magic together, you know?" She tried to smile convincingly.

Miss Spenser shook her head. "That's not what the note's implying. Maybe people assume I need nothing short of magic at my age."

Laurel shook her head. "No. You *deserve* happiness."

"Do I?" Miss Spenser said. "Falling in love is a kind of magic, but that's not what these rumors mean, is it? And I've seen girls carrying flowers around campus lately."

"Really?" Laurel said, trying to think quick. Who? "Maybe it's all part of a prank. Avondale girls love pranks."

Miss Spenser took a step closer. "Laurel, I don't want you to think I'm not grateful for all your lovely bouquets, and I know you've been through a very painful experience. I can understand how you might wish for something extraordinary to happen. But flowers are just flowers; there's nothing magical about them."

Laurel frowned. "But you're always saying that poetry can 'stir the soul.' Can't flowers, too?"

"Of course," said Miss Spenser. "Just as a Mozart symphony or a Cézanne painting does—because of artistry or beauty. That has nothing to do with magic. Promise me you'll discourage any talk of magic on this campus. It's silly."

Someone knocked insistently, and an upset student burst in. Avoiding Miss Spenser's eyes, Laurel escaped without another word. She couldn't believe her teacher didn't believe. The irony was stunning.

After practice Laurel split off from her teammates and headed to the conservatory. Kate was on her way to

Willowlawn's movie night with Tara. Laurel had given them both purple lilac and said her words, but she couldn't get Miss Spenser's comments out of her head.

"Ms. Suarez?" Laurel called out as she pushed the door open, but no one answered. Tucking the key back under her shirt, her eyes scanned the dense greenery. She recognized some leafy plants in little black containers on a table: basil. Laurel lifted one of the plants to her nose. Basil for Whitney.

There were lots of other herbs, too: lemon balm, oregano, fennel, and dill. Laurel walked the length of several tables and then paused. In the corner of the building, there was an odd metal enclosure she hadn't noticed before. There wasn't any glass in the frame, so it looked like the skeleton of a room within the larger, airy space. Lush leaves and rich colors seemed to beckon to her from inside. She stepped to its edge, marveling at several sprays of exotic blooms.

"You should *still* avoid the orchids," said a voice behind her.

Laurel pivoted. "Oh! You scared me."

"I'm sorry," Ms. Suarez said. "Did you use your key to get in?"

"Yeah, I didn't think you'd mind."

"I don't, but you left the door ajar. You need to lock it even when you're inside. I have rare and valuable blooms, and sometimes Mrs. Westfall allows gardening groups to tour the grounds. Orchids, especially, have been known to disappear at flower shows."

"Really? I'm sorry." Laurel's heart still thumped from the fright, but she sensed something else, too: the beginnings of a long and delicious vibration. It was this promise of tingling, of spinning, that turned her body back to the orchids, toward their soft petals, which were so bold, so alluring. . . .

She felt Ms. Suarez's hands grip her shoulders. "Not yet," the teacher said. "You need more control." She steered Laurel away from the enclosure.

"I—I didn't know they were orchids," Laurel protested. "They aren't labeled."

Ms. Suarez rubbed her forehead with the heel of her hand. "I'd love to chat, but I'm swamped. I'm making centerpieces for a donor brunch tomorrow, and I can feel a migraine coming on. Did you need something?"

Laurel shook her head reluctantly. "I just wanted to be with the flowers." And you, she added to herself. "Can I help out with the brunch?"

Ms. Suarez hesitated. "I'm tempted, but these arrangements are subtle. I'm afraid I'd spend too much time teaching you and not get them done."

"So, what are you trying to do? Make people donate more money?" Laurel said.

The teacher almost smiled. "Let's just say I can put them in a generous mood."

"Cool," said Laurel. "Money power."

"Yes, but with that power comes responsibility, right?" The teacher pressed her fingertips to her temples. "There's one more thing, Laurel. I wish the rumors about Sheila's bouquets hadn't spread so quickly."

"Why?"

"People who hear about your flowers—Avondale girls—will ask you to do things you're not ready for," said Ms. Suarez. "Please don't demand too much of your gift. It's fine to make a bouquet or two for Sheila, but you can't give flowers to every girl who asks. And you certainly shouldn't be playing around with basil in crowds."

Basil? Laurel dropped her eyes to the ground. How did she find out about that?

"I ran into Rose on May Day. She reeked of basil and told me you'd given it to her." Ms. Suarez put her hand on Laurel's shoulder. "Listen to me. It's not your fault, but your education is backward. Most Flowerspeakers have worked quietly and anonymously throughout history, but we are known because of one woman. She was one of us but used a pseudonym—Charlotte de Latour—to spread our secrets. *Le langage des fleurs—The Language of Flowers*—was first published in 1819. Some of us considered her a traitor. Her list was copied and translated into many languages as more and more people learned about our gift and tried to master it."

Ms. Suarez's hand hovered over the herbs on the table and pulled a leaf off. She held it to her nose. Laurel craned her neck to see which one, but the containers were so tightly clustered she couldn't tell.

"But flowers don't perform in ignorant, untrained hands," said Ms. Suarez. "When people didn't understand true meanings, they invented preposterous ones. The language became a game, and our book—our *bible*—was nothing more than an elegant coffee table decoration. That's how we're seen even now: as quaint relics of a bygone age. Not as women and men of insight and power, not as mistresses of an ancient and vital wisdom."

Wisdom. Power. The words reverberated through Laurel's head.

"Be careful not to treat this as a game, Laurel. You can memorize long lists; you can learn the powers in a bloom, but if you can't sense the right or wrong time to use your gift, it will create only heartache."

"But Miss Spenser's getting married," Laurel said. Stepping backward, she slipped on a damp spot and threw her hands out. A tall plant tottered, and Ms. Suarez lunged to catch it.

"Sorry," said Laurel as she straightened.

"Careful," Ms. Suarez pleaded. "*Please* be more careful."

"I—I will," said Laurel.

"There's one more thing. Sheila has asked me to make her bridal bouquet."

Laurel felt a sudden spasm of hollowness.

"Such an occasion requires the hand of an expert." Ms. Suarez met Laurel's eyes. "It's not for fun."

Laurel's hands tightened into fists. "My flowers aren't just for fun. My magic made this wedding happen."

"You're sure?"

"Yes," said Laurel, holding the teacher's gaze. "I'm sure."

"Uh-huh." Ms. Suarez crossed her arms. "So you're the expert now? You know *all* about the language, all that it means to have this gift and exactly how to use it?"

Panic rocketed through Laurel's body. Ms. Suarez was the only Flowerspeaker she knew, other than Grandma—the only one who could teach her more. "I mean no," she said contritely. "I have tons to learn. I know that. I'm sorry."

Ms. Suarez sighed heavily. "Socrates said that knowing you know nothing is the beginning of true knowledge." Her fingertips lifted Laurel's downturned chin. "You have *so* much to learn. Be patient with your gift."

"I'll try."

"Try *harder*," Ms. Suarez said. "In the meantime I *could* use your help with Sheila's wedding bouquet."

"Really?" Laurel blinked in disbelief. "I'd love to!"

Ms. Suarez pressed her palms together. "I don't have a minute to think about it right now, but I'll let you know as soon as I'm ready."

"Awesome." Laurel hesitated but then threw her arms around Ms. Suarez's waist. The teacher took a step back to balance and then wrapped her arms around Laurel.

"Thank you," Laurel whispered as she let go.

"It's nothing," said Ms. Suarez. "I'll see you soon."

Laurel walked toward the door and then turned to see where Ms. Suarez was. She was looking at some papers with her back to Laurel. Power, Laurel thought as she tiptoed back. Whitney needs the power of basil. Laurel was a little surprised that the senior never acknowledged her when they passed each other on the quad, but Laurel wasn't about to ignore her request. She found the label she was looking for, quickly pinched off several leaves, and stuffed them into the side pocket of her duffel bag.

That night Laurel willed herself to dream about her mom. She rubbed rosemary and said her words, but her sleep was restless and shadowy.

Both the varsity and JV soccer teams at Warrenton Prep were undefeated, the coach told them on the bus ride to the away game Saturday morning. Laurel had never played before so large and rowdy a crowd. Avondale was down by one goal, and it was nearly halftime. Heavy gray clouds hung over the mountain ridge in the distance, and the wind was picking up. A flowery scent swept across the field with every gust, but Laurel couldn't see what was blooming.

The ball had stayed on the far side of the field so far. Laurel ran up and down, up and down, waiting. Finally, an Avondale forward missed a shot and Prep's goalie boot-kicked the ball Laurel's way. She trapped it and took off up the sideline while Kate sprinted down the center of the field.

Control . . . control . . . Laurel dribbled around Prep's half-back. It was too soon to pass to Kate, but she didn't want to get stuck in the corner, either. The crowd pressed close to the field—too close. A defender was headed her way, but Laurel knew she could beat the girl and charged forward.

The sidelines were a blur of movement and color, but one bright image came suddenly into focus: a strangely familiar flash of silky pink and yellow flowers next to brown hair.

Mom? Laurel's thought caught in her chest, and she hesitated, trying to slow it all down, to focus. The ball stopped dead, but Laurel flew. She somersaulted and landed hard on all fours, jerking her neck. She blinked at the thick grass under her palms, too shaken to stand. Rolling onto her butt, she scanned the line of spectators. Her mom had never missed her games, but this wasn't possible.

"You okay?"

Laurel squeezed her stinging eyes to shut out the world.

"Hey, Laurel, you okay?"

She knew that voice. Justin, wearing a tie and a forest green blazer, was crouched in front of her. She blinked, but he was still there. Dazed, she took his outstretched hands, and he pulled her up. He held on to her hands a beat longer than he had to.

"Thanks," she managed.

"That was a spectacular flip," he said. "Are you all right?"

"Yeah." Laurel dusted some grass off her knees. "Um, why are you here?"

"We just finished a debate meet," said Justin. "Alan and I wanted to catch the game before our bus left." He pointed at her head. "You have some grass in your hair."

Laurel touched the top of her head. "Here?"

"No," said Justin. "Here." His fingers lightly brushed the grass out of her hair, sending shivery thrills through her skin.

"Thanks," she said softly, not wanting to break the spell of his touch.

"Laurel!" Coach Peters was jogging across the field. "I

was yelling, but the ref didn't see you were down." Coach put her arm around Laurel's shoulders. "You okay?"

"Yeah." Laurel smiled at Justin. "Thanks for helping me out."

"Anytime," he said.

"You need a break?" asked Coach as they walked back to their side.

"I'm fine," Laurel said. Her emotions whirled. Turning back, she waved to Justin, and he lifted his hand. Alan stood next to him now, but there was no sign of a flowered scarf anywhere on the sideline.

"Prep is tough," said Coach. "We've got to ramp it up a notch."

"Yep," said Laurel, but the ball stayed on the other side until the referee blew the long whistle for halftime. By then Justin and Alan had disappeared. Grabbing a water bottle, Laurel sat apart from everyone else. Her knee had started to bleed, so she reached into the side pocket of her duffel for a Band-Aid. Instead, her fingers found the basil leaves she'd taken from the conservatory, and she lifted them to her nose. They were still pungent.

Perfect, she thought. Maybe these can help us win.

"Hey." Kate sat down a few feet away. "Are you okay?"

"Yeah." Laurel hid the basil.

"What's up?" Kate asked. "Your eyes are, like, huge."

Laurel gulped her water. "I thought I saw my mom. On the sidelines."

"Wha-at?" said Kate.

"I thought I saw my mom." Laurel stared at the grass between her muddy cleats. "My mom had this scarf with pink and yellow flowers that she wore all the time, and she had brown hair. I saw that scarf next to that hair."

They were silent for several seconds as Kate sipped her water. "It had to be someone who looked kinda like her. Right?"

"Yeah." Laurel wiped her sweaty face on her shoulder.

"Hey . . . um . . . does this happen a lot? Seein' your mom and all?"

"No," Laurel said. "I'm not loony."

"I was just askin'."

Laurel wanted to change the subject. "How was Willowlawn last night?"

Kate smiled widely. "Alan is sooo awesome, but Tara was bummed because Everett didn't show. I think he went home for the weekend."

Laurel squinted at a man and woman coming up the sideline. "Ka-ate?" Her fingers squeezed Kate's arm. "That *is* my dad coming toward us, isn't it?"

Kate looked up. "I met him only that once. Did he tell you he was comin'?"

Laurel shook her head. They'd hardly communicated since their fight in the diner.

"Laurel!" her dad yelled and waved to her. His other arm was supporting an elegant, black-haired woman whose high heels were sinking into the turf.

Glancing sideways to make sure Kate wasn't watching, Laurel held the basil to her nose, whispered her words, and inhaled deeply. *Power.* She didn't care what the book said; basil made her feel like she was carrying a weapon.

"Girls, move it!" Coach beckoned them into a huddle. "You really okay, Laurel?"

"Fine." The basil seemed to be elevating her energy level already.

Coach nodded. "Good. Laurel, Ally, you gotta pick it up. Number sixteen is faster than she looks. Kate, talk to Laurel out there. Let's try this." Her pen slid across the board.

The referee blew his whistle, and all the girls put their hands on top of Coach's. "AVONDALE!" they yelled.

"Laurel?"

Recognizing her dad's voice, Laurel turned to walk backward toward her position. "I'll see you after the game, Dad." Stray leaves and pieces of trash scuttled across the grass, and the temperature was dropping. The clouds over the ridge seemed closer and menacing. She couldn't believe her dad had brought a date.

"We'll go out to dinner!" her dad shouted.

"Or not," Laurel said, scowling at Number 16. The girl was good, but she was also cocky, and Laurel despised cockiness. She scanned the sidelines again, but there was no sign of a flowered scarf. She rubbed the leaves so she could feel the rush and tucked them into her waistband. The scent seemed to rocket through her blood.

The referee blew the whistle. Kate passed to Ally, who dribbled around a Prep forward. Number 16 hung back, watching the action on the other side. Moron, thought Laurel. Quickly, quietly, she zipped behind the girl. The pass would be high, and she had to get to it first. Ally slowed and—*thwack!*—the ball was in the air. Laurel raced to trap it.

Kate was downfield with a Prep fullback glued to her, and Number 16 had to be close. The crowd droned in her ears as Laurel dribbled almost into the corner. She needed only a second to turn and pass. The ball lofted off her foot and arched toward the goal, but Laurel couldn't watch Kate head it in. Out of the corner of her eye, she saw Number 16 coming at her late. Surging with anger, Laurel jumped straight up and then landed on the sliding girl.

"Ow, my foot!" said Number 16.

Laurel rolled off her and stood up. "So sorry," she said. The Avondale crowd was going nuts. Kate ran toward her and touched fists. "Awesome pass! What happened?"

"That tackle was major late," said Ally. "I can't believe the ref didn't see."

Laurel glared at Number 16 as they walked back to their end. Tie game. Glancing westward, she saw darker clouds rushing their way. The referee blew the whistle, and the Prep center passed. But Ally read it perfectly, and the ball was hers. Kate hung back while Laurel shot up the sideline and then cut toward the center as if she were taking the shot. She waved her arm and shouted. "Ally! Ally!"

But before anyone could score again, a deep rumble unleashed itself overhead, and the referee blew his whistle to call the game. Laurel held her hands close to her face. Basil was a rush she wanted to keep riding.

Her dad was standing at the bus door next to Coach while her teammates jogged up the steps. "Great game, Laurel," he said. "What a pass. I just told Coach you're leaving with me. You can take the train back Sunday night or fly."

"But I didn't pack anything," Laurel protested.

Her dad waved his hand. "We'll figure something out."

Laurel put her hands on her hips. "No, we won't. I have an essay due Monday morning. The rough draft's on my laptop in my dorm room. You can't just barge in here and expect me to drop my life."

Her dad's mouth was open.

Coach spoke up. "There's another problem, too, Mr. Whelan. Unless I have prior permission from Mrs. Westfall, I have to bring back every girl I brought. Laurel didn't tell us you were coming."

"I wanted to surprise her." He spread his hands in amazement. "This is ridiculous. She's my daughter."

"I'm very sorry, sir," said Coach. "Get on the bus, Laurel."

"You can't make an exception?" asked her dad.

"If I do, I'll get fired."

Laurel could barely hold in a smile.

Her dad took hold of her arm. "Just a minute. I want you to meet someone." The black-haired woman took a step forward. "This is Madeleine Eakins. We attended a fund-raiser in Warrenton this morning and decided to swing by."

The woman extended her hand. "Hi, Laurel. You played a great game."

Her dad's hand felt heavy and insistent on Laurel's back, rubbing a circle. "Thanks," she said, rubbing her nose. "But if I were you, I wouldn't bother playing too nice. The way my dad's running through women these days, I'll never see you again."

No one said anything for several seconds, and Laurel felt a flicker of triumph.

"Excuse us," her dad said in a strained voice. His eyes were flat with anger as he pulled Laurel away.

"Mr. Whelan," said Coach. "There's lightning. I've *got* to get everyone on the bus."

"Just one minute!" he yelled back as a bolt sliced the sky behind his head. "Look at me," he said to Laurel. "I cannot believe that my own daughter just said something that rude to someone I care about. What the hell's going on?"

"It's true," Laurel said as raindrops spotted the pavement. "You've got your little sports car, and now you're going out with all these different women. I called the other night and some woman with an accent answered."

"That was Marta," said her dad. "My new housekeeper. She couldn't come at her usual time, so she asked to come one evening. Did you bother to talk to her?"

Laurel shook her head.

Her dad's lips were pulled thin. "I don't know where to begin." Madeleine walked up behind him and handed him an umbrella.

"Here," she said. "We should go now, Bill."

Laurel wouldn't look at the woman. "I've got to get on the bus."

"Fine," her dad said as he opened Madeleine's umbrella over the two of them.

Laurel walked past Kate and Ally to the back of the bus. Through the rain-splattered glass she watched her dad open the door of his car for Madeleine and then get in. His car stayed in the same place, though, for as long as Laurel could see it from the bus.

I won't regret anything, she told herself, savoring the certainty of her anger. He so deserved that.

PART FOUR
Legacy

And in the garden, as the sun arose,
She walked up and down, and, as she chose,
She gathered flowers, white as well as red,
To make a dainty garland for her head;
And like that of an angel was her song.

—FROM "THE KNIGHT'S TALE," *THE CANTERBURY TALES*
BY GEOFFREY CHAUCER, 14th-CENTURY BRITISH WRITER
(TRANSLATED FROM MIDDLE ENGLISH BY
RONALD L. ECKER AND EUGENE J. CROOK)

CHAPTER SIXTEEN
The List in the Book

For the rest of the weekend, Laurel's emotions swirled in a mixture of hope and dread. She kept imagining Justin's touch on her hands, on her hair. If she knew when she'd see him again, she'd have the perfect flowers ready. But she also had to fix things with her dad. She didn't exactly regret what she'd said, but she knew it was pretty far over the line. Her dad had sent a livid e-mail from his BlackBerry, telling her how "immature and selfish" she was being and demanding she write a note apologizing to Madeleine. She did it, even though she thought he was the one being selfish. And she sent another note to Grandma with forget-me-nots attached.

Halfway through Tuesday's lunch Laurel glanced

up from her soup to see Susan Monroe glaring at her. Laurel's stomach plunged as the table chatter quieted around them.

"You shouldn't lie about your flowers, Laur-*elle*," Susan snapped. "They're totally lame. I got an F on that chem quiz. I can't believe I thought you were for real."

"An F?"

"Why don't you say it a little louder so the whole school hears?"

Everyone in earshot was already listening. "I never promised—" Laurel whispered.

"I'm telling everyone you're a joke!" Susan shouted. "So you have to stop lying."

"I—I didn't lie," Laurel protested, but Susan had stormed away. Nicole's eyes were as wide as Tara's uncensored smile. Her head and heart pounding, Laurel stared down at her tray.

Kate put a hand on her arm. "Just forget about her." Her voice was unconvincing.

"I told you all her flowers are worthless," Tara said loudly. "Or maybe they only work in la-la land."

Laurel looked at her in confusion. "But you *know* my flowers work," she whispered.

Tara raised her eyebrows and shook her head. "I think it's time for someone to see her counselor. Or maybe a shrink."

Several girls at the table laughed. Her hands shaking, Laurel just managed to carry her tray to the conveyor belt, but Kate didn't follow. No one followed as Laurel pushed through the door and sprinted to the dorms.

Locked in her room, she called the office to say she was sick. An hour later Mrs. Fox stopped by to feel her forehead, declared it to be a twenty-four-hour virus, and praised her for not spreading the germs. Laurel spent the afternoon trying to forget her life in the pages of a novel. Later, when she glanced up at her oversized day calendar, she saw the little J in the corner and remembered it was Tuesday.

"Anytime," he'd said on the soccer field, but she'd blown it again.

On top of that, Miss Spenser's wedding was only days away, and Ms. Suarez hadn't contacted her about the bouquet. Laurel had stopped by her classroom twice but hadn't caught her there. Did she change her mind? Laurel wondered.

Several people knocked, including Kate, who tried to convince her to go to practice. Kate stopped by again before dinner, but Laurel refused to go, even though her stomach was empty. She didn't open the door until she heard Rose's voice.

"Laurel? It's me."

Giving Laurel "the Probe," Rose came in and set a rectangular box on the floor. Laurel dove back onto her bed. "Why did you skip dinner? Kate said you skipped practice, too. Just because Susan Monroe is a pea-brained hair-flipper—"

"She's telling everyone my flowers are worthless. Everyone's laughing at me."

Rose pushed some papers aside and sat on Laurel's desk. "Puh-leeeze. Anyone who's worth having as a friend knows Susan was using you. If you're stupid enough not to study, you deserve to flunk. Everyone will forget about it in a few days."

"But Tara's dissing me, too, and she saw what my flowers did to Robbie."

Rose shrugged. "She's always dissing someone."

Laurel frowned. "Can you bring me some food? I don't want to leave my room."

Rose handed Laurel a sandwich from her backpack. "Room service now, but you are not allowed to mope. That means they win."

"They *always* win."

"Wrong. Susan got an F, remember? Which was her own fault, but maybe . . ."

"Maybe what?" Laurel's mouth watered as she unwrapped the sandwich.

"Maybe you shouldn't give people flowers for tests."

"I just promised Kate and Tashi some more."

"Then swear them to secrecy," said Rose. "Otherwise

losers like Susan will blame you for everything. There's no way flowers can make you pass a test."

"Then tell me why Tashi and Kate are doing better?"

Rose tapped her head with her index finger. "Been wondering that myself. My theory is your flowers make them feel more confident. Tashi's smart, but she chokes. I read in this psychology book that if people *believe* they're lucky or blessed, they perform better. Maybe your flowers work because people think they can."

"'I think I can, I think I can, I think I can,'" said Laurel.

Rose smiled. "Choo, choo."

"What about Miss Spenser?" Laurel pressed. "Or Kate at May Day?"

"Maybe your flowers made them feel prettier or bolder," said Rose.

"And Robbie and Tara? Explain that one, Sherlock."

Rose shook her head. "That one's beyond the realm of reason. Look, Laurel, you're messing around with people's lives. All morons want to believe in magic, and then they have such high expectations."

"Great expectations," said Laurel, remembering one of her mom's favorite novels.

"Here." With her foot extended Rose slid the package she'd brought in across the carpet. "This was outside your door."

Crumpling her napkin, Laurel bent over the box. "Oh my god!" she screamed. "It's from Grandma!"

"No way." Rose hopped off the desk to look.

Laurel quickly cut the tape and pulled a leather-bound book out of shredded paper.

"Excellent," said Rose. "That looks vintage."

Laurel's heart beat deeply as she ran her fingers across the familiar title embossed in gold. "It's exactly like the one in the tower. *The Language of Flowers.*"

"How does Grandma know you're into flowers?" asked Rose.

"I wrote her notes." Laurel propped the book on her legs and opened it to the flyleaf. A list of names was written there, and a small card was stuck inside. She glanced up, but Rose wasn't watching anymore. Laurel slid the card into the back pages.

"Look at this." She turned the book to face Rose and read aloud.

Violet Evelyn Mitchell
Rosemary Louise Simpson
Cicely Jane Nelson
Lily Rose Clark

Rose squinted at the list. "Guess that's your pedigree. Your ancestral line."

"I *know* what it means," said Laurel. "But it's yours, too."

"Nope. I don't see my name on that list."

"Your mom probably has this book," Laurel said. "In the attic or somewhere."

"Nope." Rose shook her head. "She's not into flowers."

"But we're cousins."

"That doesn't mean we're identical," said Rose. "I have my own gifts."

Laurel's heart skipped at Rose's admission. "So, you really think I have a gift?"

"I guess so."

Laurel closed the book but kept it on her lap. "If you have a gift, then you should use it, right? You said that when you were talking about what a waste case Everett is."

Rose reached for her backpack. "Maybe this is more complicated than I thought. It may be time to call in the experts."

"Like who?"

"I don't know. Grandma's pretty unpredictable. What about Ms. Suarez? She knows about flowers, right?"

Laurel nodded thoughtfully. "I think she's a kindred spirit."

Rose laughed. "Kindred spirit, I like that." She mussed Laurel's hair. "Hey, I thought of another flower myth."

"Which one?"

"Persephone," Rose said in a theatrical voice. "Daughter of Demeter, goddess of agriculture."

"About the seasons, right?"

Rose nodded. "Persephone has to go to the underworld for half the year, so Demeter mourns, and that makes it winter. When Perseph comes back, spring is sprung."

"We read that one in middle school."

"But don't forget the grown-up version," Rose added. "Young Perseph was abducted by Hades when she was out picking flowers. She yanks up this beautiful bloom and out pops Hades in his chariot to deflower her."

"Deflower?" asked Laurel.

Rose smiled. "'Deflower' is one of those quaint terms for losing your virginity. It probably has to do with pollination. In other words, Hades raped her. Nice story, huh?" Rose walked to the door. "Got to run. Fare thee well, kindred spirit."

Laurel quickly locked the door behind Rose and took out the card Grandma had sent with the book. The envelope contained a sepia photograph of a pretty young woman with her brown hair in a bun and a cameo pin on her high-collared dress. Laurel turned the picture over. *Violet Evelyn*, it said. *1889*. She skimmed the note:

Dear Laurel:
Is it all happening again? My blessings.
Love, Grandma

"Blessings," Laurel repeated. She could almost feel the hands and hearts of her mom, her grandma, and her great- and great-great grandmothers reaching out to her. Across the depths of time, across the chasm of death they stretched, offering her rare knowledge and the gift of flowers. She just had to find a way to take hold of their hands.

Laurel picked up all the flowers she'd found around campus lately—more rosemary, myrtle, and fresh forget-me-nots—and bundled them together with floral tape. Now she wanted a ceremonial light. She found a small votive candle in the school-issued emergency kit, and some matches in her drawer. Standing on her chair, she lifted the top of her special stuff box and took out her mom's letter.

She shut her curtain, turned off the lights, and lit the candle. She sat cross-legged on the floor with the flickering glow at her feet. The antique flower book and the letter lay in her lap. Clutching the bundle of blooms in her right hand, she called out to the gifted generations before her.

"Violet, Rosemary, Cicely, Lily," she whispered, and

raised the tussie. "Come . . . teach me to Flowerspeak." Then she said her words—the words which her mom must have taught her, words which now belonged to her.

A gust of wind shook the windowpane, and Laurel threw her arms wide as her body began its pleasing hum. She closed her eyes and saw . . .

The luminous dream angels dancing their circle again. They danced to the humming, to a music that sang through the universe. The world around them was icy and barren, but they sang on, casting their light and harmony until a green shoot broke through the ice. Tiny leaves unfurled and stretched toward the rising sun. Higher and higher, the leaves offered up their bud, which opened into gossamer petals. Laurel leaned . . .

But something bumped behind her. Out of place, out of rhythm, it dragged her back. Laurel shut her eyes tighter, but the humming had stopped.

"Laurel? You in there? I've got brownies." It was Kate's singsong voice, but Laurel didn't want her, not now. Her arms fell to her sides, aching.

Sighing, Laurel blew out the candle and reread Grandma's note. Then she dialed Grandma's number by heart. The line rang and rang, but no one answered.

CHAPTER SEVENTEEN
Flashlights in the Garden

The next morning Laurel dug up the courage to face the hallways and found them less hostile than she'd expected. Only two girls canceled their requests for flowers, though Laurel assumed that Tara had and she didn't run into Susan. Kate even asked her to go to a movie at Willowlawn on Friday.

After dinner on Thursday she ran to the garden to gather purple lilac and lily of the valley for herself and Kate. She'd save hers until she was face-to-face with Justin. The Saturday track meet was home, so she was hopeful he'd be at movie night. On the way back from the garden, she stopped by the conservatory, but it seemed eerily dark. Ms. Suarez clearly wasn't working on the wedding tussie, and Laurel couldn't bring herself to go inside alone. Not at night.

By Friday morning, though, her spirits began a spiral descent. There was still no word from Ms. Suarez about the wedding bouquet, and time was running out. She doesn't want me, Laurel thought. When she got back from practice, she was stunned to see a single white iris outside her door. She scooped it up and hurried inside.

An iris meant "message." From Ms. Suarez, Laurel thought, and sat down heavily. If Ms. Suarez was working on the wedding bouquet, she had to be in the conservatory or the gardens. But if Laurel ran to find her, she'd miss the bus with Kate. And if she didn't show, Ms. Suarez might think she wasn't serious about Flowerspeaking.

Kate wasn't in her room, so Laurel wrote a note and slid it under her door. She wrapped Kate's tussie in a wet paper towel and tucked it into the corner. Kate would get over her absence, but Laurel couldn't miss the chance Ms. Suarez offered. Miss Spenser was getting married only once. Laurel pulled a sweatshirt over her head and sprinted toward the cedars.

As her feet pressed the fallen needles and her hand swept aside the branches, a soft and piney scent enveloped her. She felt a surge of calm and confidence, but she didn't see any flowers nearby. Up ahead the conservatory seemed dark again, as if deserted.

"Ms. Suarez?" Laurel opened the door and leaned into the darkness.

"Finally!" said a familiar voice from the shadows. "I was beginning to wonder."

"I just got your message," Laurel said, panting. "Soccer practice took forever. You want me to turn on the lights?"

"No." Ms. Suarez was standing behind a table covered with white vases. "I have a better idea." She disappeared into a storage closet.

Laurel walked toward the table. Two dozen identical vases were lined up. Each one had a single bloom or frond of greenery in it and an index card with the flower's name scrawled across it. She had time to read only a few before Ms. Suarez emerged carrying a large and tarnished candelabra.

"Let's do this the old-fashioned way," said Ms. Suarez. She set the candelabra at one end of the table and handed Laurel a box of ivory candles. Laurel placed a candle in each arm while Ms. Suarez lit them.

"I love candles," said Ms. Suarez softly.

Laurel could feel herself calming down. "It's like we're on an island of light in the middle of a great darkness."

Ms. Suarez seemed to freeze.

"What?"

Ms. Suarez rubbed her arms. "Déjà vu. I just had a

flashback—to a moment when your mom and I were girls."

"Tell me about it," Laurel pleaded. "Please."

Ms. Suarez's watery eyes shone in the candlelight. "I have to set the scene. Lily—your mom—was interested in a particular boy at Willowlawn. . . ."

"Not my dad," said Laurel. "He didn't go there."

"No," said Ms. Suarez. "Lily wanted a specific flower for a dance. Somehow she got it into her head that the bloom would be most potent if picked precisely at midnight."

"Weren't there curfews back then?"

"Of course, even stricter than now." Ms. Suarez gave her an exaggerated frown. "Mrs. Fox wouldn't appreciate me telling you this. You might get ideas."

Laurel raised her right hand. "I solemnly swear that I won't get any ideas from your story about my mom. None at all. Whatsoever."

Ms. Suarez smiled. "Guess I can't stop now."

Laurel tapped the table with her fist. "No, you can't. So my mom wanted a flower at midnight and . . ."

"And we couldn't go out the front doors of the dorm, because they squeaked horribly and our dorm mother was a light sleeper. We climbed out a first-floor window and ran to the garden. When we found the flower, Lily said something just like what you said. Something about our flashlights making an island of light in the darkness."

Laurel felt the story sink into her. "What flower was it?" she asked.

"I wish I remembered." Ms. Suarez sat down next to her. "When I first came here, your mom and I ran into each other in the garden all the time, but it took us months to discover we both had the gift. We felt so dense afterward."

"So, did it work?" asked Laurel wistfully, wondering who Justin was hanging out with at movie night. "Did she take the flower and get the guy?"

Ms. Suarez shrugged. "I don't remember. Lily must have moved on quickly."

Will he even notice I'm not there? Laurel thought, as she pulled a vase toward her nose. "Can I ask you a personal question?"

"Yes, but I reserve the right not to answer. We've got to get going."

Laurel's eye traced the tattered edge of the flower in the vase. "Have you ever used Flowerspeaking to get a guy interested in you?"

Ms. Suarez's head tilted. "And you said you weren't going to get any ideas."

"I didn't," protested Laurel. "I mean, I already had that idea—about guys."

Ms. Suarez laughed. "We all do." She straightened one of the index cards on the table. "Have you ever tried using flowers to bring about your own desires?"

Laurel shrugged. "Maybe a little."

"Then you know it's a delicate business. The flowers don't always 'speak' the way we want if we use them *only* for ourselves."

Tell me about it, Laurel thought.

Ms. Suarez turned a vase between her hands. "It seems like it should be so easy, to make another person love us forever. But then we might have perfect lives, and no one's life is meant to be perfect, is it?"

Her eyes were solemn as she met Laurel's. "I believe our gift is meant for others, not just for ourselves. And speaking of others, we've got to get to work on Sheila's bouquet. I don't want to keep you up till midnight before your flower girl debut."

Laurel's sigh made the candlelight waver. Tara will have no mercy. Ms. Suarez came back carrying a leather book—just like the one in the tower, just like the one Grandma had sent—and laid it on the table between them. The sight of it jarred Laurel's memory.

"I've been wanting to tell you," she began. "I *finally* heard from Grandma."

Ms. Suarez clapped her hands together. "Oh, Laurel! I'm so, so happy. Maybe she's ready to take her place again—with you and with all of us. What did she say?"

"Not much, but she sent me my mom's flower book. Is this one yours?"

"It belongs to the conservatory. I found it hidden with Juan José's journal."

"But you have one of your own, don't you?" Laurel asked.

Several silent moments passed. "I did," Ms. Suarez said, "but someone stole it."

"Who?" Laurel asked in astonishment. "Why?"

"My ex-husband." Ms. Suarez raised her index finger. "And that's all I'm saying. He doesn't deserve another word."

Laurel felt like she could erupt with questions, but she held them in. She wouldn't let anything or anyone spoil the magic of this evening.

"Now," said Ms. Suarez, "we're going to make this a learning experience."

Laurel sighed dramatically. "Must we?"

"We must." Ms. Suarez said with a little smile. "I've given you an array to choose from. You can look up the meaning of each bloom, inhale its fragrance, and then I want you to make a recommendation to me: should we include it or not?"

"Is this a test?" asked Laurel.

"Not at all. It's an excellent way for you to gain

experience. Now that you've aroused the love between Miss Spenser and the professor, what emotions, what feelings will help their love last until death-do-us-part?"

Laurel skimmed the first index card and opened the book to A. Alyssum's sweet scent was for "worth beyond beauty." She jotted that down, starred it, and moved to the next vase. Ms. Suarez hovered nearby, busying herself at the edges of candlelight.

"Ms. Suarez?" Laurel said when she was nearly done.

"Yes?"

"Are Flowerspeakers magic?"

"Magic?" Ms. Suarez pursed her lips. "Not exactly. The flowers have the magic. The power to awaken and arouse. The power to remind. You release those powers."

Laurel's eyebrows drew together. "How?"

"Precisely? No one knows. We're few and don't want much attention—no extended scientific studies. It's been so since the beginning of time, among people who have ever walked the gardens of the earth. When the gift is weak, people call it a green thumb. Some Flowerspeakers—the strongest—have influenced the decisions of kings and queens. Some have made potent arrangements for White House dinners."

"Really? Wow." Laurel phrased her next question delicately. "So, when you give someone flowers, do you say anything? Like special words?"

Ms. Suarez shook her head. "I don't, but your mom did. My family hums." She began the familiar strain of "Ode to Joy." "We choose a melody that expresses what we want to happen, and we hum to bring forth the magic."

"I feel like my whole body is humming when I'm with flowers!" Laurel said.

Ms. Suarez nodded. "Your gift is potent, but that means you have to be careful."

"But the magic doesn't work unless I say my words, right?" Laurel asked.

Ms. Suarez frowned. "That's a good question for Cicely. Your flowers are unlikely to work for *other* people without your words, but your nose is very sensitive. The strongest scents might affect you anyway. Which is why I want you to take this slowly, so you can figure out these things. Okay?"

Laurel nodded as she moved to the next vase.

Ms. Suarez put a hand on her shoulder. "One more piece of advice: be sure to choose a flower for faithfulness."

Laurel glanced sideways, wondering again about her teacher's ex-husband.

Ms. Suarez checked her choices. "Good . . . good . . . interesting . . . good . . . yes. Sheila will have quite a bouquet of lovely wishes."

"But there's room for one more flower, isn't there?"

Ms. Suarez pushed away the vases Laurel had rejected. "Which one? You've recommended an armful."

"Lily of the valley, for the return of happiness," said Laurel. "It's blooming now."

"But her happiness has already returned," said Ms. Suarez. "She's happy now."

"Yeah, but—" Laurel struggled to articulate the urgency she felt. "But lily of the valley was in the first tussie I ever gave her, and it's the flower my mom chose to introduce the language to me. I feel like we're *supposed* to include it."

Ms. Suarez shrugged. "There's no harm, I guess."

Laurel rubbed her palms together. "Good. Can we get some right now from the garden? We could take flashlights."

Ms. Suarez threw her head back. "Not going to get any ideas? Yeah, right."

Minutes later they were winding down a garden path, the beams of their flashlights bobbing in front of them.

"Did you know some flowers release their scent only at night?" asked Ms. Suarez.

"Really?" Laurel sniffed, but the fragrance of some nearby pines masked all others.

"Here we are," said Ms. Suarez. Their flashlights illuminated sprays of bell-shaped white blooms clinging to their stalks.

"Yesss," said Laurel. *The return of happiness.*

"Another island of light," whispered Ms. Suarez as she went down on one knee. "How many do we need? You should always arrange blooms in odd numbers."

Laurel crouched next to her. "Is that one of our ancient wisdoms?"

"No." Ms. Suarez grinned. "I saw it on a cable gardening show."

Laurel giggled as she took a stalk.

"I'm guessing one won't be enough?" said Ms. Suarez.

"Three, please," said Laurel. Happiness never seemed to last long enough. Maybe it had to return over and over and over.

"There." Ms. Suarez handed Laurel the sprigs. "Anything else?"

Laurel shook her head. "I'm good." They directed their flashlights back toward the conservatory, and she could smell sweet whiffs from the lilies as they walked.

"You can ride with me to the wedding tomorrow," Ms. Suarez said. "We should get to the bed-and-breakfast early, and there's something I want to show you, too."

"What?"

"You'll see."

Laurel didn't press her, but her steps slowed when she

saw the conservatory tower shining above the trees. Her skin trembled in the cool darkness. "Ms. Suarez?"

"Yes?"

"People say the ghost of Gladys haunts the conservatory," Laurel whispered.

"People say lots of things," said Ms. Suarez. "Too many things. What is a ghost but the presence of a strong memory? Gladys's spirit will always be alive here, and that's a good thing." She put her hand on Laurel's lower back and gently pushed forward. "Don't you think the spirit of Thomas Jefferson still walks the floors and fields of Monticello? And the spirit of Emily Dickinson still roams her gardens?"

And my mom still wanders through my dreams, Laurel added to herself.

They were past the cedars before Ms. Suarez spoke again. "Lily's ghost must be powerful, too," she said softly. "No one we truly love ever leaves us completely."

CHAPTER EIGHTEEN
The Many Gardens of This Earth

Reaching into a basket woven with ribbons, Laurel scattered rose petals—pink, red, and white—as she walked up the grass past rows of white folding chairs. The lavender dress she'd borrowed from Kate was gauzy and scalloped at the bottom, like petals sewn together. For the garland on her head, she had chosen purple violets to say "you occupy my thoughts." She added blue forget-me-nots, because she wanted to remember and be remembered.

Laurel returned the guests' smiles as she approached a vine-twisted trellis at the entrance to the Victorian bed-and-breakfast. Rose snapped a picture of her, but Kate looked away. When Laurel had gotten back from the conservatory the night before, she'd knocked on Kate's door to apologize, but no one answered. That morning

Ms. Suarez had given Laurel a ride to the bridal brunch before the afternoon wedding, so she hadn't seen Kate before she left.

Laurel's petals landed on the professor's shiny black shoes, but he didn't shake them off. She turned as the notes of "Trumpet Voluntary" sounded, and everyone stood. Miss Spenser was wearing a cream-colored, lacy dress that fell to her shins, and both her hands clutched the bouquet. Her eyes were wide, as if gaping at this unexpected twist in her own life. Laurel threw another handful of petals, which the wind spun and lifted over their heads. *Bright cut flowers, leaves of green, bring about what I have seen.*

The minister spread his arms. "Welcome to all: friends, colleagues, and students. We will begin with a blessing from one of Luke and Sheila's favorite poets, Gerard Manley Hopkins."

Justin suddenly appeared. Laurel's face warmed, but he wasn't looking her way. His black hair hung straight over the collar of his Willowlawn blazer. He held a paper steady in both hands, took a visible breath, and read.

"Pied Beauty

Glory be to God for dappled things—
     For skies of couple-colour as a brinded cow;
          For rose-moles all in stipple upon trout that swim:

Fresh-firecoal chestnut-falls; finches' wings;
  Landscape plotted and pieced—fold, fallow, and plough;
    And all trades, their gear and tackle and trim.

All things counter, original, spare, strange;
  Whatever is fickle, freckled (who knows how?)
    With swift, slow; sweet, sour; adazzle, dim;
He fathers-forth whose beauty is past change:
        Praise him."

Laurel's eyes glazed. The words were strange as they tumbled into her mind, but she felt, with a spine-tingling rush, the abundance and richness of life. It was all out there—sweet and sour, swift and slow, waiting for her. A world of everything and its opposite. Her eyes met Justin's, and a tear escaped down her cheek. She looked away. Her heart thumped, deep and full, as he walked by her and back to his seat.

After the ceremony Laurel found Kate in the buffet line. "How's it going?"

Kate crossed her arms. "I can't believe you ditched me last night."

"I didn't *want* to," Laurel said. Kate was angrier than Laurel thought she'd be. "Ms. Suarez needed my help with the wedding bouquet. Isn't it gorgeous?"

"I guess so." Kate piled finger sandwiches on her

plate. "You know, sometimes I just don't get you."

"What's to get?" Laurel said lightly, but Kate frowned.

"You're always disappearin', and sometimes you don't even answer your door when I *know* you're in there. And then last night . . . I thought we had plans."

Laurel directed Kate toward a less crowded corner of the lawn. "I couldn't help it. Ms. Suarez asked me to help her out a *long* time ago, but I had no idea it'd be last night. I couldn't miss that, not after giving all those flowers to Miss Spenser. But I really wanted to go with you."

Kate stared at her food. "I told Alan to tell Justin you were comin', and then you don't show. It makes me look bad, and what's Justin supposed to think now?"

Laurel scanned the crowd, but Justin was talking to Rose and Mina with his back to her. I need to see his face, she thought. "Did you tell him I like him?"

"Kinda," said Kate. "I told Alan, so you blew it by not showin'."

"Did you tell Justin why?" Laurel asked. Her stomach felt too tight to eat.

Kate shrugged. "I said you had to go help a teacher, but it sounded pretty lame."

As soon as Kate finished eating, Laurel took hold of her elbow. "Let's go see that bouquet." It was displayed with the wedding gifts on a table not too far from Justin.

"Only two months." A woman with white hair

whispered loudly as they passed her. "They've known each other only two months. Can you imagine?"

Laurel had to smile. How could Miss Spenser *not* believe in flower magic when this day was like a miracle? Her bouquet was inside a tulip-shaped vase, whose own petals seemed spun of lacy silver. Feet shaped like leaves sprouted from the base. It was a posy holder, Ms. Suarez had explained the night before, that once had belonged to Gladys.

"Awesome bouquet, isn't it?" said Mina. Her black hair was in a coil on her head, and she had an orange lily over one ear. "So many flowers."

"It's perfect." Laurel's eyes danced from one magical bloom to another.

Mina touched the silver filigree. "This posy holder is amazing, too."

"Posy?" said Kate. "Like in 'Ring around the Rosie'?"

"Kind of." Laurel tried to position herself to catch Justin's attention. "A posy is a little bouquet, like a tussie." But not so powerful. A voice she was hoping to hear interrupted her thoughts, and she felt like she had wings flapping in her chest.

"Hey, Laurel," said Justin. "Hi, Kate."

"Hi, Justin," said Kate. "What's up?"

"The usual." Justin glanced from Kate to Laurel.

"Uh, Mina," said Kate, grabbing her arm. "Can I ask you something? Now."

"So, you're the flower girl?" Justin said, taking a step closer.

"As a favor to Miss Spenser," Laurel explained. "She really wanted one."

"It fits, though," said Justin. "You like flowers a lot, don't you?"

"I do," said Laurel. Her violets and forget-me-nots were nearly under his nose, but she and Justin stood wordless for a few elongated seconds. "I *really* wanted to come to movie night, but something came up."

Justin shrugged. "It happens."

"And I like that poem you read. I want to read it again—when I can think about it."

"It's pretty cool," said Justin. "A lot of Hopkins's poetry was rejected when he was alive. People thought it was too weird."

"Really?" Laurel frowned in thought. "It was a little strange, but it made sense, too."

Justin's smile was wide and sunny.

"Wha-at?" Laurel's face mirrored his.

"I could tell you got it."

Her skin warmed under his addictive smile. "I love poetry. Miss Spenser reads us a poem almost every day."

Justin nodded. "Cool. Who's your favorite?"

"Laurel!" a slightly accented voice called out, and she saw Ms. Suarez approaching.

"Emily Dickinson," Laurel said quickly. "Or maybe E.E. Cummings."

"There you are," said Ms. Suarez. One hand clutched the wide brim of her hat while the other balanced a flute of champagne. She let go of her hat, and—almost immediately—a gust of wind caught it and carried it into the rows of white chairs.

"I'll get it," said Justin, running after it.

"I've been looking for you," Ms. Suarez said. "I'd like to show you something."

"Right now?" said Laurel.

Justin reappeared. "Here's your hat."

"*Gracias.*" Ms. Suarez took the hat and raised her glass toward the wedding trellis. "If there's hope for Sheila Spenser, there's hope for us all." She took another sip and laced her arm through Laurel's. "Come. I want to show you a garden I designed."

Laurel's eyes met Justin's. "But we just . . ." she stammered. "I . . ."

Ms. Suarez glanced between them. "Yes?"

"We were talking," Laurel managed. "Justin and I."

Ms. Suarez turned to Justin. "Something important has come up, and I need to speak with Laurel immediately. We'll be back in a few minutes."

"Oh." Justin took a step backward. "Okay. Uh, see you later?"

Laurel could read only confusion in his eyes, and her flowers were failing miserably. Again. "Bye."

When he was out of earshot, Laurel spun on Ms. Suarez. "What's so important? I—"

"You like him," said Ms. Suarez. "He's very sweet, but we may not have another chance to see this display. C'mon."

Your timing's horrible, thought Laurel. With a glance at Justin's retreating back she followed her teacher through a break in a boxwood hedge.

"You're entering my spring garden," said Ms. Suarez. "I also designed one for summer, fall, and winter, so each season has its own show. The owner of this B and B wanted truly unique gardens." Ms. Suarez squeezed Laurel's arm. "C'mon. You can't be moody on a day when our flowers have triumphed."

Laurel felt beyond moody. Nothing ever goes right with Justin, she thought.

Still, delicious fragrances swirled around her head with each quiver of wind. Butterflies and bees danced from bloom to bloom, intoxicated by the surfeit of nectar. Gradually Laurel's frustration dissipated as she remembered her mom's garden. Any other world, any other mood, dropped away as soon as you entered and opened yourself to the waves of sensuous delight.

In Ms. Suarez's garden the color yellow came first:

sundrops, coreopsis, and a lemony blooming vine arched toward the blue sky. Laurel turned a corner and felt doused in pink. It was stunning, but it seemed bizarre, too: such concentrations of one color at a time.

"I wanted visitors to encounter the colors of each season," said Ms. Suarez. "To contemplate color itself."

Glory be to God for dappled things, Laurel thought, remembering the first line of Justin's poem. Who's he talking with now?

Her teacher strolled to a wooden bench under another trellis and sat down. The pink blooms on the leafy vines were just starting to open. This spot was as romantic as the kissing couch.

Maybe I can bring Justin here, Laurel thought. She looked for the turret of the Victorian house to regain her bearings. Sitting down next to Ms. Suarez, she took the garland off her head and slowly turned the flowers between her hands.

"They're lovely," said Ms. Suarez. "So delicate."

And useless, Laurel thought. Then it struck her. When she'd said her words before the ceremony, she'd directed all her attention, all her energy, toward Miss Spenser and her bouquet. Maybe I could say them again with Justin. Just for me.

Ms. Suarez drank the last sip of champagne and set the glass in the grass near her feet. "Now that Cicely's back in your life, I can tell you something very important."

"Did you hear from her?" Laurel asked. She'd called Grandma again that morning, but no one had answered.

"Not yet," Ms. Suarez said. "But I think I will. I want you to know something else: your mom wrote to me when she was about to die."

Laurel's entire body tensed as she held her breath.

"Lily hoped with her whole heart that her only child would have the gift, but she couldn't be certain until you became a woman. She knew she wouldn't be around then, so she wanted someone to watch you and await the signs."

Laurel blinked in confusion. "My mom asked you to watch me?"

Ms. Suarez nodded. "If I had the opportunity."

"But she didn't know I was coming to Avondale," Laurel said. "I didn't even know I was coming here." She stood up and took several steps away from the bench. "Why didn't you tell me this *before*? Like when we first met?"

"I couldn't," Ms. Suarez said emphatically. "I had to make sure you had the gift. If you didn't, your mom made it clear to all of us that she didn't want you to know it existed."

Laurel's head was spinning. "All of us?"

"Flowerspeakers. She asked others to watch you, too: people closer to your home."

Laurel folded her arms tightly. "So, you've been watching me ever since I got here?"

"From a distance," said Ms. Suarez. "Until your first bouquet. Then I tried to contact Cicely. Your mom wanted her to be the one to explain it all—to teach you."

Laurel shook her head. "I *still* don't get it. Why didn't my mom tell me herself? She could have taught me all about Flowerspeaking before she died."

Ms. Suarez walked to Laurel's side. "No. She couldn't risk that. What if she'd told you about this marvelous gift? What if she showed you its secret paths, and then you didn't have it? And she was gone. She wanted to spare you the pain of Gladys—the pain of knowing and not having."

"But she should have known I have it," Laurel said. "She knew me all my life, and . . . and she's my mom."

"Maybe. I don't know what mothers know." Ms. Suarez's voice was hardly above a whisper. "And your mom could never have predicted the depth of Cicely's grief."

Laurel wanted to ignore the sadness in Ms. Suarez's voice, but it penetrated her own anger as she walked to a bush heavy with yellow blooms. "Was my mom one of our elders?"

"She would have been, I think."

"Will you be?"

Ms. Suarez shook her head. "I don't know. I've laid low for so long. . . ."

Laurel turned and put her hands on her hips. "So, if

my mom's gift was so powerful, why couldn't it fight the cancer? Why isn't she still alive?"

Ms. Suarez's head fell back as if she were asking Heaven the questions. "The flowers helped her for a while, especially with the pain. But we're not miracle workers. The power of life and death is beyond us."

Laurel frowned at a bee gathering nectar, and Ms. Suarez cleared her throat.

"Did you know that bees see colors differently from us?" she said. "On many petals there are distinctive color patterns that direct the bees to the nectar, like traffic signs. We can't read them, but the bees do."

Laurel batted the air with her garland, and the bee deserted the bloom in a frantic, zigzag flight. A burst of laughter reached their ears, and she pictured Kate and Alan, how they touched each other so easily. *I want to be with Justin*, she thought.

Ms. Suarez glanced at her watch. "Oh no! I've got to run. My plane leaves in a few hours."

"Your plane? Where are you going?"

"Costa Rica," said Ms. Suarez. "They're building a hotel for ecotourists and have endangered a rare orchid habitat. It makes me furious!"

Laurel suddenly felt forlorn. She wanted to hold on to someone her mom had trusted with secrets. "Can't somebody else go? How am I going to learn about my gift?"

"I'll be gone only a week. Luke—the professor—has agreed to care for the conservatory, and you can help. I left instructions."

Laurel's forehead wrinkled. "*He* has the gift?"

"No, but he's decent with flowers," said Ms. Suarez, squeezing Laurel's shoulder. "Spend time with the blooms, but make bouquets only when absolutely necessary. *Please.*" Ms. Suarez kissed her on both cheeks and hurried away.

But prom's next weekend, Laurel thought. Putting her garland back on her head, Laurel wound through the rainbowlike gardens and stopped at the edge of the gathering. A stray program lay in the grass, and she found the Hopkins poem reprinted there. She spotted Justin across the lawn with Mina. Laurel started walking, lifting her hand toward the flowers, and saying, "Bright cut flowers, leaves—"

But she stopped speaking and slowed down as she realized that Mina was seriously flirting with Justin, as she saw him put his arm around Mina's shoulder. Wearing a low-cut green silk dress, Mina looked exotic and gorgeous as she smiled up at him.

Laurel looked down at the modest dress she'd borrowed. I look like I'm twelve, she thought.

"Hey, flower-power chick." Tara was at her elbow. "Have you heard?"

"Heard what?" Laurel said shortly.

"Alan just asked Kate to prom," said Tara. "So please get to work on *my* flowers."

Laurel gawked at her. "You're kidding, right? You've been abusing me nonstop."

Tara smiled knowingly. "Of course I have. We don't want *everyone* to believe in your flowers. We don't want just *anyone* to have them, do we? They should be reserved for special people."

"Like you?" Laurel said incredulously.

"Exactly."

"No way."

Tara's face hardened. "Look, Laur-*elle*. You think you're special, but I can crush you if I want. I want some flowers to make Everett like me, and I want them by Wednesday. Got it?"

Tara walked away, and Laurel looked around for Justin and Mina. They were headed into Ms. Suarez's garden. That should so be me, she thought.

CHAPTER NINETEEN
Everything and Its Opposite

The conservatory felt light-years from campus to Laurel. An orangey fragrance saturated the bright light streaming through the glass ceiling. Clearing off some terra-cotta pots, she set her backpack on a rustic table far from the orchids. She taped a photograph of herself and her mom before the cancer to the window. It was Sunday, so she could spend the whole afternoon here.

Since the wedding Laurel had avoided both Rose and Mina. If she didn't confirm that Justin was dating Mina, she could still cling to hope. Strangely, no one had seemed to be talking about it at chapel or brunch that morning. Browsing the aisles, Laurel removed dead blooms and checked for moistness, according to Ms. Suarez's notes. Creamy blooms still graced several gardenia plants, so she made a mental note to pick some later for Tara. Laurel had managed to patch things up with Kate, but she wasn't up to battling Tara. Kate had some bizarre loyalty to that girl that Laurel couldn't fathom.

She picked up an herb marker from a container: SWEET BASIL. Moving down the row, she found another marked just BASIL. She carried one of each plant to her table, sat on a stool, and leafed through her paperback. Basil was for hatred, but sweet basil meant "good wishes." Laurel wasn't sure if it was luck or intuition that had made her pick the right one for Robbie. And she was positive her mom had cooked with *sweet* basil.

But plain basil had made her feel strong and focused at the soccer game and at the diner. This was the plant that would help her stand up to people like Tara and Susan. Her dad had just caught her off-guard, and she'd let her temper flare as never before. She rubbed a leaf and lifted it to her nose.

I'll just have to watch what I say, she thought. I can handle basil. Nothing else could be as bad as her dad betraying her mom's memory. She put the sweet basil back and grabbed another plain one to take back to her room.

A gardenia for Tara; basil for Whitney. The contrast reminded her of Justin's poem, which she reread last night along with her mom's letter. *Swift, slow; sweet, sour; adazzle, dim*—everything and its opposite. That's my life, she thought.

The handle of the conservatory door jiggled, and the door began to open. Laurel ducked behind a small tree and watched the professor step inside.

"Professor Featherstone," she called out. "It's Laurel."

"Good afternoon, Laurel," he said in his leisurely accent. His shoes squeaked across the damp floor. "It's so refreshing to see a young person interested in horticulture."

Laurel started walking toward him; she didn't want him to tell Ms. Suarez she was making bouquets. Off to one side a cascade of fuchsia-colored flowers caught her eye, and she stopped. "Wow. What's this?"

"Bougainvillea." The professor gently cupped a bright frond. "It's tropical."

Laurel's eyes drank in the carnival colors as she leaned forward.

"Alas," he said, "it has no scent."

Laurel turned to hide her smile at the exotic aroma sweeping through her.

He pushed his fingertips into the soil. "Still moist. May I show you something that *should* have an amazing scent?"

"Sure." Following him through the tables, Laurel felt a spasm of panic when she realized where they were headed.

"After you." The professor stopped at the orchid enclosure and extended his hand.

She wrapped her fingers around the cool metal framework and hesitated. Ms. Suarez had said to avoid the orchids, but Laurel's eyes danced from one extraordinary bloom to another. Small yellow flowers dotted with maroon flung themselves from a tangle of roots. Lacy pink petals pouted, like the orchid in the woods. Silky white blooms glowed ghostlike. She took a shallow breath and stepped inside.

"It's a remarkable collection," he said. "Ms. Suarez has over a hundred orchids. I have only a dozen myself. Do you understand what a hybrid is?"

Her eyes followed his finger to waxy leaves above curly roots. Purplish buds were emerging from the center. "A hybrid's when you combine two things?"

"Correct." He unwound a hose from its hook. "There are over twenty-five thousand naturally occurring species of orchid and over thirty thousand man-made hybrids. This one is a hybrid Ms. Suarez created. If the bloom is appealing, this plant could be worth thousands."

Laurel's mouth gaped. "Of dollars? For one plant?"

The professor nodded. "That one"—he pointed to

another—"is a descendent of one collected in Borneo in the eighteen hundreds for the renowned conservatory of King Leopold of Belgium. Overcollected, I should say. The species is believed to be extinct in the wild."

Laurel rubbed her nose and smelled basil on her fingertips. "If it's extinct, then why does Ms. Suarez have it?"

The professor smiled. "You've heard of Gladys and Edmund du Valle?"

"Of course." She was starting to relax; her body felt perfectly normal.

"A descendent of Gladys's sister is alive in England on the family estate and still tending that conservatory. When Ms. Suarez renovated this one, she implored the woman to send orchids to restock it. The woman sent ten, including the priceless Borneo species. Clearly she had no idea. Ms. Suarez then cross-pollinated it with a very fragrant cattleya orchid. She's waited five years for the bloom."

"Five years? You're kidding."

"No," he said. "Ms. Suarez also told me an intriguing legend about that Borneo habitat. This particular orchid is found only in a place called Mount Kinabalu. According to local lore, the spirits of the dead ascend to that mount when they depart their bodies."

A shudder passed through Laurel's body. My mom, too?

"You've heard of the Galapagos Islands?" asked the professor.

"Darwin went there?"

"Exactly. Mount Kinabalu has a similarly unique ecosystem. Species thrive there that grow *nowhere* else. We're all very excited to see this bloom. It could be breathtaking."

The lady slipper orchid in the woods had taken Laurel's breath away. *Literally.* She rubbed her nose and sniffed basil again.

"Orchids are the most complex flowers in the world," he continued. "They grow everywhere, from the tropical rain forests to the Arctic Circle. Some have the scent of chocolate. Others reek like roadkill. All to attract a specific pollinator."

Laurel pointed to the bud. "Could that one reek?"

His face crinkled with amusement. "It's highly unlikely. Both the parents emit pleasant scents."

"So this one should, too?"

"It should," he said. "If you're in the right place at the right time. Orchids sometimes release their fragrance in a quick burst, and some release only at night. It's a strange trick."

Laurel suddenly felt warm, and her heartbeat pulsed at her temples. She turned away from the orchids and passed several tables before leaning on one.

The professor followed her. "Are you feeling all right? You look pale."

"I'm just tired," said Laurel, lifting her hand to her face.

"Your generation is far too casual about sleep." The professor took out his wallet and handed his card to her. "May I ask a favor? Contact me immediately if that orchid opens. Ms. Suarez believed she'd return in time, but the bud's swelling."

On Tuesday afternoon Laurel stood at the window of her class and watched Justin walk to his with Alan. She felt her stomach drop, even though she didn't want it to, but stayed out of his sight. Kate was heading to Willowlawn every chance she got and had invited her along for Wednesday dinner, but Laurel didn't think she could handle watching Justin and Mina together. She told Kate she was busy.

On Wednesday she gave both Kate and Tara tussies with gardenia and forget-me-nots to take with them. After practice she slipped away from her teammates and headed to the conservatory until she was sure they'd left for Willowlawn.

The basil plants Laurel had brought back were thriving on her sunny windowsill. Basil made her body surge with power, and its scent must have counteracted the orchids. Still, she was careful not to say her words in her room with basil around. She'd moved one of the plants to her desk and was toying with its leaves when someone knocked.

"Hey." Kate went straight for Laurel's mom's chair. "Where have *you* been?"

"Busy. I had to check on some plants in the conservatory after practice."

"But I thought you were still comin'," said Kate. "We almost missed the bus lookin' for you."

"Nope." Laurel sat down backward on her desk chair. "Not this time."

"But you're never gonna get to know any guys if you don't start goin' to dinner."

Laurel pulled off a leaf and rolled it between her fingers. "I didn't think you or Tara really wanted me along."

Kate almost snorted. "Well, Tara won't anymore. *That's* for sure."

Laurel's skin prickled anxiously. "Why not?"

"Your flowers messed with her brain," said Kate. "She's not even back yet."

"Is she with Everett?"

"Nope. They decided she had to be feverish or high and took her to the clinic."

"They? What happened? I *told* her to be discreet."

"Hardly." Kate leaned forward in the chair. "So, Tara had the flowers in a shoppin' bag and went over to Everett and took 'em out. He smiled that lopsided grin of his. Then Tara shoved the flowers at him, but he leaned back and fell off the bench. So Tara yelled, 'Everett, honey!' And then the whole cafeteria burst out laughin'. Tara tried to get him to smell them again, but Everett yelled, 'Get off me, you frickin' lunatic!' Then the cafeteria monitor grabbed Tara's arm and wouldn't let her near him."

Laurel let her head drop forward against the desk chair. "She's going to kill me."

"Yeah, but she's the one who acted like a 'frickin' lunatic.' "

"But she'll blame *me* for it." Laurel lifted the basil leaf close to her nose. What if Tara had spilled everything to some teacher? "Did she mention my name?"

Kate was studying her fingernails. "I don't know. But there's no way Everett's askin' her to prom."

"I don't get it. My flowers should have worked." I said all the words, she thought.

"He kept turning away," said Kate. "Maybe he didn't get a good enough whiff."

Laurel rubbed her temples, and the scent of basil seemed to strengthen. "But you and Alan are still hot and heavy, right?"

Kate smiled and nodded. "He asked me to come to his track meet on Saturday afternoon. Wanna go with me?"

"Saturday afternoon? But you said you'd help me with the prom tussies then. And it's going to take all day. You can't desert me."

"I'm not desertin' you," said Kate, looking at the floor. "Anyone can help you. Admit it: you love all these girls wantin' your flowers. You love all this attention."

Laurel was stunned. That last comment didn't sound like Kate *at all*. She opened her desk drawer. "Look at all these notes. I've got to make twenty bouquets, and you promised to help. You said you'd be a hostess with me, too."

Kate stood up. "You want me to pass up a prom date so I can ladle punch?"

"I didn't say that," Laurel said. "It's just—it's just that you had a life before Alan. Remember? And now you act like he rules your life."

"He doesn't *rule* me." Kate crossed her arms. "You should be happy for me; you're my friend. Have you even been in love? It changes everything."

"Friend?" Laurel's rising anger felt clean and pure. "Puh-leeeze. You're spending all your time with Alan and Tara."

"Well, what do you expect? You're never around anymore. You're always in the gardens or at the conservatorium."

"It's conserva-*tory*." Laurel flung the word. "And you're obsessed with Alan."

"Well, you're obsessed with flowers," said Kate. "You're turnin' back into this weirdo hermit like you were when you got here."

Laurel twisted the basil leaf and tried to calm her breathing. "Look. When will Alan's track meet be over? Maybe you can help me after? Or in the morning?" It was a long shot. Kate slept until noon on Saturday unless they had a game.

Kate didn't meet her eyes. "I have to see when the bus is leavin.' Can't we just have fun? I mean, we're both goin' to prom."

Laurel snickered. "Not exactly."

"But Justin'll be there," said Kate. "I'm sure."

With Mina. Laurel looked away. "He's not really my type."

Kate threw up her hands. "How would you know? Have you even had a boyfriend?"

Laurel's anger and disappointment felt like a hot, churning mass she wanted to aim right at Kate. "Get out," she said. Snarky comments shot through her head, but she pressed her lips together.

Kate let out an exasperated groan as she threw open the door. Slamming it behind her, Laurel clenched her teeth and willed herself not to cry.

* * *

Laurel's eyes scanned the office as she waited for the principal to get off the phone. A dried, dusty flower arrangement topped one bookcase, but there was nothing fresh and living in the room. Laurel had no idea why she'd been summoned. Nervousness spread through her body like an itch. *Did Tara snitch on me at Willowlawn?*

Mrs. Westfall hung up and pressed her lips into a half-smile. "Thanks for coming in, Laurel. I'm sure you know something about the history of this school?"

"A little," said Laurel.

"Well, after the unfortunate scandals last year we now require our students and parents to sign a waiver allowing us to search rooms and lockers if drugs are suspected."

"Drugs?" Laurel was so confused she felt light-headed.

"Yes. I'll come right to the point. We received a note, searched your locker, and found this." She set a baggie of something greenish brown on her desk. "Is it yours?"

Laurel stared at it. "I guess so. Can I smell it? I think it's basil."

"It is, but what's it doing in your locker?" Mrs. Westfall pointed to another dried herb. "And rosemary, too?"

Laurel shifted in the chair. "I like the smell, and it helps me focus. My mom had a big herb garden, so it reminds me of her." There. She'd played the dead-mother card.

Mrs. Westfall pursed her lips. "It's an odd habit, though, don't you agree?"

"But it's not like I'm doing drugs." The petulance in her own voice surprised her.

"True, but we have to be careful and avoid even the appearance of drugs. These may be only herbs, but someone thought they were drugs."

"Who?" said Laurel, leaning forward.

Mrs. Westfall shook her head. "I'm sure you understand why I can't tell you that. Students are allowed to report drug use anonymously."

"But it doesn't go on my record, does it?"

"Of course not. It's only basil and rosemary." Mrs. Westfall almost smiled. "However, it's not a good idea to keep it in your locker. I'm sure there are reporters still attuned to our activities here who'd be only too happy to write an exposé."

"Yes, ma'am." Laurel started to get up.

"One more thing," said the principal. "I've been hearing your name lately in connection to flowers. Can you tell me more about that?"

Laurel practically stopped breathing. Lies could boomerang back at you, but she couldn't tell the truth. "I—I've been trying to help some girls. Everyone says I have a way with flowers and carrying them can make people feel more confident. I read that in a psychology book."

Mrs. Westfall tilted her head back. "Avondale has a long association with flowers going back to Gladys du

Valle. Our gardens truly set us apart." She paused. "You understand I must stay on top of everything that happens, Laurel. Everything."

"Yes, ma'am." But I've told you everything I can, she thought. Everything you'll believe.

For the rest of the day Laurel eyed everyone suspiciously, because someone—probably Tara—was out to get her. She couldn't help wondering if her mom had ever faced such an enemy and if she had managed victory. During practice she gave Kate the cold shoulder and then sat as far away as she could at dinner. Kate left a note on her door asking her to stop by, but Laurel crumpled it.

"'Rosemary to remember, With sage I esteem,'" Laurel recited sarcastically when she was locked alone in her room. "Thyme to be active, Parsley for the feast." Then she froze, because she'd finally remembered the last line without even trying. She flipped through her book, but it said only the same: *Parsley for the feast, festivities.*

"Lame," she said, tossing the paperback. "I need something with *real* power."

"Yo, Flora?"

Laurel recognized Rose's voice later that evening and let her in. "Flora?"

"The Roman goddess of flowers." Rose wrinkled her nose. "What smells in here?"

"Basil. I'm studying it." Tiny bits of leaf were scattered across her bed.

Rose sat down on Laurel's desk. "Is that what they found in your locker?"

"Yeah. That and some *killer* rosemary." Laurel dropped into her mom's chair.

Rose laughed. "Are you okay? You're kind of missing in action these days."

"Like anyone cares." Laurel pulled another basil leaf off a plant in her window. "I can't believe someone told Westfall to search my locker. It *had* to be Tara."

"Maybe. But she might not be the only person who's pissed off at you."

"You think Susan snitched?"

Rose picked up a pencil and twirled it between her index fingers. "You have a pretty high profile these days, so you're more likely to be a target."

"But that wasn't a prank," Laurel protested. "Westfall was dead serious."

Rose smiled. "But they can't exactly expel you for illegal possession of *basil*."

"No." Laurel folded the leaf in half. "So Mina's seeing Justin now?"

"Seeing, as in going out with?" Rose's eyebrow lifted. "Puh-leeeze. He's a freshman."

"But she was flirting with him big-time at the wedding," said Laurel.

Rose shrugged. "That doesn't mean they hooked up. Recreational flirting is Mina's favorite sport. The other guys were all dweebs or taken."

Laurel sat up straighter. "So, she doesn't like Justin?"

"Not like *that*."

Laurel felt so relieved she couldn't even smile. Still, that didn't mean Justin was hers. *Not yet*, but she felt sharp and strong, like she could make anything happen. She glanced at the notes divided across her bed into categories. "Do you have plans tomorrow night or Saturday morning? Kate just ditched me, and I have to make all these prom bouquets by myself."

"Ditched?" said Rose. "Aren't you being kind of hard on her?"

"Wait a sec. *I'm* being hard on *her*?" Laurel said. "She has no time for me. She's completely obsessed with Alan."

Rose picked up the basil plant on the desk. "He's a decent guy."

"That doesn't mean she gets to treat me like dirt."

"Does she? She says she's asked you to do stuff with them."

Laurel gestured toward the notes. "I'm busy."

Rose scrunched her nose and set down the basil. "Maybe this whole flower thing is getting out of hand. People are starting to say you're stuck-up."

"Me?" Laurel suddenly had the oddest sensation, like she was floating outside herself, watching her anger rise, hearing her words sharpen. "Whose side are you on?"

"I'm *way* too smart to pick sides," said Rose. "But you're acting like you always have more important things to do these days."

"Maybe I do," Laurel snapped, crossing her arms and legs on the chair.

Rose held up her palm. "Fine, but if that's your attitude, you're not going to have a ton of friends here."

"I've got you, don't I?"

"I'm family."

"So you *have* to be my friend?"

"That's not what I said." Rose glowered. "Look. This is exactly what I mean. We just started talking, and now we're arguing. You never used to be like this."

"Like what?"

"Argumentative. Defensive. Maybe the flowers are doing weird things to you. Have you heard from Grandma since that book came?"

"No," Laurel said sullenly. "And she doesn't answer her phone."

"What about Ms. Suarez?"

"Out of the country."

"Right." Rose threw her hands out and stood up. "Are you sleeping okay? Your personality seems . . . different."

"Maybe this is the real me," said Laurel.

"Maybe," said Rose softly. "You haven't—uh—seen your mom again, have you?"

Laurel's voice was taut with anger. "Kate has the biggest mouth on campus."

"She was worried about you. That's the only reason she told me."

"But everyone already thinks I'm bonkers." Laurel paused, waiting for her cousin to contradict her, but Rose didn't. "So, can you help me with the prom flowers or not?"

Rose shook her head. "Not. I want nothing to do with prom."

"You could be a hostess, too."

"Nope. I'm taking a moral stand. I'm protesting how people treat prom as the most important thing in their lives. In the big picture it's just one night that's never going to live up to anyone's grandiose expectations."

"Can't you protest next year? I need you."

"Nope. The time is ripe."

Laurel's anger surged like venom through her veins, and she flung her words as if they were barbed.

"You'd go if a guy asked you, but nobody has."

Rose narrowed her eyes. "I am *not* going. End of discussion."

"Someone will ask you to dance."

"Maybe," said Rose. "But I'm not playing wallflower."

"Is that what you think I am?" said Laurel.

"Whoa." Rose held up her hands. "You're being totally paranoid. I'm your friend, remember? Kindred spirit?"

"Kindred?" Laurel said. "But you can't even Flowerspeak. Your gifts are nothing like mine, not even close."

Rose opened her mouth, but—for once—she didn't have a comeback before she left the room.

CHAPTER TWENTY
Basil for Hatred

*A*s Laurel brushed her teeth Friday morning, she realized with a pang that her dreams had been dark. Even her mom had deserted her. Emptiness pooled inside her as she spit out toothpaste. She slipped fresh basil in her pocket and left for class.

All her teachers, and even Mrs. Fox, fixed her with "the Probe." Laurel forced smiles and said she was fine and knew she'd be called in by her counselor, especially after she skipped practice to start the tussies. Strapping on her backpack, she found two buckets in the dorm kitchen and half filled them with water. Then she headed for the garden.

Other than Whitney's, the girls' desires were predictable: they wanted to flirt, to dance, to be the brightest flower in a field of flashy blooms. Even Nicole wanted a tussie now. In the garden Laurel cut lemon verbena for "enchantment," double red dianthus for "pure and ardent love," and scarlet poppies for "fantastic extravagance."

As soon as she opened the door to the conservatory, Laurel knew the air had changed. There was a rich and unfamiliar scent: spicy and alluring. She set her buckets down, and when she stood up, the entire room moved in a slow, disquieting wave. *Spizzy, tinny, dingly.* She clutched a table and looked toward the orchids.

All the windows were closed. Steadying herself, Laurel opened one and leaned into the rush of unscented air. She unlatched the others and gulped breaths as she made her way toward the metal frame. Reaching into her pocket, she rubbed a basil leaf and held it to her face as she stepped inside.

Ms. Suarez's orchid seemed to glow like a setting sun, and Laurel trembled with excitement. She was the first person in the history of the world to lay eyes on its frilly, yellow petals with orange spots. *Glory be to God for dappled things,* she remembered.

Laurel took a step toward the orchid, but reality rippled again. She stumbled back, her fingers grabbing the cold metal. A yearning, deep and hollow, wrenched her body. She hugged herself tightly, but she wanted Justin there to steady her dizziness—his lips close enough to kiss. His arms will be around me at prom, she vowed.

Goose bumps pricked up her arms, and she shivered violently. The world outside was cooling and darkening, but she couldn't close the windows and stay. And there was nowhere else for her to assemble the tussies, nowhere free from snooping eyes.

"Poor Ms. Suarez," Laurel said as she walked back to her table. "Five years, and she missed it." She reviewed her list for Whitney: candytuft for "indifference" and foxglove for "insincerity." And lots of basil. The senior had basically ignored her since the flower request, but it wasn't worth ignoring her back. Yawning, Laurel folded her arms on the table and laid down her heavy head. She was suddenly, wholly exhausted. . . .

Laurel's head popped up, and she blinked anxiously at the darkness. What time was it? Her nose felt clogged, and the breeze passing over her skin was cool—too cold for the plants. She stood up to stretch but heard a strange rustling near the orchids. Dread squeezed her chest. Ms. Suarez hadn't exactly denied the ghostly Gladys rumors. Laurel ducked low and peered into the darkness, her fears multiplying with the pounding silence.

Is Gladys jealous of me? she wondered as a craving for basil pinched her. Basil to sharpen and focus. Standing quickly, she lunged toward the tabletop, but miscalculated and the plant toppled off. A window rattled across the room, and Laurel spun around.

"Mom?" she cried out. No one answered. Her mom felt nowhere near—nowhere Laurel could be in this lifetime. Her craving gnawed at her gut, and she dropped to all fours. Small rocks bit into her knees as her fingertips raked through the dust and dead leaves to find the plastic container. She ripped out the basil and sniffed, but her head was stuffy. She crushed a few of the leaves, but still nothing. She stuffed the basil into her mouth, but spat it out. Then something with lots of legs crawled across her bare knee.

"Ahhhh!" Laurel screamed and climbed onto the stool. Shuddering with disgust, she hugged her knees to her chest as tears streamed around her nose.

"This isn't it!" she yelled at the darkness. "This isn't what I want!" She wanted kindred spirits. Rooms full of scents and blossoms. She wanted to feel loved but also powerful. She reached again for the basil.

Basil is for hatred, a voice said in her head. A voice she knew. Her mom's voice. Her own voice. *Hatred.*

"Idiot." Laurel pulled her arm back. "Moron." She'd been breathing basil—and its subtle poison—for weeks. Kate and Rose weren't speaking to her. She and her dad exchanged only curt e-mails now, thanks to her basil-filled outbursts. Her face fell into her hands, and she sobbed.

Moments later Laurel sensed the air around her brightening, and she looked up at the night sky beyond. Silver light from a newly risen moon was streaming through the glass roof. She wiped her tears on her sleeve and spread her hand into the moonlight.

Sun shine, star shine, moon shine, you shine. The memory of her mom's sweet voice flooded her ears. *Shine and bloom beneath the light.* Laurel cupped her palms to capture the moonlight. Every night she'd begged her mom to sing that little song she'd made up—every night until she was too embarrassed to ask.

"'Sun shine, star shine, moon shine, I shine,'" Laurel sang softly. But she couldn't hold on to the moonlight any more than she could hold on to her mom.

A gust of cold wind jiggled the windows, and with a shiver Laurel remembered Ms. Suarez's orchid. I hope it's okay, she thought. One by one she closed all the windows, but she didn't want to go anywhere near the orchid.

"Bye, Gladys. Bye, Violet," Laurel whispered before she pulled the conservatory door shut. It was silly for her to fear Gladys or any other ghost. Her own great-great-grandma Violet had been Gladys's friend. They must have laughed and marveled over flowers and secrets in this very room. Laurel locked the door and ducked under the cedars. Then she doubled back to pull off some of the long needles.

"Cedar for strength," she whispered. The right kind of power.

Her clock said 1:36 A.M. as she opened the windows in her room to dilute the scent of basil. She tied the plants in a plastic bag and put them outside her door before playing the message on her phone: a dog barked and then a raspy voice followed.

"Quiet, Dickens. Laurel, this is Grandma. I had a strange feeling that I *had* to call you tonight. Is everything all right?"

Rain beat into the soggy ground on prom morning. The instant Laurel awoke she called Grandma back, but no one answered. Still in her pajamas, she picked up the bag of basil, carried it to the dorm kitchen, and dropped it in a trash bin.

"Good-bye, basil," she said.

On the way back Kate came out of the bathroom just ahead of her. Laurel now realized that everything that had happened between them lately was skewed by basil's influence. She hadn't been herself at all—not the self she wanted to be.

"Kate?" Laurel's voice was a congested whisper.

Kate turned and put her hands on her hips. "Well. Where have *you* been?"

"I'm sorry."

"First you skipped soccer practice," said Kate. "Coach was pissed. And then you weren't at dinner. I knocked on your door at like midnight, and you didn't answer. I thought you'd left Avondale or something. Why didn't you answer *this* time?"

"I wasn't there."

Kate stepped closer and lowered her voice. "Where were you?"

"In the conservatory. I fell asleep there."

"Nooo," said Kate. "All by yourself? Weren't you scared?"

"Terrified. I heard this noise, and I thought it was the ghost."

"Was it?"

Laurel shook her head. "No. It—it was just me. I haven't been myself."

Kate nodded, close-lipped. "I was so worried I almost went to see Mrs. Fox."

Laurel couldn't help smiling.

"What's so funny?" Kate demanded.

"I guess I'm glad that you were worried," Laurel said, blinking quickly.

Kate threw out her hands. "Of course I was, but

you've been totally hard to live with, Whelan."

"I know, I know. It won't happen again. Promise." No more basil.

Kate nodded. "So, Alan's track meet is off 'cause of the rain, but I was gonna come help you with the flowers anyway. . . ."

Laurel bit her lip to quell the quick rise of sarcasm. Basil had rooted deeply inside her, and its power was seductive. She'd have to fight herself, fight her darker side, to keep it from growing.

"Do you still need me?" Kate asked.

"Definitely." Then, before she could think twice, Laurel put her arms around Kate, who squeezed her back.

"Can you believe prom's *tonight?*" said Kate, almost squealing.

Laurel shook her head. "No. I have so much to do."

Back in her own room she pulled on holey jeans and a stained sweatshirt. She dialed Grandma's number but still no answer. She met Kate, and they sprinted through the slanting rain to grab bagels and juice before heading to the conservatory. Laurel unlocked the door as Kate shook the rain off her umbrella.

"You have a key?" said Kate.

"I'm watering while Ms. Suarez is gone." Laurel held the door open for her.

"Ooo, what's that smell?" said Kate.

Laurel's head still felt full of cotton, like her senses had overloaded the night before. "Maybe an orchid? Ms. Suarez is breeding a really rare one that just bloomed." She opened a window near her table to be safe. "But don't tell anyone about it, okay?"

"Cool," said Kate. "It smells orangey."

"That's just the orange trees," Laurel said with relief. She wasn't sure she could handle the orchid right now, especially not without basil.

Rain pattered rhythmically on the glass roof as they worked side by side for several hours. Under Laurel's guidance, Kate cut the stems evenly, bound them with floral tape, and tied neat ribbons. Laurel had simplified her plans, so the tussies had just a few flowers and some potent greenery. All except Whitney's.

"Kate?" Laurel's heartbeat leaped with her doubts.

"Hmm?" Kate pulled a red ribbon tight.

"Does Justin think I'm a total loser?"

"No—oo." Kate spoke more cautiously than usual. "I think he's confused. You're not an easy person to get to know, ya know?"

Laurel returned her smile. "I hope I didn't scare him off."

Kate shrugged. "Justin beats his own drum."

Laurel looked at her quizzically.

"Or marches to his own beat, whatever." Kate pointed

to the flowers Laurel had set aside for Whitney. "Who are those for?"

Laurel felt a quick flicker of fear. She didn't want to lie to Kate, but she'd promised Whitney her total silence. "Whitney."

"Really," Kate said, but she didn't press Laurel further. "I think all these sweet smells are makin' me sleepy. Can I see it before I go?"

"See what?"

"That rare orchid. I've never seen one."

Laurel took a deep breath. "Sure, but don't tell anyone about it, okay?"

In the daylight the yellow-and-orange orchid seemed almost ordinary, just another fancy flower showing off. "There it is."

Kate leaned into the bloom. "It doesn't even have a smell."

Laurel started to check but stopped herself. "Oh yeah. The professor told me some orchids release their scent only at night." She grabbed her head with both hands. "The professor! I was supposed to call him as soon as it bloomed."

"Want me to?" Kate asked.

"Can you? I have a few things to finish up." They walked back to her table and Laurel dug through her backpack for his card. "Just tell him it opened."

"No problem." Kate started toward the door.

"Hey, *you* need some flowers for prom," Laurel said, following her.

Kate waved her hand. "Alan's gettin' me something."

Laurel grinned. "I could make something so special he won't be able to resist."

Kate shook her head. "No, thanks. Maybe your flowers got his attention, but now he's pretty into me. I don't wanna mess with that. If it's only because of the flowers—"

"You *know* that's not true."

"But if it's only the flowers, then it's like a trick, isn't it?" Kate met Laurel's eyes. "I wanna know his real feelings."

"But the Featherstones aren't a trick," Laurel protested. "Their love is true."

Kate shrugged. "So maybe I just want Alan to give me flowers."

"He will. Definitely."

After Kate left, Laurel sat motionless at the table littered with stems and leaves. She met her mother's eyes in the photo on the window. "It's not a trick," she whispered. The Featherstones' love was deep and lasting, and any fool could see Alan adored Kate.

A squeak near the entrance of the conservatory startled Laurel. She turned and drew in a sharp breath; Tara was walking toward her.

"I'm coming tonight," Tara announced. "So is Nicole. She told me you'd be here."

Laurel jumped off the stool. "You mean to prom?"

"Duh. Whitney said we could. I'm not about to be the only freshman not going."

A craving for basil lashed at Laurel, but she tried to ignore it. I should have grabbed some cedar on the way in, she thought.

Tara shook her head at the labeled flowers. "I don't understand why people still want your flowers. They're such a joke."

Laurel took a measured breath. She had to start over—with everyone. Even Tara. "I'm sorry it didn't work out with Everett. I heard—"

Tara crossed her arms. "You can stop pretending you care, flower girl."

"I want to help you out." Laurel took a step closer. "Really."

Tara stared at her hard for a moment, but Laurel didn't back down. "He thinks I'm a freak," Tara said.

"We could try some other flowers or a different combination." Laurel pushed Whitney's flowers toward the back of the table.

"Like those?" Tara pointed to Whitney's flowers. "I didn't have any of those."

Laurel tried to sound casual. "Uh, trust me. Those aren't what you need."

Tara flipped her hair back. "Why not?"

"Because they're for somebody—something—else."

"Somebody more important than me?" said Tara petulantly.

"No." Laurel's eyes flicked to the basil in Whitney's tussie. It would make this so much easier. "They're just wrong for you. Trust me."

Tara's fingertips touched a yellow foxglove bloom. "Are they Kate's?"

"No." Laurel had to press her hands against her thighs, because the basil was so close, so tempting.

Tara lifted her nose. "What's that smell? It's fruity."

"Just the orange trees." Laurel pointed toward a corner. "They're over there."

"I don't trust you," said Tara. "So I'm going to pick my own flowers this time." She hesitated a moment near the staircase and then headed toward the orchids.

A wave of fear washed through Laurel. No, please, no, she prayed. "There's nothing good over there."

Tara ignored her. Laurel hurried after her and gasped.

Tara was stroking a ruffled petal of Ms. Suarez's orchid. "What is it?"

"An orchid," Laurel said. "It's totally rare, but what you smell is an orange tree. I swear. This flower might not even have a scent. I—I don't know."

Tara glared at Laurel. "I am sooo tired of you lying to me."

"I'm not lying," Laurel stuttered. "I—it's just—"

"It's just that you don't like me, and you don't want anyone else to like me." Tara's sudden smile was strange as she reached for something. "You think you can just walk in and take over the whole school."

Laurel shook her head. "Why would you think that?"

"Hmm. Let's see. You stole my spot on the soccer team, and you're trying to steal Kate, too. I bet you sabotaged my chances with Everett." Tara turned toward the orchid and opened the pair of scissors that was somehow in her hand.

"Stop!" Laurel yelled, waving her hands. "You can't! This is the very first time that plant has ever flowered. Ms. Suarez has waited five whole years."

"Not my problem."

Laurel lunged for the bloom, but Tara was too quick. The scissors flashed. Watching the orchid drop into Tara's hand, Laurel felt as if she'd been stabbed in the chest. "No!" she screamed.

"Yes. I'm going to wear this flower tonight." Tara twirled it between her fingertips. "Everett will just love it." She slinked past Laurel and headed for the door.

Laurel stared in disbelief at the severed stem. "Ms. Suarez is going to kill me."

PART FIVE
Matters of Consequence

"It is at the edge of the
petal that love waits."

—FROM "THE ROSE IS OBSOLETE" BY WILLIAM CARLOS WILLIAMS,
AMERICAN POET AND PHYSICIAN, 1883–1963

CHAPTER TWENTY-ONE
The Scent of an Orchid

"*It's* here! The bus is here!" yelled Kate. She dashed from the window of Laurel's room and sat down on the bed to strap on her high heels. "Oh no! I forgot to tell Alan I was gettin' dressed in your room."

"He'll search high and low to find you," said Laurel. She had French-braided Kate's hair, pinned it up, and attached a few forget-me-nots. "You look gorgeous."

"Thanks." Kate focused on her for a moment. "Now don't forget lipstick."

Laurel shrugged and reached for some pink gloss. "I'm just a hostess."

"But Justin'll be there," Kate said in her singsong voice.

Laurel held her finger to her lips. Her feelings for

Justin weren't common knowledge, and she wanted to keep it that way.

"Oh, I told Miss Sp—I mean, Mrs. Featherstone about the orchid," said Kate. "She said the professor will be back tonight. They're chaperonin'."

Laurel's insides hollowed with fear. But he doesn't know what the orchid looks like, she told herself. He can't recognize it. She wanted to tell Kate about Tara clipping it—Kate could help keep an eye on it at prom—but something stopped her. Kate knew way too much already— more than Ms. Suarez would ever want her to know.

Kate wobbled and then stood straight on her heels. "I can't believe this is happenin'. I'm Cinderella!" She hiked up her dress and raced out the door.

Laurel's head had felt clearer after a hot shower, but her stomach was twisted with worry about the orchid and all the tussies she'd given out. With all those floral scents whirling through the ballroom, anything might happen.

"Please don't let Ms. Suarez find out," she prayed. "Ouch!" She pricked her finger on a thorn as she pinned her own flowers above her ear. She'd saved the fuchsia bougainvillea—an exotic flower not mentioned in either of her books—for herself. It will mean what I want it to mean, she thought. Romance . . . and fun.

Laurel strapped on her black sandals, which were not

exactly glass slippers. If Kate was the belle of the ball, then Laurel felt more like Cinderella sweeping the hearth before the fairy godmother arrives on the scene. "Belle of the ball." That was one meaning for orchids. They could also mean "passion."

Laurel adjusted the flowers in her hair and spun around so that the silky skirt of her strapless black dress billowed out. Outside her window a bus horn honked three times. Holding her breath against the basil, Laurel took Whitney's flowers out of her refrigerator, slipped them into a shopping bag, and covered them with tissue paper. She felt a little like Whitney's fairy godmother rescuing her from the handsome prince with ulterior motives. Her phone rang just as she was shutting the door, and she ran back in.

"Hello?" she said impatiently.

"Laurel?" The voice cracked halfway through the name. "It's Grandma Cicely."

Laurel sat down in disbelief.

"Are you there? Are you all right, dear?"

"I—I'm fine. I got the book you sent. Thank you."

"It was yours."

The horn beeped again, and Laurel jumped up. "Grandma, I'm dying to talk to you, but I have to go. It's prom tonight, and the bus is leaving."

"Prom?"

"I'm just a hostess. Can I call you back tomorrow?"

"But I—"

"I love you, Grandma. Bye." Laurel threw down the phone, grabbed Whitney's flowers and flew out her door. The bus had already pulled away from the curb.

"Wait!" she screamed. The rain had stopped, but her heels sank into the soft ground.

"Please wait!" The bus lurched to a halt, the door opened, and she ran up the stairs. Kate—sitting next to Alan—waved to her from the back, but all of the seats near them were taken. Panting, Laurel scanned the rows again, but Justin wasn't on the bus.

"You can sit there," the driver told her. He pointed to the handicapped seat, and Laurel sat down, her heart sick with regrets.

WELCOME TO THE ISLANDS, MON! proclaimed a banner hanging over the entrance to the hotel ballroom. Laurel trailed her classmates through cardboard palm trees and crepe paper flowers on the lookout for Justin, but she didn't see him.

"Groovy," Nicole said sarcastically. "A disco ball." Suspended above the dance floor, the mirrored ball cast dizzying rectangles of colored light. Nicole's hips swayed to the reggae beat as she and Tara sashayed onto the dance floor.

Laurel found the refreshment table and hid Whitney's flowers underneath it. Sugar cookies and triangular sandwiches were piled high on plates. Sighing, she filled a few cups with punch and set them in front of the bowl. Some Cinderella night, she thought.

"Good evening, Laurel." Mrs. Westfall picked up a cup. "How are you?"

"Fine," Laurel said warily. "How are you?"

Mrs. Westfall looked around. "Where are all the other hostesses?"

Laurel gestured toward the spinning lights. "On the dance floor."

"Would you mind passing on some information to them?"

"Sure," Laurel made herself say.

Mrs. Westfall took a step closer. "I'm concerned that someone might try to spike the punch. Would you all keep an eye on it and let us know if anyone's acting suspicious? We don't want any car accidents on prom night, do we?"

"No, ma'am." Laurel scowled at the punch bowl as the principal walked away. Mrs. Westfall wanted her to snitch, as if she had friends to spare. A craving for basil flitted through her body.

"What's wrong?" Whitney held out an empty cup. She was wearing lots of makeup and a low-cut red dress that glittered when she moved.

"Nothing," said Laurel as she tipped the ladle over Whitney's cup.

"You've got my flowers, right?"

"Yep," said Laurel. Nicole was coming toward them.

Whitney hiccupped. "When they announce king and queen, bring them right to me, okay? I'll be surrounded, but I'll watch for you."

"I'm sure you'll be the queen," Nicole gushed. "I voted for you."

Laurel coughed to hide a giggle, because she'd written Rose's name on the ballot as a joke. Her delight fizzled as she remembered her cousin wasn't speaking to her.

Ricky walked up and slipped his arms around Whitney's waist. "Whit, c'mon."

Laurel couldn't help staring. Ricky was movie-star gorgeous, and Whitney reached for his hand as they walked away. "They *look* like the perfect couple," Laurel said.

"He is sooo hot." Nicole took a sip of punch. "By the way, Tara's pissed."

"At me? Why? *She* stole the orchid, and *I'm* going to get busted."

"But that flower doesn't smell like anything. I gave her some of my stuff."

Laurel frowned. She wasn't up for dealing with Tara. "What stuff?"

"This one." Nicole pointed to the lemon verbena—for enchantment.

Passion and enchantment, thought Laurel. Pretty potent. But she hadn't said her words tonight—not over anyone's flowers—and she wasn't sure she would. There's no point if Justin doesn't show, she thought. She wished she'd never mentioned Justin, even to Kate.

"What about you? Who's your target?" she asked Nicole.

Nicole shook her head. "Nuh-uh. I know better than to make public pronouncements about my personal life."

Laurel bit into a sugar cookie. A redheaded senior stumbled and nearly fell into her date as he grabbed a sandwich from the pile. "Hey, um, Mrs. Westfall wants us to make sure the punch doesn't get spiked and to report if anyone's drunk," she said.

Nicole shook her head again. "I think that's her job, not mine."

Frowning at the happy crowd, Laurel noticed the professor threading his way toward her. Her stomach clenched. "I have to go to—to the bathroom."

"Laurel!" He called out before she could escape. "May I have a word with you?" The professor guided her away from the table, but she could feel Nicole's eyes on them.

"Sheila gave me your message," he said, his hand on

her elbow. "I'm so eager to see it. We would have gone directly to the conservatory, but there wasn't time."

Laurel felt like she was sitting in the first car on a monster roller coaster ascending an alpine peak. In a moment she'd feel the drop into nothingness.

"Would you like some punch?" she asked, not meeting his eyes.

"No, thank you," said the professor.

"Sandwich?"

"No. Thank you." He paused. "Is something wrong? You seem agitated."

Laurel's stomach was a massive knot, and she couldn't draw a deep breath. "I have to tell you something," she said. "About the orchid."

His breath was minty as he leaned close. "It does have a pleasing scent?"

"I think so. It's just—" Laurel paused, but nothing intervened to stop the difficult flow of truth. "It's just somebody cut the bloom."

The professor stepped back as if struck. "Cut?"

"It wasn't me," she added, shaking her head. "I know how much that flower means."

"You have no idea." His eyes passed back and forth. "Somebody cut it? *Why*?"

"She wanted a prom corsage." Laurel's voice was fast and squeaky. "She followed me into the conservatory."

"A corsage?" he repeated with disdain. "Ms. Suarez will be livid. She was hoping to win awards with that hybrid."

"But I didn't do it!" Laurel protested. She flinched as cool hands came up from behind and covered her eyes.

"Didn't do what?" Kate giggled behind her.

Laurel pulled the hands off and spun around to see Justin standing directly behind Kate. His hair was down, the way she liked it best. She met his dark eyes but couldn't copy his smile.

"Look who I just found." Kate bumped Laurel playfully.

"Hey," said Justin. "Hello, Professor." Justin leaned forward to shake hands with the older man, and his body seemed to tug on Laurel's with the confidence of gravity.

I need to touch him, she thought. Soon.

"Hello, Justin," said the professor. There was silence for an awkward moment, then he and Kate spoke simultaneously.

"Well, I—"

"You wanna—"

The professor bowed his head to Kate. "Please. After you."

Kate glanced from Laurel to Justin. "The DJ's awesome. You two need to dance."

Laurel met Justin's eyes again. "Want to?" he asked.

"Yes." Laurel couldn't keep the happiness off her face, even as she glanced over at the professor.

"Go ahead and dance," the professor said gruffly. "It *is* prom."

"Thank you," said Laurel, but she felt the professor's hand grip her arm.

"I have one question," he whispered. "Is it here?"

Laurel nodded once. She slipped her hand into Justin's, and a sweet shiver rippled through her body.

His head bent toward her. "What's he talking about?"

"Nothing," Laurel said. "Just a flower."

"Do you always wear flowers?" Justin asked.

Laurel touched the petals above her ear and laughed. "Not always. This is a tropical plant that grows in the conservatory. I work there sometimes." At least until Ms. Suarez finds out about the orchid, she thought.

"Sweet," said Justin.

As Laurel followed him through the crowd, she spotted one of her bouquets. Her words began to spill out in her head. *Bright cut flowers, leaves*—but she froze the thought and stopped walking.

Justin turned around. "Something wrong?"

Laurel smiled up at him. "Nothing's wrong." She had another chance with Justin, and she'd make sure it was perfect. It was too noisy for him or anyone else to hear her voice as they neared the disco ball. Holding her right hand near her flowers, she spoke her words and pictured him holding her . . . kissing her. *Again and again.*

The tangy burst of sweetness made her stumble. She tugged on Justin's arm while her tingling hand pushed on someone's bare back to stay standing.

"Watch it!" Tara spun around so the orchid tied on her wrist was just below Laurel's nose. Laurel stared down at it, open-mouthed. Oh no, she thought.

"I should have known it was you," said Tara. "You're such a klutz."

"I—I tripped." Laurel couldn't take her eyes off the sunny petals, even though she knew she shouldn't breathe its perfume—not after saying her words.

Justin put his arm around her waist. "You okay?"

Tara's eyes flashed up to him, and her voice sweetened. "Hi, Justin. We just bumped—no biggie."

"Yeah. That's all." Laurel gulped a breath, but her senses were drowning. Was it the bougainvillea or the orchid? Or the lemon verbena?

"C'mon." Justin tugged on her arm. "This is a great song." He led her to the very center of the dance floor and let go of her hand. She looked around self-consciously, but surrounded by the crowd, they were nearly invisible. The music was fast, and the beat was strong. No one was watching her, not even Justin, who danced confidently, loosely, singing along to the lyrics. Her head seemed to clear, and she relaxed as the persistent beat seeped into her bloodstream.

Maybe this will be my Cinderella night, Laurel thought. She raised her arms and swayed her hips to the beat.

The song ended too soon, and nearby a senior couple kissed. Other couples stood side-by-side, waiting for the first notes of the next song to cue them into motion. Laurel heard a burst of Kate's laughter. A couple jostled through the crowd, and Laurel stepped closer to Justin to get out of their way.

"Hey," he said softly. His fingertips grazed the length of her arm.

"Hey," she echoed, and reached up to tuck his hair behind one ear. He laughed and shook it loose.

The DJ's smooth voice interrupted. "I usually don't slow it down this early, but I got ladies here who want to get close to you guys. I got one thing to say. Awwriiight!"

It was a love song played by a hard-rock band. Justin put out his left hand, and their fingers intertwined. His other hand pressed the small of her back as a soulful voice rose above a strumming guitar. Laurel had never felt so alive, so aware of her heart pumping. So aware of his body brushing hers as they turned under the glittering ball.

"You smell so good," he whispered. Her neck tingled with his warm breath.

Then the tempo of the song quickened, and Justin loosened his grip. Grinning, he stepped back and spun Laurel around and then around again. One hand grasped hers in an arc above her head while the other lightly trailed across her back and stomach to steady her as she twirled. Above her, around her, the rectangles of light were spinning . . . spinning . . . and she felt like she was dancing at the center of the world. Like the entire universe was spinning in sync. She ached with happiness.

"Nice of you to show." Tara was behind the punch table, her arms crossed tight.

"I was here earlier," Laurel said breezily. She couldn't be angry with anyone, not tonight. At this moment she loved everyone on the entire planet.

"You and Justin were gettin' cozy out there," Nicole said.

"I—we—" A syrupy scent flooded Laurel's nose. It was too sudden, too strong, and the ballroom swam before her.

"Earth to Laurel," Nicole said, snapping her fingers. "What are you on, girl?"

"Huh?" Laurel inched away from Tara and the orchid.

"Laurel is a full-time resident of la-la land," Tara said. "Okay, you and Nicole stay here. Mrs. Westfall said two hostesses at all times. I'm ready for Everett."

"He's here?" Laurel asked.

"Duh. You just walked right past him." Tara smirked.

Laurel downed a glass of punch and grabbed a sandwich as Tara disappeared into the crowd. The sugar on her tongue seemed to dull the orchid's scent.

"LADIES AND GENTLEMEN. MAY I HAVE YOUR ATTENTION, PLEASE?"

The DJ was waving an envelope above his head. "I hold in my hand the answer to someone's lifelong dream. Who will be king and queen of the prom? Senior prom court, please ascend the stage."

Lifelong dream? Puh-leeeze. Rose's eyes would practically roll out of her head. Nicole's eyes were fixed on the court, so Laurel grabbed Whitney's flowers and tried to push through the crowd toward the stage.

"A DRUMROLL, PLEASE," said the DJ. "THIS YEAR'S PROM KING AND QUEEN ARE . . . RICKY PAVOTTI and ASHLEY SMITH!"

The crowd cheered and clapped but almost immediately started whispering about the outcome.

"Oh my god. How could they do that?" a senior said.

Laurel watched as Whitney, her face tight with anger, hurried off the far side of the stage, across the dance floor, and out of the ballroom. Ricky was spinning Queen Ashley on the stage.

"Excuse me," Laurel said, trying to follow Whitney's trail. She ran out of the ballroom and saw Whitney disappear into the ladies' room. Laurel followed and found the senior leaning against a huge marble sink, studying herself in the mirror. She scowled at Laurel's reflection and covered something with her hand.

"What do *you* want?" Whitney said.

Laurel held up the bag. "I have your flowers."

Whitney turned her back to the mirror, and tears pooled in her eyes. "Are you blind? I don't even need them. Ricky was all over that Ashley slut."

"I—uh—" Laurel said. "Maybe he's just excited to be king."

Whitney smirked. "I'm sooo happy for him. God, I can't believe this crap!"

Laurel set the bag on the sink. Whitney dabbed at her face with a balled-up tissue, and her eyes met Laurel's in the mirror. "You don't have other flowers with you? The kind that attract guys?" She was staring at the bougainvillea above Laurel's ear.

Laurel shook her head. "Not anymore." The night was already too complicated.

Whitney pursed her lips. "I don't need them. I can get any guy I want."

Amanda burst into the room. "I can't believe this, Whit." Her hands sliced the air frantically. "This is sooo wrong. How could they?" Whitney leaned on Amanda and started sobbing.

Laurel stared at the bag that contained hours of her work and worry. Should I take it back? she wondered. Shrugging, Laurel left the bag and the seniors behind.

Halfway down the hallway, she froze on the patterned carpeting. A girl with a curtain of long black hair was sitting on a guy's lap. She'd recognize that backless dress anywhere, but who was Tara making out with? One of his hands was buried in her hair while the other spread across her thigh, just below a long slit in her dress. Her wrist was draped over the guy's shoulder and still had the orchid tied to it. Laurel dashed behind a large potted plant and gawked through its leaves at Everett Buchanan, whose lips were slowly moving up and down Tara's neck.

"But you don't even like her," Laurel whispered. Or do you? Passion and enchantment, belle of the ball. The heavy scent infused the hallway.

A tall boy sauntered by. "Get a room," he cracked at the couple.

Holding her breath, Laurel crept close and yanked, but the corsage didn't budge.

"Hey!" Tara pulled her arm back and stared at Laurel. Her eyes seemed glassy. "It's *my* flower."

"I just want to show it to someone," Laurel said sweetly. "I'll bring it right back."

"No way." Tara giggled as Everett kissed her bare shoulder.

Someone cleared his throat loudly behind Laurel, and their heads all turned. Mr. Rodriguez, the towering Willowlawn headmaster, had appeared. Everett stood up abruptly, and Tara slid off his lap, thumping onto the carpet.

"Ow!" she yelled, thrashing her arms.

Laurel stood wider to steady herself against the waves of fragrance.

Mr. Rodriguez helped Tara up. "I'm disappointed, Mr. Buchanan. You don't seem to remember any of our earlier discussion."

"Yes, sir. I mean, no. I—I—" Everett's lips were red and smeary and sparkly.

Mr. Rodriguez sniffed and looked around. "What's that smell? Perfume?"

"Yes, that's it," said Tara. "Exactly. Excuse me, sir." She took hold of her long skirt and walked somewhat unsteadily toward the dance.

Laurel nodded at the confused headmaster. "Excuse me, too. I'll go . . . make sure she's okay." She had to follow that orchid.

Tara had already merged onto the darkened dance floor when Laurel reached the ballroom. Walking along the edge of the crowd, she spied Tara standing with Kate and Alan. Tara was leaning toward Alan, holding the orchid just below his nose. She stroked his cheek with her fingertip and then pulled him onto the dance floor.

"Nooo," Laurel whispered. "You can't do that to Kate." Now she really wished she'd told Kate everything. Laurel started toward her, but an arm caught her. Irritated, she turned to shake free and then gasped.

"Laurel, dear," said Ms. Suarez. "It's so good to see you." She kissed Laurel on both cheeks. Her hair was long across her shoulders, and her crystal earrings sparkled. The Featherstones were right behind her, looking pinched and anxious.

Laurel tried to swallow the expanding lump in her throat. "You surprised me. W-when did you get back?"

"Just now. Mission accomplished: the orchids are safe!" said Ms. Suarez. "We convinced the Costa Rican developer to create a garden and leave the habitat in place."

"That's great." Laurel frowned at the dance floor but couldn't see Tara or Kate.

". . . possibilities for cross-pollination," said Ms. Suarez.

Laurel blinked at her blankly.

"The orchids." Ms. Suarez stepped closer. "We'll study them soon; I promise."

Laurel met the professor's stern eyes and realized he hadn't told her yet. But the scent—the truth—couldn't be hidden. "I need to talk to you," Laurel began. She had to regain Ms. Suarez's trust even before she lost it. "It's—"

"It's like nothing I've ever encountered." Ms. Suarez's face lit up as she looked around the ballroom. "What is that marvelous fragrance?"

Laurel knew exactly what she had to do. "It's an orchid," she said. "*Your* orchid."

Ms. Suarez stared. "Mine? What do you mean?"

Laurel held her gaze. "The rare hybrid."

"Geneva." Mrs. Featherstone put her hands out. "Someone—a misguided student—got into the conservatory and cut the first bloom for a corsage."

Ms. Suarez's hands covered her mouth. "No!"

"But we think the plant's fine," added the professor. "There will be other blooms."

Ms. Suarez's mouth hung open in disbelief. "How did she get in?" When her eyes shifted to Laurel's guilty face, they filled with disappointment.

Laurel took a deep breath. "She was mad at me. And I didn't check the door."

Mrs. Featherstone hugged Ms. Suarez with one arm. "Let's get you back to campus, Geneva."

Ms. Suarez stepped closer to Laurel. "My orchid's here? In this room?"

Laurel nodded, and Ms. Suarez sniffed again.

"Hey," said a now-familiar voice. "Where've you been?" Laurel spun around to see Justin's carefree smile.

"Does *he* know about this, too?" asked Ms. Suarez.

Laurel shook her head.

"About what?" Justin's hand rested comfortably, deliciously on her lower back.

Ms. Suarez looked from one to the other, as if making up her mind. "Do either of you know what an aphrodisiac is?"

"Something about Aphrodite?" Laurel was afraid to look at Justin now.

"She's the goddess of love," Justin added. "So, an aphrodisiac is something that inspires love."

"No, no, no." Ms. Suarez waved her hands. "Not love, necessarily. Lust. There's a huge difference. Excuse us, please." She pulled Laurel several steps from the others. Laurel's back felt cold without Justin's hand.

"Listen closely, Laurel. You have to understand," Ms. Suarez said, squeezing her arm. "My orchid shouldn't be here. Many cultures have used orchids as aphrodisiacs, and this bloom comes from old and potent stock."

"Oh." Her flower books had said nothing about aphrodisiacs. "Uh-oh." Tara and Everett's public display made sense now. *Merde*. Where was Tara?

Ms. Suarez shook her head. "Laurel, what happened? I *begged* you to be careful."

Laurel shut her eyes. Too much was happening too fast, and her head was starting to pound. "I'll bring her to you. I promise."

"Go," Ms. Suarez said huskily. "I'm *dying* to see her."

Laurel walked away from the teachers and tried to breathe clearly, but the scent was inescapable. Even the music sounded exotic now, with a pounding, irresistible beat.

"What's going on?" Justin's hot breath on her ear made her shiver.

"It's complicated," she said, reaching for his hand. "I have to find that orchid."

"Wh-y?" Justin turned her to face him.

She trembled as his hands slid slowly from her bare shoulders to her wrists. His voice, his touch, were hypnotic. "It belongs to Ms. Suarez. And she needs it back."

"Why?" Justin said again, and he stepped even closer. Laurel felt like she was moving through water—warm, pulsating water that pushed her against him. His face bent toward her, and she lifted her chin to meet his lips.

The kiss was perfect. Her fingers threaded through the silky hair at the back of his neck. She held on to him because her world was spinning and not just because of the orchid. She wanted to let go and lose herself in the magic of his lips and his arms around her, but a small, stubborn part of her wouldn't. I can't let Ms. Suarez down again, she thought.

"I have to find Tara." Pulling away reluctantly, Laurel scanned the dance floor and nearly gagged in amazement. Ricky Pavotti's crown was on Tara's head, and his hands were on her swaying hips. The orchid was perched on his shoulder as Tara grinned up at him. The song was fast, but most of the couples were slow dancing. Laurel shook her head to try to focus.

Justin put his hands around her waist. "C'mon. Dance with me. Now."

Laurel hesitated. The heavy scent made everything seem slow and shivery and unreal. Justin leaned to kiss her again, but she turned away. What if it's *just* the orchid? she thought.

"What's wrong now?" asked Justin.

"You—you have to trust me." She pressed her fingers to his lips, and he kissed them. "We have to get the orchid out of here. Everyone's acting drunk." She pointed at the dance floor. Whitney was making out with Everett. Nicole was French-kissing some tall guy. Ricky's hands were moving all over Tara's body. *What if he takes her back to his hotel room tonight?* "See? Nobody's acting normal."

Justin's hand slid down Laurel's back, releasing a cascade of shivers. "What *is* normal?" he said.

"Not this," Laurel said, biting her lip. "I am not going to be responsible for this." She frowned at the dangling orchid. "I need scissors."

"Scissors?" Justin reached into his trouser pocket. "My dad gave me this Swiss Army knife when I was nine. It's got everything." He pulled out the little pair of scissors and handed it to Laurel.

"They let you carry this?" she asked.

"Not on planes." Justin shrugged. "But somebody's got to be prepared."

"You're such a Boy Scout," Laurel teased. "Can you catch?"

"You know I can," said Justin. "Why?"

Stifling an impulse to kiss his earlobe as she told him, Laurel outlined her plan.

"But I—" he started.

She pressed her fingers to his lips. "Shhh. Trust me. It'll take only a minute."

Justin grabbed her wrist and kissed her fingertips again. Laurel wished she could forget about the orchid and jump into his arms, but he walked away as instructed. She felt a light tap on her arm.

"Laurel, what's up?" Mina's nose wrinkled. "I keep—"

"Nothing," Laurel said shortly, pulling away. "Everything's under control." She didn't want yet another person involved. Hiding the scissors behind her back, she wove toward Tara and the prom king. Swiftly, silently, she grabbed the ribbon and pulled. She felt a responding tug but held tight, snipped, and caught the orchid as it fell. Tara shrieked, but Laurel was off: running toward the entrance, where Justin was standing on a chair.

Please, God, please. She set her feet and threw the orchid. High over the heads of the crowd it tumbled, but Justin caught it deftly with one hand, like it was a Frisbee. He leaped off the chair and was out the door. Laurel quickly zigzagged off the dance floor, picked up the end of a tablecloth, and crawled underneath to hide from Tara's wrath.

"Everyone can get their own damn punch," Laurel said, after her breathing had slowed. The rest of her evening was dedicated to Justin. Lifting an edge of the tablecloth, she saw a distraught Tara across the room and dove for another table. Laurel scampered from table to table until she reached the one closest to the door, where she could see Mrs. Westfall frowning and vigilant.

The crowd gradually grew quieter. Laurel was wondering when the scent would dissipate when Whitney's bouquet flashed into her mind. Basil, she thought. The antidote. It had been hidden under a table when she said her words, but all these flowers in one place seemed like Pandora's box. Laurel had no idea what she'd released into the world. She lifted the tablecloth again to see the professor now standing in the principal's place. She crawled out and smoothed her dress.

The professor shook his head. "You, young lady, are full of surprises."

Laurel kept her back to the dance floor. "Where's Justin?"

"I believe he's on his way back to campus."

"What? *Why?*"

"Sheila and I thought Geneva should get some fresh air, and Justin went outside the hotel to give her the orchid."

"I don't understand," she cried. "Why did he go back to school?"

"He had no choice," said the professor. "Anyone who departs the site of a dance may not return. Those are the school regulations, and this has been an odd evening."

"But he wasn't drinking or doing drugs," Laurel protested. "You know that."

"I'm sorry, Laurel, but Mr. Rodriguez saw him go *outside* the hotel. He can't make exceptions, not even for Justin."

Laurel wanted to scream. He could have thrown the orchid in a trash can, but she'd whispered for him to give it *only* to Ms. Suarez so she could see it and keep it alive longer. Laurel trudged toward the bathroom, where she'd left Whitney's bouquet.

"How dare you?" a familiar voice shrilled behind her.

Every cell in Laurel's body tensed as she turned around.

"How *dare* you take my flower?" Tara's face was red with anger.

"It wasn't *your* flower," Laurel said. "You stole it."

Tara was on the verge of tears. "I was dancing with the prom king," she said. "He was kissing me and—"

Laurel stepped closer. "You don't even know him. He's not what you think."

"Shut up!" Tara's fists were tight balls. "Just shut up!"

"Is there a problem here?" Mrs. Featherstone was at Tara's elbow. "May I help?"

Tara let out an exasperated groan and ran back toward the ballroom.

"Thanks," Laurel said. "She's—uh—a little upset."

"You'd better come back to the dance, too," said Mrs. Featherstone. "Luckily Mrs. Westfall missed some of the excitement, but she's asking about a flying flower."

"Great," said Laurel under her breath. "May I use the rest room first? Real quick?" She walked into the ladies' room, but Whitney's bag was gone. Laurel met her own eyes in the mirror and touched the blooms in her hair. Romance and fun. She couldn't believe what she and Justin felt was only lust. I'll keep this alive as long as I can, she thought.

CHAPTER TWENTY-TWO
Petal by Petal

*D*aylight pressed against her eyelids, but Laurel's body still buzzed with the vibrancy of her dream world. Closing her eyes, she pulled the pillow over her head and . . .

pushed open a wooden door, which was carved with flowers and vines. Her bare feet stepped onto the cool bricks of a courtyard. At its center a fountain gushed, and its splashes tumbled like laughter through the air. She plunged both hands into the warm water and cupped it to her mouth. Redolent of honeysuckle, the water streamed into her body. Its energy radiated to her limbs and zapped out from her fingertips. In a flash the courtyard was transformed. Two staircases opened before her. One descended into a cool, dark cave. Gnarled brown roots and yellow leaves covered the railings, and down there someone was crying.

The other, a white staircase, ascended into swirling mist. Vines heavy with red and white blooms twined around its railings, and strains of lively music beckoned from above. Laurel had had enough of tears.

She grabbed hold of the rising banister and climbed the smooth marble steps. At the top a huge white blossom hung just above her nose. She stood on her tiptoes to breathe its fruity essence . . . and the mist was blown away to reveal an enormous ballroom.

Ladies in billowing gowns waltzed with men in black tuxedos. Vases brimming with flowers hung from every wall and decorated every tablecloth. The dance floor was paved with rose petals that spiraled up with each spin of the dancers. Bright blooms adorned the women's hair, and the men had flowers in their buttonholes. Laurel's lungs swelled with the scent of lily of the valley.

One, two, three . . . one, two, three . . . The couples danced to music full of light and structure. One, two, three . . . One, two, three . . . An elegant woman, her chestnut hair swept up, emerged from the crowd and extended her white gloved hand.

"Come, Laurel," Violet said. "Come dance with us."

One, two, three . . . Laurel took her hand and entered the ballroom. The pastel gowns swished and glided. The rose petals swirled, but the dancers spun by her without pausing. Laurel held out her hand, but no one took it. She stepped forward and backward, turned this way and that, but she couldn't merge into the pattern.

She left the dance floor and met Violet's eyes through the whirling bodies. Violet blew her a kiss, and when she mirrored Violet's smile, Laurel was transported into an enormous light-filled room.

Music rang through this house—her music—both loud and soft, swift and slow, measured and unpredictable. Flowers cascaded from nooks in the walls, and Laurel took a deep breath of the richly scented air. She knew without looking that every person she cared about, every person she would ever care about—was somewhere in this sprawling, scented home. But she had to find them all, to make sure they'd stay. . . . They wouldn't leave her alone . . . on the dark staircase . . . down. . . .

Laurel woke up panting and squinted at her clock. It was almost noon, but they were allowed to skip chapel twice a semester. She rolled onto her side and hugged her knees close. It had been ages since she'd dreamed about the big house.

"The house that you dream is your life," her mom had once explained. "Picture your own life like a house with many rooms. You always dream of a huge one, so you're capable of loving many people, of filling many rooms." But this morning Laurel's rooms felt lonely. She might have driven everyone away.

A scent was strong in her memory: lily of the valley. It was the fragrance of Violet's long-ago world, but it was also part of Laurel's here and now. And she desperately wanted happiness to return. Outside her dorm room someone ran down the hall giggling, but Laurel's head pounded.

As she filled a glass with water, Laurel wondered if anyone she loved would speak to her today. She could blame the mess on basil, but that wasn't entirely accurate. Flowerspeaking didn't create something from nothing. It drew out and magnified the feelings and emotions that were already there. She usually kept her ugly parts better masked.

Laurel dialed Grandma's number, but no one answered. Turning on her computer, she typed a quick e-mail.

> Justin: I'm SOOOO sorry about what happened. I had no idea you'd have to leave. Can you come here for dinner tonight? I'd really like to see you.
> Laurel

Her words seemed ordinary, nothing like the drama she was feeling inside. Justin liked poetry, so she pasted part of the E.E. Cummings poem that reminded her of him:

your slightest look easily will unclose me
though i have closed myself as fingers,
you open always petal by petal myself as Spring opens
(touching skilfully, mysteriously) her first rose

"Petal by petal": it was perfect, but did she have the guts to send it? She didn't know if he ever wanted to touch her again. She squeezed her eyes shut and clicked *send*.

The buzz of her dream was fading, but Laurel didn't want to forget it. She found a blank notebook and wrote down every detail. Yet, even full of words, the page looked bare. Grabbing colored pencils, she quickly sketched a bunch of blue flowers in the corner: forget-me-nots. She tucked the book into her special stuff box. Then she climbed the steps to Rose's room, rehearsing what she'd say.

"Who *is* it?" Rose asked in a high, fake voice, but Laurel said nothing until her cousin opened the door wide enough for her to slip in.

"I'm an idiot," Laurel said. "You've got to be one of the top ten cousins in the entire history of the planet, and I treated you like crap. Please forgive me."

Scowling, Rose twirled a pencil between her fingers. "Yes, you did. You aimed for the jugular."

"I'm sorry," Laurel took a small step toward her. "I promise it won't happen again."

Rose stared at her for several seconds. "Look, Laurel. Anybody can be a bitch. That takes no skill at all. It's all about self-control. Do you have any idea how many times a day I hold my tongue? It's *not* easy."

"I know." Laurel bumped her gently. "So, we're okay now?"

"Okay," said Rose. "But I'm putting you on probation,

and you have to do everything I say for a week. And don't even try to use any of your flowers on me."

Laurel pressed her palms together and bowed. "Your wish is my command."

"Excellent. First, let's do brunch," said Rose. "Second, tell all. What's this I hear about you kissing Justin on the dance floor? Major PDA. I want details."

Laurel's face felt hot. We might be history already, she thought, but she forced a shrug. "We danced. We kissed. Who told you?"

"I'm not about to divulge my sources . . . but Kate says you're—"

"Please don't tell anyone," Laurel whispered, following Rose out the door. "I *really* screwed up. He may despise me now."

"Highly unlikely." Rose shook her head. "Young love. I'll try not to be nauseated."

There were a few stragglers in the dining hall. Their voices, the whole campus seemed muted, as if everything the night before had been too loud, too colorful, too much. Rose and Laurel filled their trays and sat at an empty table.

"So, spill," said Rose.

Laurel shook her carton of orange juice. "I've heard that prom never lives up to anyone's expectations. It's totally overrated, especially if you're just a lowly hostess."

"Okay, okay," said Rose. "I deserved that. Now shut up and tell."

Kate came over and slid her tray next to Rose's, and Laurel unburdened herself of every last detail, including the orchid's history and Justin's abrupt departure.

"So, that's why Ricky was all over Tara." Kate threw up her hands. "He was bewitched. How'd I miss that?"

"You're in love," said Rose. "Being in love decimates your powers of observation." She tapped a spoon on her tray. "Okay, so you smooched and played catch with an heirloom orchid, but are you in love, floral Laurel?"

Laurel wanted to bask in Justin's smile. She wanted to know his thoughts, what books he adored—every last detail of his amazing life. She wanted to touch him and be touched. "Maybe. I invited him to dinner tonight."

"Awesome." Kate clapped her hands once. "I'll call Alan. We can—"

"No," Laurel said forcefully.

Kate's face fell. "Why not?"

"Because I'm not sure we're together," said Laurel. "It's all my fault he had to leave." And if it was just the orchid. . . .

"Puh-leeeze," said Kate. "I saw you two dancin'. Alan can explain it all to him."

Laurel shook her head. If they were going to be a couple, she didn't want it all grapevine and gossip. "I need to talk to him first. Alone. Don't tell Alan anything."

"Uh, Laurel, hon?" Rose drummed her fingers on the table. "How are you going to 'be alone' in the Avondale dining hall?"

A purple note was taped to Laurel's door when she returned from brunch.

Please come to the conservatory at 4:30.—G. S.

Her stomach plunged; the tone sounded so formal and distant.

"Are you in trouble?" Kate asked.

"I hope not." Laurel pulled the key from under her shirt and rubbed it.

"It wasn't *your* fault Tara cut it." Kate shook her head. "I still can't believe she went after Alan."

"I should have been more careful." Laurel folded the note into a tiny purple square.

Kate squeezed her arm. "Everything's gonna be all right, okay?"

"Okay." Once inside her room, Laurel quickly dialed Grandma's number, but there was still no answer. There was a new message in her in-box, though. Her stomach plunged, and she steeled herself before opening it.

OK. See you at 5.—J

Laurel reread it, but there were hardly any lines to read between. And Justin had said nothing about the poem. I have absolutely no idea what he's thinking, she thought. She showered, finished some homework, and decided that Ms. Suarez would have to lecture her earlier than four-thirty, because Laurel *had* to be at the bus stop when Justin arrived. She was leaving the quad when she heard a guy's voice call out. Her heart jumped, but it was Everett who ran toward her.

"*Merde*," Laurel whispered, feeling panicky again. He had to be furious about the Tara episode, and he was a master of wicked pranks.

"Laurel, wait up!"

At least he got my name right, she thought. She stopped and turned around. "What?"

"Top o' the morning to you, too," Everett said in an Irish accent. "A little hungover, are we?"

"Hardly. But I'm supposed to be somewhere."

"It can wait. I have an amazing business proposition. Let's chat." He sat down on a bench and patted the space beside him. Laurel sat at the far end, but he scooted closer.

Everett pushed his shaggy blond hair out of his eyes. "Last night was frickin' unbelievable," he said. "I was totally into Tara, and normally I can't stand her."

"Yeah. I'm sorry about that." Laurel stumbled for an explanation. "It was all part of this—this huge prank. It didn't go exactly as planned."

"Prank?" Everett waved his hand. "No way. It was sweet, a total high. See, Tara just explained your flowers to me. I stopped by to see if the effect had—uh—worn off."

"Had it?" Laurel couldn't help asking.

"She looked like hell." Everett did a fake shudder. "She *scares* me."

Laurel bit the inside of her lip. She had to find a way to stop all this gossip about her flowers. "So, what do you want?"

"I told you: my awesome business proposition." Everett rubbed his hands together and leaned forward. "Get this. We're going to sell your fussy-wussies on the internet."

"What?"

"It's genius. We're going to make a frickin' fortune. I've even got a name: Laurel's Florals. I'll register the domain as soon as I get back to my room. We can start with a web-based, mail-order business and build. It'll be our own little cottage industry."

Laurel looked around for a video camera. She'd heard about some Willowlawn guy who uploaded his prank to YouTube. "You're insane."

"No, I'm genius." His hand was on her shoulder. "People are always lookin' for *luv*. If your flowers can make me jump Tara, they can make anyone do *anything*."

"That's not how they work," Laurel protested. "My flowers can make your feelings stronger or draw them out, but they don't create something from nothing."

Everett squinted at her and pulled back. "Wait a sec. So you're saying the flowers don't work unless a person is actually *attracted* to another person."

"Exactly," said Laurel. "At least a little." Tara was a total pain, but she wasn't ugly.

Everett shook his head. "That's troubling."

"See what I mean?" Laurel stood up. "It's sooo much more complicated than it seems. I have to think about tons of things before I can even begin to make a tussie for anyone—ever again. And definitely not on the internet for people I don't even know." She started to walk away, but Everett jumped up and followed.

"You have to see the potential here." He grabbed her arm. "All we need to do is make people *think* your flowers will work. Most crap on the internet is a hoax, anyway. Hell, people will buy pheromone aftershave—like that's going to get them laid."

Laurel twisted away from him. "I really don't have time for this."

"Then how about some flowers for me?" he said. "You know, just to hook up with someone. Other than Tara, I mean?"

Laurel had to turn around. "You want me to make you a 'hook-up' tussie?"

Everett nodded. "Yeah. Why not?"

Laurel felt her anger rise. "You think I feel no sense of responsibility?"

"Well, you gave all those girls flowers for prom. Isn't that what they wanted?"

"No!" Laurel said. "They wanted love, not some cheap, one-night freebie."

"Hey. Don't knock it till—ya know," Everett said.

Laurel wanted something sharp to throw at him. "Rose was right. You *are* scum of the earth."

Everett spread his palms wide. "And here I thought we had a thang goin' on."

"Not in this lifetime, Ev." Laurel turned and ran toward the conservatory.

"Think about it!" he yelled after her. "It's brilliant."

Laurel's thoughts were a confused tangle. She didn't want to be a hot topic on the sometimes vicious gossip grid. She didn't want a blip of popularity just because Everett was using her and her magic. Had he told any other guys yet?

She slowed to a walk. Maybe—with Rose's and Kate's help—she could convince everyone that flower magic *was* a huge prank. That might at least buy her time to master her powers. Surprisingly, Laurel felt a twinge of regret about Tara, too. Tara had to feel like she'd lost everything: soccer, Kate, and now Everett. He'd probably been harsh with her. Now that Laurel was free of basil, she had to find a way to call a truce.

As she ducked under the cedars, she yanked off some needles. She lifted them to her nose—*cedar for strength*—and slipped them into her pocket. She knocked on the conservatory door and almost fell off the step when she saw who answered.

CHAPTER TWENTY-THREE
Raspberry for Remorse

"*Grandma*?" Laurel said, breathless with surprise.

"Laurel, dear."

"I can't believe you're here!" Laurel stepped into open arms, but Grandma was frail now, almost papery thin. She pulled back to study the lined face, as if she feared the petite, white-haired woman might vanish. "When did you get here?"

"A few hours ago," said Grandma.

"But I called you this morning," said Laurel. "Tons of times."

"I left quite early to drive down," said Grandma.

Laurel's hands moved to her hips. "But why didn't you call when you got here? Why didn't you come straight to my room?"

Grandma leaned against a table. "I needed to see Geneva first."

"Surprise, surprise." Ms. Suarez walked toward them with a plant in the crook of her arm. "We weren't expecting you this soon."

Laurel forced herself to meet Ms. Suarez's eyes. "I'm sorry. About everything."

"You should be," said Ms. Suarez. "But I have some good news. Come and see." Her bracelets jingled as she gestured for them to follow.

Laurel held out her arm for Grandma to lean on as they walked, but a silence fell over them. I don't know where to begin, she thought as they entered the orchid enclosure. She looked around anxiously, but several windows were open.

"See." Ms. Suarez pointed to a small bud. "My baby will bloom again soon, and then I will harvest the seeds."

Laurel felt a rush of gratitude, but she wasn't sure she ever wanted to see that orchid again. She sniffed but smelled only orange. The bloom was still tightly wound. Grandma let go of her arm with a squeeze and walked to the far end of the enclosure to examine another flower.

Laurel moved closer to Ms. Suarez and whispered, "I'm really sorry."

"I know you are," she whispered back.

"It won't happen again," said Laurel.

"It can't." Ms. Suarez rubbed her temples. "Maybe I should be furious, but I'm not going to ruin this reunion. It's too important. Cicely just showed up on my doorstep, like a gift." They both stared at the older woman, who was cradling a pink orchid.

"I couldn't believe it when I saw her," Laurel whispered.

"Me, either. This may be our only chance. She's so fragile."

Laurel nodded solemnly. "I know."

Ms. Suarez cleared her throat and spoke louder. "I'll be here all summer tending my orchids, and you can stay here, too, as my apprentice."

"Really?" Laurel gazed out an open window toward the cedars. Avondale was her home now more than any other place on earth. She could stay and master Flowerspeaking side-by-side with Ms. Suarez, but then she might not be able to patch things up with her dad. They needed time together for that. Time without basil.

"With powers like yours," Ms. Suarez went on, "you need serious training. Soon."

"But my dad," Laurel began. "I think he *needs* me to come home this summer."

Grandma turned back toward them. "Besides, you'll be visiting me." Her hand rested on Laurel's arm. "Let's go to the gardens—just us. I need to find you something."

"What an excellent idea, Cicely," said Ms. Suarez. "Laurel can show you what's blooming."

"I think I know what's blooming," Grandma said. "I'm not senile, you know."

"I didn't mean—" began Ms. Suarez, but Grandma waved her apologies away.

"Let's go now!" Grandma threaded her arm under Laurel's. "I've been cooped up for too long." They walked out of the conservatory, careful with each other. Sunlight flashed through the cedar needles as Laurel held the branches out of their way. Cedar for strength, she thought. I'll share mine with Grandma.

"I haven't been here for ages," Grandma said when they reached the garden's entrance, "but I think the plants I want are that way." She led them down a path Laurel had never taken because the plants just looked like unkempt brambles.

"There they are." Grandma reached into a tangle of purplish branches and broke off a cluster of small white flowers. "Raspberries. Can we find a place to sit?"

"Sure." Laurel led her back to a stone bench where the sun shone golden on their shoulders and the garden around them buzzed. Nectar-drunk bees and butterflies with stained-glass wings flitted from flower to flower. Laurel had prayed and waited so long for this moment

that it felt strange to speak. She had to start with something ordinary.

"Grandma?"

"Yes?"

"My dad said you wrote a letter for me. Did you sign
me up for Latin, too?"

"Of course." Grandma nodded. "The majority of
botanical names are in Latin. You need to know them to
master your gift."

"But you didn't know I had the gift then," Laurel
pointed out. "Nobody knew."

"You're right." Grandma pursed her lips. "I suppose I
still had hope. Sometimes hope keeps living—even when
we starve it."

She swiveled toward Laurel and held up the raspberry
branch between them. Laurel watched as Grandma raised
her hand, closed her eyes, and whispered, "Bright cut
flowers, leaves of green, bring about what I have seen."

A sudden breeze swirled Laurel's hair from her neck.
The hum of the garden—the bees, the butterflies—cre-
scendoed and suffused her body.

"Raspberry is for remorse," Grandma said. "I'm
ashamed that I neglected you, but I'll make up for it."
She held out the branch to Laurel. "I promise."

Laurel's hand wavered, because she knew Grandma's
Flowerspeaking would be irresistible. She wanted to

voice her own thoughts first. She took the branch—its energy made her hand shake—and set it down between them. "But I don't really understand. Why did you come *today*?"

"It was time," Grandma said. "*Past* time. Your lovely notes helped me see it's not my time to die. And Geneva wrote, too. I guess the world still needs me for something."

Laurel hesitated. She didn't want to inflict pain, but this might be the only time Grandma would answer. "But how could you burn your garden? I *loved* it."

Grandma's head drooped. "You can't garden when you're dead inside."

Laurel shook her arm gently. "You're not dead!"

"No." Grandma almost smiled. "And neither is my garden. My bulbs, the deepest ones, came up this spring. The green shoots poked up through the cinders and ashes."

Cinders and ashes, Laurel repeated in her mind as she looked at the raspberry branch between them. Warmer days would come soon, with sun enough to transform flowers into glossy fruit. She lifted the branch to her nose, and Grandma's gift surged through her veins. Laurel squeezed her eyes against the muddy, churning depths of sorrow and regret. Her mouth twisted with an agony she never wanted to feel again.

Then Grandma's hands enclosed Laurel's, and the sadness slowly ebbed. She was beginning to understand why Grandma hadn't come to her earlier.

"What flower is for forgiveness?" Laurel asked.

Grandma shook her head. "Forgiveness takes time, child."

"Not always. Not if I understand."

"A white tulip speaks forgiveness."

Tulips were past blooming, but Laurel vowed to find some white ones. "You have to help me," she said. "I want to use my gift. I want to be who I'm supposed to be."

"Who you're *supposed* to be," Grandma echoed. "Mmm. Your mother was supposed to be one of the great ones, but she—"

Grandma's voice caught, and Laurel sensed the weight of grief descending. Slipping to the ground, she knelt before Grandma and grabbed hold of her hands. The bluish veins were prominent, pulsing her fragile life.

"Do you know the story of Demeter and her daughter Persephone?" Laurel didn't wait for an answer. "Demeter was the Greek goddess of the harvest, and she wanted to die when Persephone was kidnapped into the underworld, but she couldn't. She had to make the world flower and grow again every time her daughter returned. There had to be food and trees and flowers. This world has to keep living and blooming no matter what."

"Yes." Grandma's voice was husky with emotion.

"You *have* to teach me all about Flowerspeaking." Laurel gently shook her hands. "I have to know everything about the gift and the magic."

Grandma looked past her into the garden. "Whenever anyone gives anyone else flowers, there's magic."

"But mine are different," Laurel insisted.

"Yes. From what Geneva has told me, your gift will be exceptional. Like Lily's." Grandma paused and raised her eyebrows. "She also mentioned the debacle last night."

Laurel's shoulders dropped. "Ugh—I didn't mean for that to happen."

"Of course not. All of us make mistakes," said Grandma. "But it sounds like there was no permanent damage."

Unless it's with Justin, Laurel thought. "Will you help me use my gift? The right way, I mean?"

"We'll *all* help you," said Grandma. "There are Flowerspeakers in every country of the world, and each has a special mission."

"Really?" said Laurel. "What's mine?"

"That, my dear, you will have to discover yourself."

A familiar laugh, high and musical, wafted toward them, and Laurel stood up quickly. The voices grew louder as the Featherstones turned a corner and came into view.

"Sheila?" Grandma's eyes widened. "Sheila Spenser?"

A large white flower was perched above Mrs. Featherstone's ear, and she held more blooms in the arm draped over the professor's. "Cicely! I didn't know you were here." She took Grandma's outstretched hands and kissed her cheek. "It's been too long! What a surprise. I was just telling Luke a story about Great-grandma Gladys—but you haven't met my husband, have you?"

"Your husband?" Grandma stood up to shake the professor's hand. "My congratulations."

"Thank you," said Mrs. Featherstone. "Laurel made a beautiful flower girl at our wedding."

Grandma tilted her head at Laurel. "I really do have to catch up."

"Isn't Gladys's garden lovely today?" exclaimed Mrs. Featherstone. "If only she could see it now."

The professor nodded. "This garden is one of my favorite spots on earth."

"Mine, too," Laurel said.

After the Featherstones walked on, Grandma sat back on the bench, a smile lighting her face. "Now *that* is something. Sheila has found love at last."

"I gave her flowers," Laurel said. "For happiness and romance. My very first tussie and a few other bouquets."

"Really?" Grandma reached for Laurel's hand again. "It's a wonderful thing to coax love into this world. The ghost of Gladys is happy at last," she said half to herself.

"What?" asked Laurel.

Grandma waved her hand. "It's just something we used to say when I was a schoolgirl here. Whenever something strange or bad happened, we'd blame the ghost of Gladys. But your gift has brought happiness to her great-granddaughter at last, and her garden is alive and lovely. Gladys must be ecstatic."

Tree leaves, young and green, billowed above her head while Laurel waited for Justin near the bus stop. Many of the spring blooms had withered, but it was too early for the fullness of summer. Laurel was going back and forth about what to tell him. She could say that her mom was dead, that their bond had been flowers—that the world had possibilities he hadn't imagined. But he might not understand.

Grandma had gone out to dinner with Rose and Robbie, and Laurel had promised to meet them later. When Laurel had led her cousin to the bench where Grandma waited, Rose was truly astonished. Together they would keep Grandma from descending into melancholy again.

Laurel heard the bus before she saw it and was gripped

by doubts. He changed his mind. He's not coming. When he stepped off, her insides seemed to cartwheel.

"Hey." Laurel held her breath to slow her reckless heartbeat.

Justin was wearing an untucked red polo shirt, khaki shorts, and a ponytail. "Hey." He stopped about three feet away and slipped his hands into his pockets.

"Want to take a walk before dinner? If you're not starving now? The dining hall's pretty crowded until later." Laurel giggled nervously.

"Yeah. Sure." Justin shrugged. "I haven't seen a lot of Avondale."

"It's really beautiful," Laurel said. An image of the gazebo and kissing couch flashed into her mind, but she dismissed it. That's not me, she thought. She pointed beyond the conservatory toward the path she'd taken with Ms. Suarez to see the wild orchid. "There's a great view of the mountains that way if you don't mind a hike."

"I like hikes," said Justin.

"Great." Laurel pointed out her dorm window as they walked across the quad.

"What's that?" Justin asked when they emerged from the cedars.

"The conservatory," said Laurel.

"Awesome architecture," said Justin. "It looks like a cathedral."

A cathedral for flowers. "See the gargoyles?" Laurel said. "Aren't they cool?"

When they reached the uphill path, Justin walked at her side, occasionally electrifying her arm with an accidental touch, but he didn't reach for her hand.

"When's your first—" She stopped herself. *Geek alert!* She'd been about to ask for his exam schedule. "When's your next cross-country meet?"

"Next Saturday," he said.

"Is it home?"

"Yeah, but they're pretty boring for spectators, except right at the finish line," he said. "Not like soccer."

"Maybe I'll come," Laurel said, hoping for an iota of encouragement. Her heartbeats were almost painful with aching to feel his touch, but she couldn't take his hand. She'd hoped the daylight would throw everything into clarity, but it felt so different from the dance floor. I knew more about him in the dark, she thought.

They reached the crest of the hill, and Justin raised his hand to block the low sun. "Awesome view. Do you come here all the time?" he asked, his eyes roaming.

"I should. . . ." But Laurel turned a circle until she found the source of a fresh and energizing scent. Mountain laurel, *her* plant, had finally come into bloom. She broke off a cluster of the cup-shaped flowers that looked like striped peppermint candies.

Scampering up some rocks, she found a spot with room enough for Justin, but he didn't seem to notice. Her eyes traced the rise and fall of the blue-gray horizon. Soon the sun would slip down, releasing its arsenal of colors between the tatters of cloud.

"I'm really sorry you had to leave prom last night," she started. "I had no idea that would happen."

Justin turned to face her. "That's just it. What happened? I remember dancing and catching some flower, but it's kind of like a dream. Some guys are saying the punch was spiked. Did you have any?"

"No." She tried another tack. "So, did Ms. Suarez say anything about that flower? On the way back?"

Justin shook his head. "Is she always that weird? She made me tie it up in a plastic bag and promise to wash my hands. I felt like I was five."

"She's certainly unique." Laurel forced a laugh, even though her high hopes were crashing. Justin didn't seem the slightest bit interested in touching or kissing her now. It was all the orchid. His feelings weren't real.

He turned back to the view. "Did I tell you I'm going to New Zealand for the summer? My uncle's there doing some research, and I'm going to hang out with him."

"Cool." Laurel hugged her knees to her chest. There was no point in starting a relationship now, with school ending in a few weeks and him headed to the other side of the world. She twirled the flowers between her fingers. *Mountain laurel for ambition.*

Small stones skittered down the mountainside as Justin sat on the edge of the rocks closer to her. "Yeah, he's got a boat and . . ."

Justin talked on, but she lifted the mountain laurel to her nose, closed her eyes, and inhaled its vibrant aroma. She felt her spirit rise up and up, like a red-tailed hawk gliding, sailing on wind currents in the cloud-marbled sky, and crying out. *I can do anything. . . .*

"Laurel?" Justin's voice summoned her back to earth. "Hey!" His hand pressed and gently shook her knee.

She blinked up at him.

"You still with me?" he asked. "Where'd you go?"

"Sorry. I—um—daydream sometimes."

"Me, too." Justin shook his head. Strands of hair were falling out of his ponytail.

"Whaaat?" she said.

"You know, you're kind of hard to read."

Laurel smiled mischievously. "Lots of good poetry is."

Grinning, Justin took the mountain laurel out of her hand and gently tucked it behind her ear. His hands were warm as he pulled her to standing, as his fingers twined with hers. He was so close that every cell in her body pulsed . . . warm . . . waiting. He hesitated, his black eyes solemn and honest. So honest she wanted to stare into them always. He smelled of fresh grass and mint and possibility. His head tilted, and she closed her eyes to capture the sweet press of his lips.

EPILOGUE
Feast of Flowers

"In the cherry blossom's shade there's no such thing as a stranger."
—KOBAYASHI ISSA, JAPANESE HAIKU POET, 1763–1828

Winding through the foothills of the Blue Ridge Mountains, Ms. Suarez's compact car passed farms and fields turning rusty and gold with autumn. Laurel didn't know where they were going, but she trusted Ms. Suarez. At the end of the summer, the teacher had welcomed her back like a dear friend. Avondale felt like home, but so did Grandma's cottage, and so did her dad's row house. If Laurel felt at home within herself, she was home everywhere.

"Cicely and I have a surprise for your birthday," Ms. Suarez had said when she invited Laurel. This day, her fifteenth birthday, promised to be perfect in nearly every way that her fourteenth hadn't been. At four o'clock she was meeting Justin for a hike. After months of e-mail-only contact from opposite sides of the world, they were both a little shy. But between practices, papers, and tests, they were finding some time together, and Laurel was beginning to introduce her world of flowers to him.

So far, sophomore year was substantially better than freshman. Except for Tuesday afternoons when she met Ms. Suarez in the conservatory, she hung out with Kate and Ally, and sometimes Nicole and Tara. Three of them—Laurel, Kate, and Nicole—had called a truce and powwowed whenever Tara got up to her usual tricks. It wasn't perfect, but Tara seemed to be trying, and Laurel didn't feel like she was a lone target anymore.

Ms. Suarez's car turned down a long driveway lined with symmetrical, red-leafed trees. They arrived at a brick, Federal-style house and circled around to the rear to park, but Laurel saw no signs of life at the manor.

"What *is* this place?" She closed her car door.

Ms. Suarez raised her eyebrows and handed Laurel an empty basket. "You'll see." Their path was lined with thick boxwood shrubs whose musty scent made Laurel think of antiques stacked in an attic. Tiny stones crunched under their footsteps. Over the summer break Laurel and her dad had toured five Virginia estates and their gardens. Her dad was attentive to the history and lineage of each place while Laurel didn't miss an heirloom bloom. Madeleine came along twice, and Laurel was gradually accepting her as the woman her dad needed in his house, in his life.

The boxwoods ended, and the garden opened out against a backdrop of autumn mountains. Laurel and Ms. Suarez followed a straight promenade toward a stone fountain where water was sparkling high into the air. A white-haired woman sat at the edge of the fountain. Laurel dropped the basket and ran.

"Grandma!" Laurel threw her arms around her neck. Grandma had grown stronger over their summer month together, more substantial and firmly rooted in this life. By the end of their visit, the three of them—Rose, Robbie, and Laurel—had managed to replant much of her garden. It would take years, but her garden would be itself again.

Grandma held Laurel's face between both hands and kissed each cheek.

Laurel felt giddy with anticipation. "Who lives here?"

"A friend." Grandma patted the seat beside her, and Laurel sat down. Ms. Suarez placed the empty basket at their feet.

"First," said Grandma. She took an envelope out of her purse. "I have kept this a secret, but it's time to share. Your mother entrusted me with the letters she wrote to you. Happy birthday, Laurel."

Laurel drew in a quick breath. "You sent her letter last year?"

"Yes, and there are many more. I have them all."

Laurel turned the heavy paper over in her hands, but

she couldn't open it now. She wanted to be alone. "I'll read it later." She tucked it into her jacket.

"Of course," said Grandma.

Laurel looked around the garden. Symmetrical paths radiated from the central fountain like the sun's rays. Lifting her nose, she recognized the scent of mums on the air and detected something more complex, too. "I'd love to explore," she said.

Grandma stood and raised one arm. "Not yet," she said. "Listen."

Someone began to play a flute. The silvery music seemed old but familiar, like a song Laurel once heard in a dream. The notes journeyed through the octaves, singing of both heavy sorrows and fleet-footed joy. Everything and its opposite, Laurel thought, as her body hummed along.

Ms. Suarez handed Laurel the basket and motioned for her to stand. "You'll need this now."

A young woman with deep brown skin and braids was walking slowly, ceremonially, up one of the paths toward them. She held a small leafy branch in her hand, stopped in front of Laurel, and offered it to her. "Here's mountain laurel for ambition." Her large brown eyes smiled as she kissed Laurel on the cheek. "Welcome."

"Thank you." Laurel took the branch, and her hand tingled with its potency. The girl stepped aside, and there was a chubby boy a few feet behind her who had red hair, freckles, and a Willowlawn jacket.

"A white chrysanthemum for truth," he said with a lisp. He, too, kissed her once on the cheek. "Welcome, Laurel."

She lifted the white flower to her face and glanced at Grandma. Grandma nodded, and Laurel breathed it in. I'll be truthful, she promised.

Laurel glanced around before the next person reached her, and her mouth widened in wonder. Rows and rows of people were coming toward her from every direction of the radiant paths. Each person carried a single flower or a branch, a gift to her on her birthday. A gust of wind sprinkled fountain water on Laurel, and it felt like a baptism.

"Jasmine for amiability," said a girl her age.

"Clematis virginiana for beauty of mind," said an older guy.

"Parsley for the feast," said another.

The line of kindred spirits seemed to be endless. She'd been surrounded by these people since her birth, she realized. Throughout her life her gift would be nurtured by their presence, sustained by their gifts. Together they had power in this world, the tremendous power to coax and nurture love.

Laurel beamed at the next person, at the next flower. She never wanted it to end.

ACKNOWLEDGMENTS

Forget-Her-Nots is a dream come true. My friends and family members have offered encouragement and enthusiasm throughout the journey that was this novel. In particular, I want to thank my husband for putting up with me through the mood swings of writing and publication. My three kids—Ian, David, and Samantha—were curious, loving, and supportive throughout their mama's drama. I can't thank my agent, Steven Chudney, enough for being there just when I needed him and believing in the magic of this novel. I also want to thank Sarah Cloots, Virginia Duncan, Martha Mihalick, and Lois Adams for their insightful editing and guidance, Paul Zakris, for the loveliness of this book in your hands, and the whole Greenwillow family for general awesomeness.

Many others have been great readers and cheerleaders. My sisters—Elizabeth Brecount Norton, Julie Brecount

Patel, and Margaret Burleigh Brecount—offered their comments and persistent optimism. Thanks also to my brother, David Brecount, for his techie know-how. Special hugs and thanks to my great friends Barbara Kanninen, Carol Ritchie, Kathi Reidy, Carol Bernstein, Margit Nahra, Susan St. Ville, Anne Marie Pace, Pam Calvert, and Jan Callies Foster, who read, asked questions, and listened whenever I needed intelligence and kindness. I also want to thank Beth and Becky Andrews for a boost in the early stages. A special shout-out to my fab teen readers, Jenna Anders, Audrey Bowler, and Ian White, who give me hope. Thanks also to novelist Dennis Danvers, who offered excellent criticism of my earlier work and believed that I could do this. And thanks to my mom, Mary Brecount Bernhold, who didn't get mad at me if I couldn't talk because I was writing. Thanks to my dad, David Jacob "Jack" Brecount, who always loved words and a good prank. Lastly, I am grateful to God for the true wonder of flowers and for my own gift of writing.

Thanks to the Folger Shakespeare Library for allowing me to research Shakespeare and the language of flowers in those hallowed stacks, and sorry, I really thought my phone was on vibrate. Thanks also to the Botany and Horticulture Library at the Smithsonian Institution for sharing your holdings with me.

Laurel's flowers (and a few more) and their meanings

alyssum *(sweet)* ∿ worth beyond beauty

amaranth *(globe)* ∿ immortality, unfading love

azalea ∿ temperance

basil ∿ hatred

basil *(sweet)* ∿ good wishes

bellflower *(white)* ∿ gratitude

bluebell ∿ constancy

bougainvillea ∿ romance and fun *(according to Laurel)*

buttercup ∿ ingratitude, childishness

cabbage rose ∿ ambassador of love

camellia *(red)* ∿ unpretending excellence

camellia *(white)* ∿ perfected loveliness

candytuft ∿ indifference

carnation *(striped)* ∿ refusal

carnation (*yellow*) ⌒ disdain

cedar ⌒ strength

chrysanthemum (*white*) ⌒ truth

cicely (*sweet*) ⌒ gladness and comfort

cinquefoil ⌒ maternal affection

clematis ⌒ beauty of mind

columbine ⌒ folly

coreopsis ⌒ always cheerful

coriander ⌒ hidden worth

creeping willow ⌒ love, forsaken

crocus (*saffron*) ⌒ mirth

daffodil ⌒ regard

daisy ⌒ innocence

dead leaves ⌒ melancholy, sadness

dogwood ⌒ love undiminished by adversity, durability

fennel ⌒ worthy of all praise, strength

fern ⌣ fascination

flowering reed ⌣ confidence in heaven to come

forget-me-nots ⌣ forget me not, true love

forsythia ⌣ anticipation

foxglove ⌣ insincerity

gardenia (aka cape jasmine) ⌣ ecstasy and transport

grass ⌣ submission, utility

holly ⌣ foresight

hollyhock ⌣ ambition, fecundity

honeysuckle ⌣ generous and devoted affection

hyacinth ⌣ sport, game, play

hydrangea ⌣ a boaster, heartlessness

iris ⌣ message

ivy ⌣ fidelity, marriage

jasmine ⌣ amiability

jonquil ⌣ I desire a return of affection

lady's slipper ∽ capricious beauty

laurel ∽ glory

laurel (*mountain*) ∽ ambition

lavender ∽ distrust or devotion

lemon verbena ∽ enchantment, attract the opposite sex

lilac (*purple*) ∽ the first emotions of love

lilac (*white*) ∽ youthful innocence

lily of the valley ∽ return of happiness

lily (*orange*) ∽ coquetry

lily (*white*) ∽ purity, sweetness

live oak ∽ liberty

magnolia ∽ love of nature

marigold ∽ grief

marjoram ∽ blushes

mint ∽ virtue

morning glory ∽ affection

moss ∽ maternal love

myrtle ∽ love, pleasing reminiscences

narcissus ∽ narcissism, egotism

orange tree ∽ generosity

orchid ∽ belle of the ball, passion

pansies ∽ thoughts

parsley ∽ feast, festivities

peony ∽ shame, bashfulness

peppermint ∽ warmth of feeling

pinks (*double red*) ∽ pure and ardent love

pinks (*single*) ∽ pure love

poppy (*scarlet*) ∽ fantastic extravagance

quince ∽ temptation

raspberry ∽ remorse

rose ∽ love

rose (*yellow*) ∽ decrease of love, jealousy

rosebud (*white*) ⌣ girlhood

rosemary ⌣ remembrance

sage ⌣ esteem

snowdrops ⌣ hope

sunflower (*tall*) ⌣ haughtiness

sunflower (*dwarf*) ⌣ adoration

sweet William ⌣ gallantry

thyme ⌣ activity

tulip (*red*) ⌣ a declaration of love

tulip (*yellow*) ⌣ hopeless love, friendship

tulip (*white*) ⌣ forgiveness

violet (*blue*) ⌣ faithfulness

violet (*purple*) ⌣ you occupy my thoughts

zinnia ⌣ thoughts of absent friends

DA FEB 2 4 2011